The Stranger and the Star

This book is a work of fiction.
All characters, organizations, locations, and events are imaginary or used fictitiously. Any similarity to real persons, living or dead, is coincidental and unintended.

THE STRANGER AND THE STAR

Copyright © 2026 by L. N. Clarke

All rights reserved. This book or any portion thereof may not be reproduced or used in any manner whatsoever without the express written permission of the publisher except for the use of brief quotations in a book review. This book or any portion thereof may not be copied into or used to train ML, AI, GenAI, or similar technologies without the express written permission of the publisher.

Published by Naughtobelus Books LLC

www.naughtobelus.com

Developmental Editor: Connolly Bottum
Professionally Copy Edited via Reedsy
Sensitivity Reader: Rowan Pierce
Sensitivity Reader: Mel Carubia

Cover Fonts:
Hero Beam by Alit Design
King Edward by Burntilldead Studio

ISBN 979-8-9862466-5-9 (paperback)
ISBN 979-8-9862466-6-6 (hardcover - dust jacket)
ISBN 979-8-9862466-7-3 (ebook)

First Edition 2026

Library of Congress Control Number: 2026900071

To those

who still wish on shooting stars, dandelions, and birthday candles.

Never stop dreaming.

One

Breaking and entering is not something I meant to make a habit of.

If I were to categorize myself as a character in a classic heist novel, I'd be the hacker in the van at best. That's my comfort level with the bad sort of trouble. Yet, here I am in the dark of night, gripping a chilly Realtor's lockbox and sliding my thumbs across its keypad.

I regret the day I bragged to my bestie that I can tell which buttons are part of the code by how worn down the numbers are. At the time, I felt like a clever detective pointing out a clue that others had missed. Turns out, not everyone is satisfied knowing *how* they can break into an empty old house. Some folks actually want to do it.

Hands trembling from the cold, I punch in the familiar numbers, pluck out the key, and let myself in. It's late, so most of my neighbors are asleep, but I still flinch when the door sticks and I'm forced to bump it shut with my hip. The first few seconds in the moonlit foyer are always the most unsettling.

Despite its beauty, the historic home has been unoccupied my whole life. Which means in addition to fear of the law, I'm also worried that every shadow contains a malevolent

Victorian ghost, structural damage, or worst of all—spiders.

I whip out the closest thing to a flashlight I can use without drawing attention: my phone. The last text I sent is still on my screen. *Help. I messed up. How do normal humans flirt?*

The encoded response reads: *OVX*.

X is the time to meet. Ten o'clock—for which I'm already late. OV is the Old Victorian: dream home on the outside, construction site on the inside, and the only private location available in my suburban neighborhood. My nostrils burn from the stench of every flipper's favorite gray-beige paint.

"Greige," I mutter as I climb the stairs. "The official color of giving up."

On the top floor, I climb a ladder to a hatch that opens onto a flat roof. There, on the moonlit widow's walk, a shadowy figure sits on a bucket, backlit by fog-hazed streetlamps below. It bothers me that I'm used to this.

"It's been an hour," Alex complains. "I almost left. What took you so long?"

"Sorry," I mutter, hunting for an excuse that doesn't make me sound pathetic. Too bad the truth comes out instead. "My parents wouldn't leave me alone. They thought I had a bad day at school and getting in my face might fix it."

"Did you? Do you need some space?"

That's the great thing about Alex. They can be totally livid with me for leaving them waiting on a cold rooftop and still care about my needs. It almost makes up for their risky choice to use the Victorian as a clubhouse. Almost.

"It's fine," I say out of pure habit, then follow up with "The space. Not my day."

Everyone says I don't know how to lie, but if misspeaking counts, I'm a pro.

Alex stands, striking an iconic silhouette with their wavy pixie cut and cargo pants. It never ceases to amaze me how they only become *more Alex* over time, while I struggle with my identity. This year, I have ocean-blue hair with bangs—not because the look is trendy, but because the part of me that wants to stand out is at war with the part that wants to blend in. Predictably, I accomplish neither.

"Well?" Alex asks. "What happened?"

I cringe and brace myself for the reaction I already know I'm going to get, but start at the beginning anyway. "Last weekend, Jayden posted a picture of this old car he's fixing up."

They cut me off. "Ugh. Okay, step one of flirting is the talking stage. Liking photos doesn't count."

"Actually, I read—"

"June." They hold up a finger. "Please tell me you didn't look up flirting on the internet before coming to me."

"Ahh." I strategically stare at Alex's finger rather than make eye contact. Technically, I've had boyfriends before, but they approached me—not the other way around—and I hate going into things unprepared.

The finger drops. "Starting over. Step one of flirting is erasing that auto-generated clickbait nonsense from your brain immediately. Step two is getting to know the guy. Three is telling him how you feel. Guys like *Jayden* won't notice subtle hints. He's got the emotional maturity of a doughnut."

I stifle a smile despite my foul mood, and that only encourages them.

"He's like an orange cat in a tight T-shirt, sharing one brain cell with his friends. I honestly don't get what you see in him."

I hold my hands up in surrender. "Mostly the tight T-shirt. But let me finish, okay? I saw the picture and I thought, well, my art commissions are making enough to afford an auto shop gift card. And if I give him one in person, that's flirting he'd notice, right? Step three?"

Alex crosses their arms and squints as if a confession is

tattooed on my forehead. Their grandmother was an actual psychic—the kind with a legit small-town business—and sometimes I wonder if it's genetic. They know I've already given him the card. "What did you say when you did it?"

All the levity drains from the conversation as my imagination helpfully re-creates the scene: Me, gripping the plastic card so tight the sharp edge slices into my skin. Him, chatting away with a friend, oblivious to—or ignoring—my presence.

Suddenly, I can't muster a smile.

I had prepared the night before, but there's nothing on earth that can stop my mind from blanking when Jayden looks at me. He has chin-length hair with soft waves like a prince in a fantasy movie, and muscles that are always on display, thanks to his skin-hugging metal band shirts. I was doomed before I opened my mouth, so—

"Um, I said. . . sort of . . . nothing."

Alex uncrosses their arms and throws their head back dramatically. "You should have told me you were doing this. I could've helped! I could have been there."

I sigh and glance nervously over the rooftop, wishing they would keep their voice down. It's not like the flimsy wooden railing will hide us from anyone looking up.

To be fair, though, Alex has been protective of me since we were practically babies, and my text already gave away the tragic ending to my story. It's no wonder they didn't want to have this chat within earshot of their dad. He does not appreciate creative swears.

I sigh. "I thought I was good, but then I froze. He was talking to Gabe, and I had to get to my next class, so I just kind of gave it to him."

It's impossible to explain—even to Alex—why social interactions that are easy for others make me panic so badly I can't speak. Everyone tells me the simple solution is to *just stop caring* what other people think. But it's more than that. They might as well tell me to stop fearing spiders—or *become someone else*.

Still, I need an outside perspective, or the spiraling will keep me up all night. Did I read the situation correctly? I'm pretty sure I did, but hope I didn't.

"And? What did he do?" they prod while pausing to check something on their phone.

They're missing out on Friday night gaming—adding guilt to my heartache and confusion. I wait for them to finish and steady my emotions by digging my fingernails into my palms. This is the hardest part to share.

"He said thanks."

Their eyebrow lifts. "That's not so bad. What did you—"

"Then he showed the card to Gabe, and Gabe laughed."

Alex goes eerily still. "Laughed how?"

I re-live the wave of humiliation that had washed over me as I watched the two leave, snickering and elbowing each other. "A snorting laugh, like it was a private joke. I'm not sure they were laughing at me, though. I might have missed something. Was the gift . . . weird?"

Most folks have a bad side that other people try not to get on. Alex is more like a twenty-sided die, with many subtle ways to fall out of their favor. The shadow that crosses over their eyes says Jayden just rolled a natural one.

"Stop giving your attention—and money—to that loser," they order, no longer joking. "You should be the one laughing at him."

"So, you think—"

"Let me introduce you to my guild mates in my game. They'd lose their minds over a girl like you."

Welp. At least this confirms my suspicion that Jayden is just not into me. Now I'm free to stress about all the possible reasons for his laughter. Yay.

Alex makes a show of calming down and putting on a concerned expression. Thankfully, unlike my parents, they don't try to give me a comforting hug. "I know you hate internet diagnosis or whatever." They pause while I groan and shake my head. "But I saw a video that said sometimes folks treat crushes like a special interest. You know, something to study and imitate. I kind of get that vibe here. Maybe you just need a new hobby."

I pull my hands into the sleeves of my oversized cardigan and fidget with the soft yarn. "It's not like that. He's cute, that's all."

Hobbies don't make my chest ache and my breath catch in my throat. It's not like I daydream about illustrations or lie awake in bed at night pondering puzzle solutions. Okay, fine. Sometimes I do.

Alex gives me a look that says they don't buy it for a minute. "The other day you brought up camping, and I assume it's because Jayden said something. I can't see you sleeping in the woods with spiders and snakes unless someone ties you up and drags you."

I open my mouth to deny it, then give up. They know my phobias too well. "I don't know. Living in the woods sounds better than facing him at school next week."

"*That* is also something I can help with." They flash their teeth to show me their help will likely leave Jayden cowering in fear, then glance at their phone again. "I have to check out the latest patch with Sudo and the guild in fifteen." It makes sense that they'd want to get back to their partner and video games after waiting an hour, but they offer an excuse anyway. "It's Saturday morning in Tokyo, so basically everyone is online. Plus, I think you need some sleep."

"I'll be fine," I mutter.

Alex strolls to the hatch on the roof and throws their legs over the side. "Tomorrow, we'll meet up and get your mind off this. I promise. You coming with?"

They gesture toward the hatch, and I shake my head. My parents have some kind of superpower where they can detect if I so much as sniffle, even when they're fast asleep. The last thing I want is another prying conversation about my day.

Alex looks worried for only a moment, then their phone buzzes and their expression sets. They nod and drop down the ladder. A minute later, a shadow darts from the front porch and across the street, cutting between two houses. They're not even trying to hide where they've been.

"What's it like fearing nothing?" I wonder as I settle onto the still-warm bucket.

They were right about one thing, though—I hate when people try to diagnose my problems after watching a few neurodivergent social videos, as if an experience being *authentic* means it's also universal. The worst part is that it makes me question myself every time.

Which means I'm on a construction bucket, atop a cold roof, wrapped in a sweater—because grabbing my jacket would have made too much sense—wondering if I'm heartbroken or if I've misunderstood my own brain.

Now that I think about it, my only comfortable conversations with Jayden have been the ones inside my head, like a mental fanfic of a real guy. Maybe Alex is right, and I've been treating him like a subject to study from afar. I was the *hacker in the van* all along, getting close to love without taking any risks—until today.

And now I'm spiraling again.

Maybe I do need some sleep.

I lean back and rest my arms on the railing, staring up at the night sky. It's cloudless, and despite the streetlamps, tons of stars are visible—including one that streaks through the sky so fast I almost miss its tail.

A meteorite!

It's totally childish, but I jump to my feet and try to think of a wish. Yes, I also wish on birthday candles—and dandelions if no one's looking. I can use all the luck I can get.

What to wish for, though?

A relationship with Jayden? *Apparently, he's a bully and a loser.*

Assurance that I'm not the loser? It's a star, not a therapist.

"I wish I could understand love," I say. "Thoroughly, like a mental blueprint or a doctorate. I want to know when my feelings are real, and how to attract someone I like."

The wording is awkward, but the logic is sound. I want to forge my own happily ever after, with all the meet-cutes and will-they-won't-they of my favorite romance novels—except, without the real-world risk of misunderstandings and mockery.

The sky responds to my ridiculous wish with a streak of light in the opposite direction. That's surprising, since I'm pretty sure most meteorite showers are predicted in advance. I raise my phone to catch a video, just in case more of them appear, but when I check out the screen, I get a shock that makes me stumble back and trip on the bucket.

Another star—or possibly the same one—travels halfway across the screen before coming to a halt and changing direction. Its bright tail is now directly behind it, and I swear it's angled straight toward me.

Several curses escape my mouth as I drop my phone and watch it skitter across the roof. If it shatters, I won't get a replacement. The meteorite, meanwhile, does not care about my phone. It continues its advance, growing closer by the second.

There is a brief, morbidly hilarious moment where I realize

I'm not even trying to run. Thing is—I'm very good with patterns, and I notice when expected patterns change. The meteorite, or whatever it is, is *slowing and shrinking* as it nears the house. That's the only explanation for the fact that it's maintaining size and hasn't squished me like a bug.

As a science fiction fan, I'm fascinated. As an artist, I'm insulted by its blatant disregard for perspective. There are rules, you know? As a sack of meat in the path of a star, I lose track of which dots in my vision are caused by staring at the light and which are caused by forgetting to breathe.

The shooting star continues to shrink and dim as it approaches the Victorian's rooftop. It's about the size of a basketball when it stops and hovers in front of my face, giving off a faint golden light. My breath catches. This is unreal.

Unsure what to do next, I watch it lengthen into a noodle-like shape that vaguely resembles a glowing python. It wraps its impossible, glittering body around the railing of the widow's walk. I don't know the actual laws of physics, but I'm pretty sure it's breaking several. White eyes flick open on its serpentine head.

"This is new," it says.

Two

I scream. Or rather, I make the mouth shape that normally accompanies a scream. The actual sound that comes out is more like the hiss of my spirit fleeing my body. The physically impossible star lengthens to encircle the widow's walk. It glistens, glows, and expands in a way that resembles particles of sand in water.

When it speaks, its voice is two-toned: a smooth baritone sound paired with something sultry and femme. "No one has ever asked me for the same thing I ask of them before."

Again, my face shrieks, but my voice, not so much.

"What would you wager for your wish?"

"You're an alien!" I blurt, surprising even myself. "I thought you were a shooting star."

I mean, obviously it's an alien, right? Shooting stars don't fall out of the sky to answer wishes in real life. The universe is huge, though, and as far as I know, aliens might actually be real.

But wait. Did it say wager? Like it wants me to gamble for a wish? What does that mean, exactly?

I should breathe.

The serpent head closes its eyes as if in thought, then opens them again. "That is somewhat correct. By your definitions,

I am an alien and, technically, a shooting star—and you are a human in distress. I must know what that feels like."

"What do you mean *feels like*? And I'm not in distress."

Okay, I might be. But to be fair, that's my default state.

The alien-star tilts its head like an inquisitive puppy and says, "I do not experience human emotions, as I am not built the same as you. But should you consent to a competition . . . no." It blinks. "Tournament? No. Escape room . . . no. You do not have a precise word for it. But should you—"

"Absolutely not."

Oxygen returns to my brain, along with the certainty that whatever this is, it will not end well for me. I've read enough books in my life to know *escape room competition hosted by an alien* is a plot I might find in the horror section.

"Very well," the star says, unwinding itself from around the rail. "I will depart."

"Good. I'm not joining some gladiator battle for your amusement."

It halts, blinks slowly, and shakes its head. "There is no danger of physical harm, and I will only feel amusement if you do. These trials are opportunities for me to vicariously experience authentic emotions exclusive to different interstellar species."

That is a lot of words to process together, so I take my time digesting them. "You make people compete in escape rooms, and you feel what they feel while they're going through it?"

I guess that explains why it thought I wished for the same thing that it wants from me. It thinks we both want to learn about emotions. Which is kind of true—and a little sad, seeing as I'm a real human. But can it do it? Can it objectively learn love and teach me in a way that makes logical sense? How wild would it be to have accurate knowledge instead of vague symptoms and bad advice?

The star seems encouraged by my question. "For a broad definition of *people*, correct! I reconstruct your physical bodies in an environment that I create and control—and I study your responses to stimuli. The competition should only last until daylight, based on previous experiments."

I shift back to the science fiction section of my mental library. Reconstruction implies deconstruction, which is the opposite of *no physical harm*. Yet, the star makes it sound like it does this all the time. Plus, it's asking for permission. Sci-fi aliens do not typically ask their victims if they would like to be abducted.

"Why?" I ask it. "What's the point?"

"The point—" It halts its motion again, light flickering in its eyes. "One moment, the translation is complicated."

The pause gives me time to breathe and acknowledge the reality of what's happening. I'm chatting with a real space alien while standing on the roof of a stranger's house. On the one hand: What? And what? And *what*?! On the other: For the first time in my life, I'm the least awkward speaker in a conversation. Somehow, it's much, much worse.

"The point," it continues, "is scientific knowledge. I have traveled far and learned much, studying physical and biological science. Over time, that study grew tedious. I found I am more interested in the native experience of a world than its physical composition."

"You don't want to be a tourist."

The star shakes its scaly head. "Apologies, the translation is—"

"Complicated, yeah." Maybe it's the star's awkward desire for clarity that makes me want to trust it—or maybe the continued defiance of physics is too interesting for me to ignore—but I find myself considering the offer to enter a space competition. The prize is tempting, and this is certainly the most interesting thing to ever happen to me, but there has got to be a catch. "You said something about a wager earlier. What was that?"

The star coils on itself, sprouting limbs that make it look like a gecko. I watch and wonder if my body will be made of the same material if I compete. If so, will the change be permanent? I'd love to sprout wings or extra arms when a situation calls for them, but I don't want to change who I am. Not for any guy, no matter what Alex thinks, and certainly not for a sparkly snake.

"I have discovered," it says, "that there must be a risk of loss in addition to potential for gain before participants will fully invest."

There's the catch. This is like negotiating with a trickster. I need to be careful how I respond. "So, if I fail to escape, I lose . . . what?"

"You haven't said. But if you allowed me to decide, I would keep you."

"*Keep* me?" I take a step back, then wince as I slam my calf into the bucket. "What does that mean?"

"I would maintain your body as is, permanently, within a world crafted to your tastes, an asteroid in any form you desired, full of anything necessary to stimulate your mind. For my research, and—as I said—your enjoyment."

It takes a couple tries for me to find my next words. "You can create anything? Any *place*? Like, if I wanted a library with every book ever written and all of time to read them, you could make that happen?"

The star nods. "Correct."

"Some might call that a good outcome."

A mysterious being carrying me off to an alien world of over-indulgence is more escape fantasy than sci-fi or horror. I'd be lying if I said I never wondered if such a fate was so awful. After all, I rarely feel like I belong in this world, how could a magic one be worse? Just once, let me see a fantasy hero wind up in a wealthy, beautiful kingdom with delicious food and lush gardens and say, "This is pretty nice, actually."

At the same time, I would miss everyone here. And what's the point of trying to learn about love if I'll never see a human again? I can't play roleplaying games by myself, and I doubt this alien will appreciate my art. There's too much risk, even for a loner like me.

"Some might call it a good outcome," the star admits. "I suspect most would not."

No kidding.

I consider the words and tug at my sleeves, thinking of more possible gotchas. "So, if I succeed in your trials, you'll give me blueprints for love. *How* will you do that?"

The star seems momentarily flustered, but composes itself, quite literally, and answers, "I do not have the data necessary to answer your question yet, but would commit to fulfilling the bargain, should you win."

I take a deep breath, imagining all the horrors a matter-manipulating alien could cause—deliberately or accidentally—while attempting to fulfill a vague wish. This is definitely like negotiating with a trickster. The star may be doing its best to be clear, but it doesn't understand human needs. Isn't that the whole point of this?

"I don't want you to change anything about me," I declare, "even if it's the only way for me to understand. I like who I am."

"In this, we are the same."

Creepy response. Or profound. Whatever, as long as it gets what I'm saying.

A chilly breeze penetrates my sweater, reminding me that I'm trespassing on a rooftop lit by a glowing alien like a birthday party with string lights. I need to either go with the star or get out of the old Victorian before one of my neighbors looks up and spots me.

"So, if I don't escape," I ask, while searching the street below for gawkers, "I'll be stuck with you forever. And if I do, you'll grant my wish. That doesn't sound like a great deal. What are the odds of escaping this thing?"

"Ah," the star says, with a rattling breath. "Correction. If you escape, you return here as you are. To win, you must be the *first* to escape. Your odds are one in six to win, and failure to escape is rare."

Oh.

I do some mental recalculations. This wouldn't be me versus five people all competing for our freedom. It would be all of us escaping together and competing to be the first to get out. Like one of my roleplaying games, but in real life! It might even be fun.

"How long do I have to decide?"

"The competition started two minutes ago."

"*What?!*"

Now I have to add to my mental calculations the fact that I'm several minutes behind, and that the alien can apparently run the game while chatting with me on a rooftop. What *is* this thing?

"You refused, and I began without you. However, there is time to join the others, if our conversation has changed your mind."

My brain offers several unkind responses but eventually lands on "Fine. I agree."

It's probably the worst decision of my life, including that time I glued my thumb to the hem of a costume at a renaissance faire. But I have a secret weapon: I *love* logic games. Video, board, or roleplaying games, brain teasers, or puzzle boxes—anything normally chucked into an escape room, I've attempted in some form. I'm ready for the competition . . . I hope.

"Very well," the star says, and snakes itself around my legs, making me shudder at its touch. It coils upward, covering my body and face with its warm, slithering sand. "Please prepare yourself. I'm told deconstruction can be alarming."

"You know," I whisper as the light begins to blur and streak across my vision, "I'd be more concerned if it wasn't."

The lights go out, and I soar through space.

Three

My descent onto the surface of the asteroid world—an eerie floating chunk of a planet upon which, I assume, the competition will take place—can only be described as undignified. The star lowers me slowly toward the surface, allowing me a view of the fractal-patterned landscape, before releasing me several stories above the ground like a child dropping a hamster into bedding. I land, less painfully than I expect, in pink grass that smells of lavender.

I hate lavender. In my mind, it's permanently linked to perfumed soaps that break me out in hives. I quickly rise to my knees to get away from the allergen but can't help plucking a tiny blade and twirling it between my fingers.

It feels real, not grainy as the star had been, but smooth and solid as real grass. It even gets damp and soft when I crush it. The alien wasn't lying. It can make *anything*.

"Yer late!" a snarky voice shouts so suddenly I nearly swallow my heart.

"Yes, yes, upsetting the balance!" a lighter voice adds, far too close to me.

My head reflexively snaps up, and I find myself staring into the bulging yellow eyes of a gangly creature with a lemur-like face. The creature, which apparently speaks English, is three feet tall with scraggly fur and curved horns sprouting out of its head. I make an awkward attempt to stand, and instead teeter backward and fall on my bum.

I guess I hadn't thought much about it when the star had said "a broad definition of people." This is indeed very broad—even factoring in the humanoid beings my friends like to play on roleplaying nights. For a moment, I wonder if that's what this is, but one look at a familiar freckle on my palm banishes the thought that we're avatars.

For better or for worse, I'm me.

The creature waves hands with knobby fingers and cries, "We must protect the balance! We must adhere to the schedule, as the star has decreed! Do these things, and the Wondrous Grapefruit shall show us the path to victory! We shall all emerge unharmed!"

I scrabble ungracefully to my feet, more to get my face out of biting range than anything else, and take a step back. "The what? Grapefruit?"

"There are some . . . translation errors," says a man standing a few paces away.

He likely also has alien features, but they're all overshadowed by the unavoidable fact that he is almost entirely nude. I immediately avert my eyes, not because I'm some kind of prude, but because I have no desire to see a middle-aged dude in leafy hot pants.

"Yeah," says the snarky alien beside him, who has large scales, a thick tail, and a button-down shirt that barely contains its round belly. It looks almost like a pangolin, if they stood like humans and wore business attire. "The star thing's not great with nuance. You say something without a direct translation and it picks the closest word it can find. For example, everyone got my meaning when I said I'm not a flocking man to mess with, but they didn't get the expletive.

Disappointing. I pride myself on my puns."

Noted. The pangolin is a guy, flocking is a swear, and I probably shouldn't mess with him.

"So," I venture, "you aren't speaking English."

It feels like I'm stating the obvious, seeing as I'm speaking with inhuman aliens on an asteroid with no atmosphere. Surprisingly, though, I'm not concerned about the way I come across to the others. After all, there are far more pressing problems.

For starters, the whole sky is pitch black, despite visible chunks of floating rock and a sun-like star shining down upon us. How are we breathing without any air?

"See?" the pangolin says with a chuckle. "Right there, I don't think I heard the word you meant. The one I heard was hilarious, though."

Well, I'm glad he's amused. I'm completely lost. Assuming these are my competitors, how exactly are we competing? It looks like they've been standing around inside a stone circle waiting for me. What have I missed?

"The schedule!" the rodent-looking thing howls, as if in answer to my question. It seems to only be capable of speaking like a drama student auditioning for Shakespeare.

"She's right," says a velvety voice to my left, making me jump nearly out of my sweater. "Our new competitor should take a number before time runs out."

I blink, then blink again. Anthropomorphic creatures are one thing—children's TV prepared me for that—but the fourth competitor is an empty tuxedo sitting on a boulder with their feet in the air. A pair of spectacles float above their collar, and a hot-pink beverage swirls in a glass next to their empty sleeve. Are they . . . a ghost?

I shudder, rub goose bumps from my arms, and scan the boulders for a number to take, as well as competitor number five. The star said my odds were one in six, after all. To my relief, number five appears human—plus fully visible and clothed, which is apparently a bonus in outer space. He's standing a distance from the rest of us and wearing a preppy navy blazer. I think I even spot some kind of logo on the pocket.

The sight of him brings me more relief than I anticipate. I'm not alone. There's another human, and he even looks my age.

"Nah! We don't speak to that one!" the pangolin scolds, catching the direction of my gaze.

The lemur nods. "That one is a scarecrow. A bad omen!"

I raise a brow at that, assuming it's another mistranslation, but none of the other competitors react.

"It's obvious in the eyes, y'know?" the pangolin agrees. "They don't look right."

The guy in the blazer storms toward us, and I can't help but move my gaze from his dark curls to his even darker eyes. I like dark eyes. Paler ones feel more aggressive to me when I make eye contact. But I'm accustomed to dark irises and light sclera, not the other way around. His gray eyes with black sclera are difficult to look at *and* away from—causing my brain to crash like an app.

"There's nothing wrong with my eyes," the guy growls, as if continuing an earlier argument. "Everyone here looks unique. We're different species, from different planets."

"Nah!" the pangolin says again, waving a stubby hand in his direction. "It's not the color of your eyes, it's what's behind them. You're not real. Don't bother trying to convince us you are."

As far as I'm concerned, everyone present seems fictitious, but I take a calming breath and ask, "Not real?"

The mostly naked man, who I still refuse look at, explains in a haughty fashion that almost comes across as bored,

"That one can't remember what he wished for or wagered. We don't think he's a real competitor. We suspect he was fabricated by the star to sabotage us."

Fabricated? Can the star do that? I mean, it said it can make any thing or place. Can it also make anyone? If so, how do I know anybody is real? How are they so sure?

I shake my head. They're messing with me. Distracting me from whatever I'm supposed to be doing. I need to find the number that the invisible person mentioned. Where is it?

"Scarecrow," reiterates the lemur—a woman, I guess, since the others called her "she." "He is a stranger to himself! As fake as the rocks and trees around us. Be wary of that one, for he will divert you from the path of success and lead you to doom! The Wondrous Grapefruit—"

"Time's running out," the invisible person says again, silencing them all.

I spin around to better observe my surroundings, and realize how they're gauging time. There's an hourglass at the center of the stone circle, and very little sand remains at the top.

"Where is the—" I blurt before spotting an antique ticket dispenser lodged in a nearby stone. I only know what the oxidized box is because it's embossed and says as much. That's an embarrassing start to a competition of intellect, but it's clear what I have to do, so I walk over and turn a crank until a ticket pops out. "Six. I got number six."

"Course you did!" the pangolin says. "You were late!"

My brow furrows. "What's the point of pulling a number if they're all in order of arrival?"

"We don't know," the pangolin says, folding his arms.

"We *don't* know!" the lemur repeats, but in a much more joyous tone. "Isn't it wonderful not to know? To rely entirely on the senses and free ourselves of preconceptions?"

I bite my tongue. In roleplaying games, where there are no real consequences, it can be fun to meander about and discover things as I go. In the real world, I panic without plans. Thus, how I ended up here in the first place.

It's at least a relief to know I understand as much as the others do. That suggests they don't have an advantage. But nothing so far has met my expectations for an escape room. There isn't even a room.

"Not really," I mutter when I realize the lemur is expecting a response.

The invisible person goes back to drinking the hot-pink beverage in their invisible hand, liquid vanishing disconcertingly upon contact with their nonexistent lips. The gesture signals the end of their engagement, and everyone else falls silent in turn, focused on the sand in the hourglass.

Grains tumble down unbelievably slowly, and several painful minutes go by while we all fidget and stare at the thing. I hate initiating small talk, because it's hard to think of relevant subjects, and I hate when others initiate it, because I never know the expected response. But it feels like I should be strategizing now. This is free time to form alliances or work out my competitors' strengths and weaknesses. I can't just stand here watching sand.

"So," I begin, while tugging at my sweater, "should we introduce ourselves? Share where we come from?" Everyone with visible eyes stares in silence, but I continue anyway. "I'm June, from planet Earth. I'm an artist and a student and, uh, my hair isn't naturally blue. In case you thought it was."

"Councilor Yvit Squirntoes, Alpha Four, Second Quadrant," declares the pangolin.

The mostly naked man turns to face Yvit, and a pair of fuzzy wings growing from his back conceal the rear of his plant-based hot pants. I check out the patterns on the wings, which imitate angry animal eyes, and note antennae sprouting from his head. He reminds me of a cartoon fairy: tall, slender, and insect-like.

"Names have power," he spits at Yvit. "You should not give yours away so freely."

That's a weird thing to say, but the fact that he scolded Yvit and not me suggests I'm falling behind in the alliance department. Everyone else has had time to form opinions of one another, and I'm still gaping like a fish.

Yvit shrugs, and the gesture untucks a corner of his dress shirt. "I'm a career politician. Anything anyone was gonna do with my name's already been done. Trust me."

"I am Meela Cast-Stones, formerly Meela Clock-Mender, and I am an aspiring abecedarian of the Order of the Wondrous Grapefruit," declares the lemur-like creature.

I smile politely and nod. There's no way I'll remember all that, but I'll at least try to remember *Meela*. Yvit, Meela, and . . . mostly naked fairy who isn't likely to give me his name. That's three of five. I turn to the invisible person.

"No," they say before I can ask.

"Okay." I scrunch up my nose. "But can you at least tell us your pronouns? I'd rather not just guess, if that's all right."

They take a sip of their drink before responding. "Interesting question. Can I tell you? That depends. It's unlikely the star can translate the exact words. But perhaps your cultures have something similar. Feel free to use they/them pronouns, unless those inexplicably translate to grapefruit."

"That made sense to me. Thanks! And how about you?" I ask the guy everyone says isn't real. "What's your name?"

He shakes his head. "I can't remember."

"Scarecrow! Empty head!" Meela shouts, and the fairy silences her with a gesture.

"That one's name is irrelevant," he says. "I consider myself an expert in the delicate art of unfair bargains, and I assure you, it's common to plant fake participants in any contest worth manipulating. The hard part is getting away with it."

The guy presses his fingers to his face and groans. "You're all obnoxious. And if anything, my head feels too full, not empty. Finding memories is like searching through a thick layer of fog."

I frown. He doesn't sound fabricated to me. He sounds like maybe he has a concussion. Unfortunately, I have no idea what the symptoms of a concussion are, or what to do if someone has one. All I can think of is testing basic knowledge like a nurse in a bad hospital drama.

I shift my cardigan aside to expose the graphic tee beneath. "Do you know what this is called?" I ask him, pointing to it.

The guy's expression grows even colder, lips curling in a disgusted manner I've only ever seen on conceited bullies. In fact, now that I'm up close, his whole look screams *wealthy and better than you*, from his over-styled pop idol hairdo to his pristine shoes and tailored trousers. Even his blazer is partly unbuttoned to expose a designer belt buckle.

It's like he's cosplaying a wealthy jerk.

I consider myself too mature to let the garbage opinions of snobs affect me, but feel a familiar chill, nonetheless. Spending one summer in a robotics camp full of local prep school students taught me that there are certain people who can criticize *anything*. Defending yourself only makes it worse.

"It's a shirt," the guy says through his teeth, as if I've spit on his spotless shoes.

My face goes cold and hot at the same time, and I shake my hands to calm myself down. This is mortifying. Why did I get cocky because half the competitors are animals?

"Not the shirt," I reply. The words sound too desperate. Too rushed. "I mean the design. The thing on the shirt."

"A narwhal."

O-kay. I guess I never really thought through what I would do if he answered correctly—or incorrectly, for that matter. I nod and attempt a pathetic smile while observing the way his jaw clenches when he's barely concealing incandescent rage.

Anything to avoid those creepy eyes.

The self-consciousness consuming me now is not the kind I experience around Jayden. This is a guy who could chew Jayden up, spit out his bones, and drive off in a supercar while everyone gushes about his fit. His looks aren't soft and natural; they're *honed*, like he went to an expensive salon with the best photos of every teen idol and told them, "Make me look like this." His intimidation factor is somewhere between "eating in front of your celebrity crush" and "staring contest with a grizzly bear."

However, just as I decide to surrender to my urge to flee, his snarl drops into something that looks more like a stifled laugh. "Are you checking me for brain trauma with a sea mammal quiz?"

Oh no. That's even worse. I'm not going to have a single ally if he mocks me in front of everyone. "I realize that's probably not how you diagnose—" I begin.

"I appreciate that someone here is rational." He shoots a dirty glare at Meela. "But I'm not injured. In fact, I don't believe these bodies can be injured, seeing as you dropped three stories from the sky and landed without so much as a wince. I think the reassembly process went wrong."

Is that true? Are we invulnerable? If so, that is a very literal interpretation of "can't be physically harmed."

"Except," Yvit interrupts, "if you two aren't from the same place, how do you know what that animal is? I've been to a lotta planets, and I've never seen a jousting water cow."

"I have," says the mostly naked fairy, who has turned back

around, forcing me to look away. "My realm is adjacent to many others, and I have seen all manner of things. However, the physical appearance and arrival time of these two did not go unnoticed. What worlds did you say you were from?"

"Earth," I repeat.

"Leave me alone," says the preppy guy.

The fairy snorts. "That is the plan."

From the corner of my eye, I see the invisible person rise and hurl their glass at a boulder. I wince, expecting it to shatter, but it bounces and rolls in the soft grass. They stretch, notice my attention, and point a sleeve toward the hourglass—just as the last grains of sand slip through.

The stone circle and surrounding environment burst into glowing particles like the star's morphing serpent body, but more rapid and unbound. I take a deep breath and brace myself for the moment the chaotic tornado hits me.

I haven't even formed a strategy.

Four

Before I agreed to the competition, I had envisioned the "disassembly" process as something instant on a molecular level—like a sci-fi teleportation device. Current events have me slightly more concerned about the fate of my original body.

Let's just say there may be a mess waiting for the latest owners of the Vic.

Now that the hourglass has run out, I'm being treated to a shapeshifting alien's version of a theater scene change. Every inanimate object in sight is shattering into tiny bits and changing properties while whizzing through the air. It feels like I'm standing in a pot of stew while a giant stirs it with a massive ladle.

Eventually, the shards of landscape finish their dizzying transformation, and I find myself standing in a combination walled garden and iron birdcage. The star is either being dramatic by caging us inside the structure or has vastly overestimated our desire to escape into outer space.

The good: This is exactly the sort of fantasy world I was hoping for: bricks made of shimmering peacock ore, neon flowers with twisting vines, and decorative old wrought-iron fencing above and throughout the garden-cage.

The great: The lavender scent is gone, replaced by something muskier, like sandalwood or patchouli.

All five of my competitors are here with me, examining the new environment. There are no windows on the brick walls, but there is a tall gate in the center of one, through which we can see an identical garden. It's full of what look like fancy gravestones.

Goose bumps prickle my skin. Okay, maybe this isn't *exactly* the fantasy world I had hoped for. Sorry to all the characters I mocked for trying to escape such a place.

"Are those oversized playing cards?" asks Yvit as he ambles toward the wrought-iron gate. The business-pangolin walks on two legs, holding his tail up off the ground behind him, but keeps his shoulders hunched forward. I find myself wondering—for artistic reasons—how his trousers accommodate his tail.

The lemur-like Meela scurries after him, waving her knobby hands before her. "I believe they are tools of divination!"

She also has a long, furry tail, but her clothes—if you can call them that—look like random cloth draped over her body, rather than human attire.

I move closer to the gate as well, to see what the two are talking about. Sure enough, the objects I mistook for gravestones are carved stone cards shoved into the ground—each about the size of my bedroom door.

"They're both, depending on who you ask," agrees the mostly naked fairy in a know-it-all tone that irritates me—irrationally, I admit. "I've seen them before."

Weirdly, so have I. The exact images carved onto the cards are different from any I've ever seen, but the basic layout and familiar names are ones I know from back on Earth. The star—the largest, most prominent card—stands on a pedestal above the others. To its left and right are three cards each, the same number as there are competitors.

Sus.

Alex is the tarot fan in my friend group. I'll illustrate one from time to time if someone requests it as a commission, but I always have to look up the meanings on my phone. Still, I'm pretty sure some of the six represent better outcomes than the others.

For example, an emperor, in any context, is probably a better card than death. Or is it the other way around, and death is one with a tricky meaning? I wish Alex were here to advise me.

The invisible person, who I have to admit is probably the most practical in our party, locates a plaque beside the gate. It confirms what I already suspect. "We have to select one card per person to determine our roles going forward—and we have to do it in numerical order. Who has ticket number one?"

"That would be the councilor," says the mostly naked fairy, gesturing toward Yvit.

The pangolin waves his clawed hands in protest. "Wait a minute. Before we select things, we should understand what we're selecting, right? What are the rules of this game? What cards are better?"

The fairy snorts. "This is the part where I remind you that we are competitors in this event. I have no clue what the star intends, but if I did, I certainly would not tell you which card was better *before my turn*."

Yvit's shoulders slump even farther. "Right. Gotcha."

He looks deflated but walks up to the gate and gives it a little rattle. It doesn't open. He searches around for a handle or lock, then straightens, looks back to the party, and shrugs.

"Show it your number!" Meela urges while wriggling her eerily long fingers. I swear some of them are longer than the others, but she moves too quickly, and I don't want to stare.

"Show *what* my number?" Yvit snaps back, but he digs the faded ticket from his pocket and holds it up to the iron gate. When nothing happens, he lifts it toward the massive card labeled *The Star* and shouts, "Hey! I'm number one! Let me in!"

The gate unlatches.

Yvit nudges it open, steps inside, and jumps in shock as it slams shut behind him with an ear-splitting clang that reverberates around the garden. The star may not know what bricks are made of or the right word for an escape-room competition, but it knows what an aging metal gate sounds like when someone slams it shut. I get some serious haunted house vibes.

"All right, listen up," the pangolin declares, as if he's some kind of hired guide. "On the left here, we've got the fool, the hanged man, and death. Pretty straightforward imagery. Guessing these are the bad options."

"Oh, moons, no!" Meela howls, as if insulted. "Not straightforward. Not at all! There is significance to all aspects of sacred designs, from the overall palette to the filigree! Why, the numbers themselves could—"

"The other side's got the hierophant, the emperor, and the magician," he interrupts.

Her hands clasp together. "A hierophant, you say?"

All of us shoot Meela a judgmental look, except for the invisible person, who could be sticking their tongue out, for all I know.

Yvit continues, ignoring her. "All three of these, they look powerful. Emperor and hierophant are dressed pretty fancy. But this magician seems like he can do real magic, where the hierophant's kinda preachy looking. Plus, the magician is numbered one, and so am I. Think I'm leaning toward that one."

A pained sound escapes the fairy's throat.

"All right," Yvit says, even louder. "How do I pick this? Do I just—"

His stubby hand brushes the card, and light bursts from within him so bright it's like staring into a car's high beams. I wince and turn my head away, missing whatever happens next. The pangolin shrieks, and I spin back around, afraid the star has done something to him.

"Nuh-uh!" he cries. "I don't do robes. Do I look like a flocking magistrate? Get this ugly thing off me."

He wriggles out of an indigo robe that had not been on him a second before, revealing a tunic and trousers beneath, plus a leather bag that hangs at his hip. It makes him look like a ren faire attendee.

I'll admit. I kinda like it.

"The card disintegrated. Fascinating," the mostly naked fairy observes before strolling up to the gate. "Hurry up, it's my turn."

"Yeah, yeah," Yvit mutters, stomping toward the gate and nudging it open. He looks miserable, and I feel guilty for enjoying his new clothes better than his suit.

The fairy does not wait for the gate to close behind Yvit. He grabs for it and holds up his ticket, then swoops inside to claim his role. Surprising no one present, he marches straight for the so-called good options and slams a hand on the nearest one.

Again, the intense light flashes, and this time I'm not fast enough to look away. It takes a moment for the spots to clear from my vision, but when they do, it's obvious which card he selected.

Crimson regalia with intricate trim, a golden circlet of delicate leaves that complements his bedazzled bun, and a scepter clutched in one hand: He's chosen the emperor.

As pleasant as it is that he's found trousers, a knot of panic forms in my gut.

"I don't understand how this is a choice," I say, more to the star than anyone present. "I'm number six, so I get whatever role is left over. That's not fair. That's not even a challenge."

The fairy emerges and glares down at me over a slender nose and glitter-dusted cheeks. I liked him better when I was looking away. "That sounds like life to me," he says coldly before sauntering off.

I scowl. Now there are two competitors who look at me like I'm less than garbage. Great.

"I'm number three," the invisible person says with a sigh, like an exasperated teacher dealing with an unruly class. They stroll to the door, flash their ticket, and wander inside, weighing options.

Meela fidgets, knobby fingers fluttering again. "Leave me the hierophant, please! I have a strong sense that card is intended for me!"

"I'd take it just for you saying that," the invisible person replies, "but I already know which one I want."

Unexpectedly, they approach the card labeled *Death*, eliciting a high-pitched gasp from Meela.

"Not that one! You will surely doom yourself to a gruesome fate!"

The invisible person groans. "We're picking our roles, according to the plaque. By that logic, I'm becoming death, not dead. Frankly, that seems like a solid plan."

Their sleeve moves toward the card, and in a flash, their tux becomes black leather armor that seems more decorative than protective. Selfishly, my favorite detail of the fit is the black gloves that make it obvious where their formerly invisible hands are.

"Tinted glasses," invisible Death says, pushing a finger against said frames. "They don't really go with the new outfit, but I suppose it's too much to ask for vision correction from a being that can create anything it wants."

So, they're practical, tactical, and witty. I'm not ready to lump them in with the preppy guy and the emperor, but I do make a new mental box for competitors who might threaten my win.

Meela scurries to the door and bounces like a kid with an energy drink. "Hurry! Hurry! Number four! That is I!"

She squeezes between Death and the gate as they emerge, impatiently bumping both aside. As quickly as her little legs can manage, she runs with one hand extended toward the hierophant card and shouts, "I do robes! I do robes!"

A blink later, she has her robes—along with colorful beaded medallions and a leather waist-pouch of her own. That's apparently not enough swag for her, so she crouches by Yvit's discarded robe and bundles it up beneath an arm.

"Well," the fairy emperor says while she stumbles back toward the gate, "looks like we have a fool and a hanged man left. Do you think a noose is the accessory for the hanged man, or will they be hanged as part of the trials?"

He sneaks an un-subtle glance toward me like he's confident I'll get that card—or trying to influence the outcome. In a moment of miraculous clarity, I finally understand why no fantasy heroes want to live with a fairy king. Fairies are *very annoying*.

A heavy sigh comes from behind me, where the preppy guy has been silently lurking. Without a word to any of us, he proceeds to the gate and raises his ticket. Meela gives him a wide berth as she exits, as if he has a virus.

"I told you the scarecrow was a bad omen," she whispers to me as she trundles past. With several layers of robes and dangling jewelry, she appears somehow older and wiser than before. "His presence has upset the balance. I fear you shall be his first victim."

"I can hear you," he calls back. "You're not exactly quiet."

Meela cringes and hobbles farther away, mumbling, "Oh dear. Oh dear. Oh dear."

I don't yet know how to feel about her. On the one hand, she's been pleasant to me and less competitive than the rest. On the other, she comes across like some kind of wacky doom-spouting cultist. I mean, sure, that guy is intense, but I'd be grouchy if I lost my memory and everyone ganged up on me, too. Her behavior almost makes me feel a little bit sorry for him.

Not enough to say something, though. It's too early to risk upsetting her.

With only two cards remaining, the preppy guy makes his way to that side and stands between them, examining their artwork. It seems to me, regardless of imagery, there's an obviously superior choice. Yet, he rolls his shoulders before reaching for the option I never would have in his shoes.

The customary light show commences, and when it concludes, he's alive and unharmed. In place of his designer clothes, he now wears an outfit in midnight blue: a fitted jerkin with embroidered stars, loose sleeves, and modern-looking boots. One boot has a golden ring painted around the ankle like jewelry.

The guy examines his mud-splashed boots, scowls, and heads back for the gate. I stand in shock, the hairs on the back of my neck rising in suspicion of his motives. Not only did he pick the worst card, leaving me with the better option, he transformed from a stuck-up trust-fund baby to a fairy-tale rogue in the blink of an eye.

I don't like what it says about me that I appreciate the

change almost as much as I appreciate the emperor covering up. The star is even better than the guy's tailor when it comes to making clothes that complement his figure, and the costume makes me think of secrets and hidden depth, instead of cartoonishly shallow smugness.

"Get a move on, girl!" the emperor shouts while waving his golden scepter around. "Some of us still hope to win this thing."

I frown but stomp over to the gate and fish in my sweater pockets for my ticket. Up close, details in the iron stand out: curved bars shaped like meteorite tails and stars in place of fleurs-de-lis. For a being with supposedly inhuman emotions, the star enjoys its Earthlike art.

That is, assuming we weren't all chosen because we live in similar worlds.

The thought echoes in my head as I hold up my ticket and grab for the gate. Everything happening to and around me is happening because the star wants it to. The jarring personalities of my competitors, the unfairness of the challenge so far, even the nasty lavender grass all exist to get a reaction from us.

Now that I recognize that fact, it seems uncomfortably invasive.

"You're the fool," I whisper to the star, even as I set my fingers on a card with an image of a figure stepping off a cliff.

The flash of light that follows is expected, but I'm entirely unprepared for the sensation of my clothing rippling across my body. It's quick, yet I feel each section shift like ants swarming over my skin. When it completes, I look down to see what I'm wearing.

Like the others, it seems I've been given an outfit that's part historic and part modern. My linen shirt is surprisingly comfy—not scratchy like the costumes I have at home. It's puffy-sleeved, laced up at the neckline, and cinched with a sash like a swashbuckling pirate. My boots are floppy and fashionable. My trousers, however, are modern fabric—some kind of faux leather that hugs my skin—and I feel more exposed than I prefer. Heavy straps on my shoulders tell me I'm also wearing some kind of backpack.

I glance up and shrug. It's no suit of armor, but I enjoy a medieval costume that makes me feel like a sword-slinging hero. Not that I don't also love the wench look. It just doesn't feel right on me.

"Now what?" Yvit asks from beyond the gate. "What do we do next?"

"I suppose we experiment," the fairy emperor says, waving his scepter around again. "We don't yet know what these roles provide us."

Yvit crosses his arms. "I know I have a sack of nothing. What information does that provide?"

The emperor shakes his head. "You're a magician. You're meant to conjure something from the bag."

"I dunno where you come from, but my job experience includes reading things, deciding things, and getting yelled at. I can't even conjure a bathroom break some days."

"It'll come to you, I'm sure," the emperor says, half listening.

"It better." Yvit notices me exiting the gate and waves. "Hey, you! What's in your bag?"

Good question.

I heft the leather backpack—a satchel-like thing painted blue and speckled with silver stars—off my shoulders and unbuckle the top flap. Tugging it open, I'm both excited and nervous about the potential contents. But when I paw through the items inside, my heart sinks.

"It's my own stuff. Is this some kind of joke?"

The bag has makeup, toiletries, and art supplies—stuff I pack for game nights and trade shows. At the bottom is one of the old skirts I hand-made for a renaissance faire.

The emperor, predictably, snorts with laughter, but the preppy guy crouches beside me and peers into the bag. Again, the hairs on my neck rise. I don't like him so close—or judging my things.

"Does any of it have your name on it?" he asks.

I open my mouth to snap at him. Why would my name be on my stuff? Does he think I'm in grade school or something?

But then I notice his pinched brow. I'm really bad at reading expressions, even though I study faces in movies. The look he's wearing reminds me of one my mother always has after raising her voice.

Regret.

He regrets giving me this role. He's looking for a clue to his identity and thinks he would have found one if he had my bag. But why didn't he choose this role in the first place?

"What about you?" Yvit asks, jarring me away from my thoughts.

Meela shuffles through her layered robes and pulls her leather bag from beneath them. She crouches, tugs the strings apart, and dumps a small pile of rocks on the ground.

"Hah! You got rocks!" Yvit laughs.

The rodent narrows her eyes at the pangolin. "These are tools of divination!"

"Is everything a tool of divination?" he snarks.

"Oh, moons, no. But these . . . these are special. I can feel it. Ah, let me see. Let me see."

Meela flattens herself to the ground, examines the stones up close from every angle, and declares, "I understand now!"

"Care to share it with us?" asks Death.

"Certainly!" She points to her rocks, then to the garden wall behind me. "They're telling me not to leave through *that* door."

Five

The doors are new. I'm certain of it.

Earlier, when the environment exploded and we found ourselves caged inside the garden, every brick wall except the one with the gate had been solid. Now the wall directly behind me has three ancient-looking wooden doors with different scenes carved into the wood.

As the nearest to the new doors, I feel obligated to inch forward and examine them up close. Each is painted a different color, though the paint is fading and peeling in spots, exposing weather-worn wood beneath. Above them, carved directly into the stone, is the word *trial* and *1/9*.

I wonder if that's one-ninth, or one of nine? Hopefully, I won't be expected to do a bunch of mental fractions in public. In addition to blanking in front of Jayden, my mind also helpfully blanks any time I'm called on by teachers.

"Don't touch them yet," Yvit says, as if I have any intention of touching them after what happened with the other cards.

"I'm just looking," I reply, instead of rolling my eyes like I want to.

The carving on the first door looks like a party: a bunch of dancers with goblets and gowns. At the bottom, it says *Three of Cups*.

The second door has a balcony overlooking a crowd, like someone's about to give a speech. That one says it's the three of wands, but it takes me a moment to spot them in the scene.

The image carved into the third door is strange. Maybe it's some kind of preschool? There's a teacher, but the class is sitting on the ground. Again, if I hadn't read *Page of Cups* and searched the image for a drink, I wouldn't have known which card it was.

To me, that says the images are showing something other than the suits—like, for example, what trial is in store if we choose one of them.

Which means the three options are social engagement, public speaking, or school.

I sigh and turn back to the others. "Is the star picking on me, personally?"

It's a rhetorical question, but the fairy emperor takes it seriously. "Why? What exactly did you wish for?"

I flush. "I'd rather not say."

How could I even begin to explain that if the star won't provide me instructions for love, my brain will tie itself in knots trying to understand how my day went so poorly? The emperor looks like someone who goes through partners like I go through movie popcorn—barely enjoying one indulgence before he's reaching for the next one.

He doesn't hesitate to roll *his* eyes. "Fine, then. What did you wager?"

My flush deepens. "The star said it would keep me if I lost."

He nods solemnly. "You incentivized it to make you fail. That explains a lot."

"Yeah," Yvit agrees. "That wasn't wise."

Wait, what? What did they wager? I thought the whole point was that it had to be bad. The wish is the carrot, and the wager is the stick. I guess maybe they didn't wager things that would benefit the star. Crud.

"I didn't mean to!" I argue. "It didn't give me time to think. Before I even understood the deal, I was already two minutes late."

The emperor huffs and bends forward to examine the three doors himself. "You should have prepared your answers in advance, like I did."

I scrunch up my nose. "What do you mean *in advance*? The star showed up out of nowhere."

"Do you not have legends where you live?"

"Like fairy tales?" I bite my lip, realizing that may have been a faux pas, but the emperor doesn't react at all. "None that we actually prepare for. They're only stories."

"Well, there's your problem," he scoffs. "Hmm. Meela, dear. Is this one the door you said not to choose?"

I frown. The lemur-like hierophant had mentioned a door she was not supposed to pick. But if each door leads to a different location, are we meant to pick one and go together, or take different paths?

Meela looks up from where she still sits, fussing over her bag of stones, and the emperor gestures toward the public-speaking door. She shakes her head.

"That one is acceptable, as is the classroom one to the right. We should avoid the one on the left."

"All of us, though?" Yvit asks, echoing my unspoken concerns. "I mean, I hate to be obnoxious, but we don't know enough about this place yet to assume we can skip a door and all make it out."

That makes total sense. What if we need to combine things from each of the three trials in order to escape? This doesn't feel like the right time for assumptions.

"Agreed," says the fairy. "Someone here must go through that door. But not I. I choose the one in the center."

Yvit shrugs. "I opened my mouth, so I guess I can—"

"No. You're coming with me."

The pangolin puts his hands on his hips, a gesture that probably looks intimidating rather than adorable wherever he's from. "Pardon?"

"I'm rather skilled at manipulating a crowd, but at home, I require multiple advisers to ensure the decisions I make are grounded. You appear to be an experienced strategist. It only makes sense for us to work together."

"But—"

The preppy guy steps up, interrupting their debate. "I'll take the left door. None of you care what happens to me, anyway."

An uncomfortable silence stretches over the group as he moves to the door with the three of cups. My chest tightens a little with guilt, because I know what it feels like to be excluded. The sensation grows worse with every second that no one contradicts his statement.

What if I was too quick to judge him? Worse, what if I judged him *entirely* on his clothes? Isn't that something that makes me angry when I think others are doing it to me?

"I'll go with you," I blurt, and hurry over before I can second-guess myself. Third-guess myself? Whatever guess I'm on now.

It earns me a raised brow from the guy, and I cringe, realizing what I've set myself up for.

The fairy harumphs. "You make terrible decisions, girl. Anybody ever tell you that?"

Other than myself? Yes. Often.

"I choose the school!" Meela cries, scurrying over to that door. "We should all be seeking enlightenment. Perhaps the education inside will unlock spiritual abilities or meditative healing."

"Or algebra," I mutter.

"I," says Death slowly, as if considering every word, "do not think anyone should be on their own until we know what the rules are. I'll follow the hierophant for now. I suspect we'll be allowed to choose different partners for the eight trials that come after."

So, it *was* one of nine! That's a relief.

"It's decided, then," the fairy emperor says, licking his lips and reaching for the handle of his door. "Shall we find out what's inside?"

Everyone winces as he opens the door to the sound of an already-roaring crowd, just as depicted on the outside. He partially closes it, takes a deep breath, then flings it wide and strolls through with his arms raised above his head.

"My people!" he shouts before Yvit hurries after and slams the door behind him, silencing the garden.

"We should go, as well," Meela says, opening her much more subdued door.

Wind-chime music and scribbling noises waft out, along with the scent of burning incense. She and Death slink through the door and shut it respectfully behind them.

This means I'm now alone with the fellow Meela called "a stranger to himself"—though he's technically the least strange competitor, if appearance is the only metric. It's far too late to dwell on whether I've made a huge mistake, so instead I dwell on all the ways I might make things even worse for myself.

For example—should I attempt to small talk the alien who looks at me like a stain on his shirt? Or should I let the awkward silence drag on for the duration of the competition? Decisions, decisions.

"You ready?" he asks, setting a hand on the knob.

Am I ready to go into an escape room created by an alien who's psychologically torturing me just to see how I'll react?

Not really.

I nod, shake my head, and nod again, eliciting an unwelcome chuckle from the guy before he tugs the door open. Loud, warbling music spills out, making all the muscles in my shoulders tense, but I follow him through and into a space I would never associate with escape rooms.

On any social media app, if you follow enough artistic accounts, eventually you'll encounter someone sharing photos of old palaces. Many such posts feature massive ballrooms with ornate columns and chandeliers. The room on the other side of the door makes all those spaces look restrained.

The round ballroom I enter is so tall, it could be the courtyard of a fancy hotel if not for the lack of balconies. I'm awed by the intricate detail in the hand-carved molding and repeating archways. Two stories above, a thin layer of transparent film stretches wall-to-wall, separating the floor from the domed fresco ceiling. On the film, a ridiculous amount of glitter pulses and bounces like boiling water.

"Whoa," the preppy guy says, taking another step into the room.

I follow him, grimacing, and note that the doorway vanishes behind us the moment we're through. We're trapped—for now.

Above, the glitter vibrates across the film to the droning of instruments and boom of drums, obscuring painful spotlight beams. The result is an effect like rolling storm clouds projected on every surface below—including eight crystals taller than I am, with silver bowls resting at their bases. Apparently, spotlights, glitter, and crystals weren't painfully bright enough for the star, so it felt the need to add mirrors to the mix.

"This is gonna make me sick," I moan, backing away from the ballroom floor—which also has dozens of dancers upon it, all decked out in formal wear and creepy masks.

Fortunately, between each of the eight crystals are archways that exit into a ringlike hall. It encircles the entire dance floor and provides a tempting escape from the chaos. The preppy guy scowls as I flee to the hallway, which muffles the music well.

"I wasn't finished looking around," he says, as if my overwhelm is an inconvenience. "Let's go back."

"I'm not stopping you," I snap. It's kinder than what I want to say. I'm not taking orders from some snob, no matter what he's used to back at home. "I need a minute. The star's overwhelming me on purpose so it can feel what it's like to be dizzy, or whatever."

The preppy guy doesn't walk away. His strange eyes sparkle as he watches the multicolored clouds roll over the walls. "You don't think it's amazing in there?"

I take a deep breath and glance back. Now that I'm outside looking in, I recognize the ballroom for what it is—beautiful chaos. "Only accidentally. It's pretty because nature is pretty, not because the star knows what it's doing."

He raises his voice to be heard over a parade of dancers holding singing bowls. One at a time, they step into the hallway, turn, and march out again. The change in volume makes him sound even more hostile than he seemed before. "This is natural to you? What's your planet like?"

Great. Now the preppy guy thinks I come from a world of glitter parties. Not that there aren't glitter parties on Earth, but they don't, like, spring whole from the ocean.

"No. I mean—" I pause to organize my thoughts. Too much noise and movement can make it hard for me to concentrate. "It's like a grade school science project. Vibrations and reflections with interesting effects. I think the star learned about dances from watching our worlds but doesn't know how they're supposed to make you *feel*. So, it's just barfing light and sound all over the room."

He pauses to watch, and I brace myself for the dismissal I'm accustomed to when sharing my ideas with strangers. Something about being awkward and female renders my theories automatically invalid. In fact, I'm so sure he'll *well actually* me, I'm caught off-guard by his next question.

"What's a dance normally feel like?"

That's a good question. How a dance makes me feel has a lot to do with my company. They can be thrilling, fun, intimidating . . . or romantic.

But shouldn't he know that?

I pause the ideas I'm processing so I can re-evaluate him. He no longer wears the clothes that convinced me he was a stuck-up trust fund baby, but he still looks like someone popular, someone others would invite to events, even if he felt the events were beneath him. Assuming his planet has dances, there's no way he hasn't been to one. Dressed as he was, I wouldn't be surprised to learn his parents have a ballroom in their house.

"Are you asking what it feels like to me, or in general?" I probe.

His brow pinches. "In general. I understand everything in this room, but I can't remember experiencing anything like it before."

Two thoughts flash rapidly through my mind.

First, and most ridiculously, I imagine for a moment that the others are correct, and he's made of star stuff—in a different way than I am. However, it's much more probable that my assumptions about his planet are wrong. Though, what kind of wacky comic book world has blazers with logos and no dances?

And for that matter, how did a pangolin wind up with a button-down shirt and tie?

"I'm not sure I'm the right person to explain how things are supposed to feel," I admit. "If I were, I wouldn't be here. I'd be in a very different place with a very different guy."

His eyes narrow. "I don't follow."

The glare sends goose bumps down my arms. He's like the human equivalent of watching a nurse prepare your shot. Everything he says either catches me off-guard or puts me on edge, but I can't seem to shut up.

Oh well, it's not like I'll see him after this. Might as well be direct.

"When the star came to me," I tell him, "I was having a really bad day. A guy I'm into was a jerk, and it left me kind of confused. So, I wished for instructions to understand love—that way, next time I'll know if it's real and how I'm supposed to act."

That explanation managed to gloss over almost all the embarrassing details, so I'm grateful when he accepts it and returns his attention to the ballroom. "Are you feeling any better, now?"

"A little." It's technically true. I've traded dizziness for social discomfort, but that only further motivates me to escape. I squint into the ballroom in search of clues. "Any idea what we're supposed to be doing? Do we need to solve puzzles, or just look for an exit?"

He wiggles his fingers in a decent imitation of Meela. "Isn't it wonderful not to know?"

"It isn't," I say, trying my best not to smile. I'm not sure if he's being intentionally funny, or just mocking the hierophant. "All right, I'm ready."

I can do this. I think.

The shift in lighting and acoustics as I step through the archway and among the dancers feels like a direct punch to the face. Gazing at my feet to avoid the glare, I follow a curved bit of inlaid metal in the floor, hoping it will lead somewhere. Unfortunately, it leads me directly into a singing dancer in a taffeta gown. She rounds on me, furious, and I gasp.

Her mask isn't just bizarre. It's unnerving. The eyeholes on it number six, and it's not clear if only two contain eyes. She's shouting something nasty at me, punctuating every other word with malice, while jabbing taloned fingers at my chest. I can't make out a word in the din.

Even worse, more dancers have gathered to gawk, all wearing the same style mask. Some shout along with her, and others snicker. Their mocking laughter is eerily familiar, as if the star has lifted and replayed a sound bite from my failed flirtation with Jayden. My face heats. Meanwhile, the other revelers continue their dance as if I'm not even here.

Drummers drum. Horns drone. People of all different shapes and sizes—some humanoid and some alien—march and weave and spin around me as my mind empties like a beach at high tide. It's too much. I need to break away.

"Take the chalice," the preppy guy commands, close enough to hear over the droning.

"Chalice?" I shout, but hold out my hands, unsure what chalice I'm taking, or why.

Frustrated, the woman yells again and shoves a golden chalice into my hands. She waves one arm toward something in the distance, and when I turn, I spot a refreshment stand tucked into the hallway across the room.

"Oh!" I cry as understanding dawns, and I'm handed another dancer's cup.

The preppy guy accepts a chalice of his own and tilts his head to indicate we should go. This time, I don't mind taking his lead. The relative calm of the circular hallway is a massive relief to all my senses.

"They think we're waitstaff?!" I holler before catching

myself and lowering my volume to match the quiet of the hall. "You think it's because we're not in costume?"

It feels ridiculous to say after receiving the equivalent of a wardrobe swap only a couple minutes ago, but we both have relatively plain outfits on compared to the revelers—and no masks to blend in. Unless . . .

"Over here," I say, darting around the hallway to a secluded area between two archways. An end table and elaborate mirror decorate this portion of the hall.

"Did you notice any clues in there?" he asks as he follows. "Anything that looked like part of a puzzle, or a door?"

"I noticed way too much noise and light again." I leave out the embarrassment and reminders of extremely fresh wounds.

"I'm sorry," he says, and I almost believe it, even though he's the one who dragged me in there. At least it helped me form a plan.

I shimmy out of my leather backpack, set it on the end table, and rummage through the contents for the costuming supplies I saw earlier. While I hunt, he leans over my shoulder as if he's judging my stuff again. I glance up at his reflection in the mirror, ready to accuse him of being a pest, and realize he's staring at himself.

One hand moves up to his pop-idol hairdo and brushes at a loose curl. From there, his fingers drift down to his cheekbone, just below one of his inky-black eyes. The gray iris moves side to side, and the corners of his mouth twitch downward.

It strikes me this may be the first time he's seen himself since his arrival, and he may have no memory of his face. I'm torn between empathy for his situation and concern that if he likes what he sees, he's going to be intolerable.

Either way, it feels nosy to watch, so I return my attention back to the leather bag and tug a layered skirt from inside.

It's something I made from scraps of colored cloth for a ren faire and re-used for roleplaying nights. Recently, I've been playing a magic-wielding dryad, and the skirt helps me get into character. It's not as fancy as anything the dancers have on, but I'd feel smothered in their dresses any—

"Does my appearance make you uncomfortable?" he asks, staring directly at me this time.

I freeze, one foot already in the skirt. I should lie. This isn't the time for oversharing. He's in a bad place. I've been in a bad place all day. Nothing good can come from—

"Not for the reason you think," I blurt.

Betrayed! By my own mouth. I thought we agreed we were going to lie?

"Why, then?" he asks. He doesn't look mad.

I tug the skirt up to my hips. "I know it's wrong to judge people by their clothes, but some folks dress how they want to be seen. You know what I mean?"

"No."

Whoof. I suck in a breath and break eye contact, digging in the backpack for my leaf-shaped leather mask. Again, it's nothing like the ones on the dancers, some of which have animal faces and antlers, but it's all I have. It has to work. Meanwhile, I can feel the guy's stare burning a hole in the side of my head. He's waiting for an explanation, and I can't fidget my way out of it.

I give up.

"Where I come from, people who dress like you were when we met are trying to show off wealth. It's insensitive to boast that you can drop car money on a belt while normal folks are struggling with rent. So, when I saw you—"

"You assumed I was cruel."

Suddenly, it's difficult to breathe, and I can't swallow the guilt in my throat. It's one thing to think something mean about someone, and another to say it to their face. I can't look at him. His odd eyes crease with hurt or shame—or some other emotion I can't read. What's wrong with me? Why can't I shut up?

Desperate for any change in topic, I set my mask down on the table and frantically fish for a sketchbook and marker. We need to re-focus on the trial. That's what we're here for, isn't it?

"I've only got one mask," I begin, ready to rattle off my plan, but he cuts me off.

"Let me try something."

He lifts both hands to his perfectly coiffed hair, watching himself carefully in the mirror, and rapidly scrubs his fingers through it, undoing all the pop-star styling. The result is a mop of messy black curls that reminds me of a cocker spaniel. Once done, he repeats the process with his brows, which are shaped and gelled into place. I bite my lip. Does he have eyeliner, too?

"Is that better?" he asks, after rubbing his whole face. "Does it make you more comfortable if I don't look so artificial?"

It kinda does, and that makes me feel even worse. It's not like I'm repulsed by conventional beauty. It's just that the work required to maintain it suggests priorities that differ from my own.

"You didn't have to do that," I mutter.

"Eh. I didn't like the way it looked, either."

I blink. "Seriously? I wonder why you did it in the first place, then."

"Same." He frowns and takes a deep breath. "What do you think all this says about me? Do I care more about other people's opinions than my own?"

Hey, you, guy. Stop stealing my lines. Overanalyzing is *my* thing.

"Hold still," I tell him, and lift the marker horizontally in front of his face.

I slide my fingers along its length to measure the distance between his pupils, then rapidly sketch out a mask in my sketchbook. On it, I doodle wolf-like features with scribbled fur and pointy ears. It's kind of a long shot.

"What if I *am* cruel?" he asks as I hunt for my emergency sewing kit. "What if I'm a jerk and don't know it?"

Memories of spiraling when Alex called Jayden a special interest replay in my mind. It was *so easy* to question my own feelings when someone I trusted had questioned them first. Not that I wouldn't have spiraled anyway—but Alex's pep talk sure didn't help. And here I am, doing the same to this guy, who doesn't know himself well enough to object.

I'm the jerk here, not him.

I cut the paper mask off its page using painfully tiny sewing scissors, then thread a needle and poke it through one side. "Maybe everyone dresses like that on your planet, or you were wearing some kind of costume. Either way, this is the only *you* I'll know, unless the star fixes your memory."

"If I'm cruel, maybe I shouldn't be fixed."

I frown. "That's a horrible thing to say."

"It's true, though. I can see the hatred when you look at me."

That's a trap. I'm not responding to that. There's no way to explain that I don't really hate him without confessing that on Earth he'd look down on me. A guy who can afford tailored trousers and a girl who buys dye at a pharmacy? We'd be from different worlds even if we were both Earth-human.

Come to think of it, that may explain my attraction to Jayden. Sure, he's scruffy, car-obsessed, and appreciates exactly none of my hobbies, but he comes to school each day in the same T-shirts he uses when he changes his oil. He doesn't care what anyone thinks of him. Maybe that fooled me into believing he'd accept me for who I am as well.

I hold the paper mask up to the formerly preppy guy's face and loop the thread around his head, securing it to the paper on the other side. Once the band is tight, I snip the thread and point him toward the mirror to get his opinion. His expression doesn't change.

"No offense, but I don't think I can wear this, and it won't fool anyone out there," he says.

Okay, he has a point. The mask makes him look like a cartoon villain, not a fancy ballroom dancer, and that's probably not how he wants to be seen with the way everyone is treating him. It's the best I can do with what I have, though, so I shrug and tug my leather one on.

"I'm hoping the dancers are, like, preprogrammed or something, and any effort we put in will go a long way. Otherwise, I don't know how we're expected to— What?"

He gapes at me, wide-eyed. "How did you do that?"

"Do what?"

"You don't even look like yourself."

"It's just an old—"

I spot my reflection in the mirror, and it steals the rest of my words from my lungs.

The woman who stares back looks nothing like me.

Six

I raise a finger to prod my cheek and watch the woman in the mirror do the same. To my relief, my skin feels like mine—soft, plump, and thinly coated with hypoallergenic products. The woman in my reflection, on the other hand, has sharp cheekbones, hollow cheeks, and makeup straight out of a tutorial.

There's perfect eyeliner beneath her catlike mask.

Berry-kissed lips under its feline nose.

I'm kind of smitten with her . . . and a bit jealous.

If I really looked like that, I'd have a sponsored influencer channel and my own studio apartment. Not only would Jayden stop laughing at me, he'd have to fight ten guys for my attention. Guys with names like Val and Huntsley. Guys who look like the one beside me.

A little shiver runs down my spine, and I check to see if he's still staring. He is, but not in an ogling way—more like he's seeing a creepy ghost. And no wonder; even my hair has changed from blue to white with opalescent glitter. I look like some kind of fantasy snow queen.

Out of scientific curiosity, I reach up and slide the leather mask to my forehead, marveling as the illusion fades, revealing my real—and less glamorous—face.

He removes his paper mask and crosses his arms. "Well, that's settled. You'll have to mingle to gather clues. I'm stuck on beverage duty."

I pale.

The only thing more intimidating than joining a dizzying dance with a stranger is joining a dizzying dance by myself. I *can* dance—and sing—if I'm with my friends. But these are not my friends, and this is not my sort of dance.

Then again, if I'm wearing the mask, it won't be me everyone is laughing at if I elbow someone and cause a scene. It'll be that woman with white hair and berry lips.

"Maybe we should circle the hallway first," I suggest, hoping my desperation isn't showing, "before we head back into the center. For all we know, there could be a hidden exit."

He glances toward the nearest archway. "The star's put a lot of effort into the dance for it to be a red herring, but you could be right."

I sigh and shove my crafting supplies back into my backpack. He can see right through me. I don't know why he's playing along.

"Never mind," I say. "I'll go in. I guess I'm just a little nervous. If something happens and I need you quickly, what should I shout? Have you remembered your name?"

He shakes his head. "No, but I feel like it was short. A single syllable, maybe."

"Fred?" I ask half-jokingly.

He shakes his head but makes a motion as if encouraging me to try again.

"Maybe Jack? Kai? Dan? Luke?"

He shrugs, then stares absently through the archway. "It could have been any one of those. Hey—do you see something shiny in the glitter?"

I look, wince, and look away again. Everything in the

glitter is shiny.

"Maybe you should pick a temporary name," I suggest, "so I have something to call you."

"If I must. What were my options again?"

I grimace. None of those names feel right for him. Maybe I can try to pick something more fitting. I eye him. Despite the rogue-like jerkin, he's not gritty, edgy, or super-swole. With the makeup gone, his face is less striking, handsome, but not abnormally so. There's nothing distinguishing about him. Except—

"How about Cole?" I ask.

"I don't hate the way it sounds. But why that one?"

Oh, wait.

I realize far too late that I've stepped in it again and need to stop talking. Meanwhile, my mouth continues to betray me. "Well, where I come from, there's a rock that's black and—"

"Oh, right. Coal. I get it now."

He's not amused.

Blood drains from my face, and I consider fleeing to the dance floor, where I can apparently do less damage. "Sorry. I'm sorry. That was offensive."

He leans out into the ballroom space, examines something in the glitter above, and leans back into the hallway to respond. "It's a little *insensitive*, as you would say, to nickname someone after a physical feature just because it looks different to you."

This is it—the worst moment of my life. If it were possible for a human to combust from shame, I'd be ash. I'm terrible. I deserve Jayden's laughter, and then some.

The guy smiles, and it almost seems genuine, though his words drip with satisfaction, as if he's just beat me at a game of cards. "I know you didn't mean it that way, though. That's not the kind of person *you* are, or you wouldn't think so poorly of me. So, you must think my eyes are attractive."

Hah! Joke's on him. I'm incapable of thought. I'm waves of despair, personified. I'm terror so bright, it could power a planet. I'm standing here with my mouth open and failing to respond, again.

"Sorry," I repeat. "I've only ever named pets and game characters before, and you don't look like a Mister Fluffy Boots."

His smile widens. "You don't know that. I might enjoy Mister Fluffy Boots. But how do you feel about Sol? Is that a decent name?"

Humor. He's not offended, just tormenting me. I try to get my breathing under control and ask, "Sole? Like a shoe?"

"No, like solar." He points to the fresco above the glitter. It has a vaguely sun-shaped outline that is almost impossible to look at through the lights. "It's similar to Cole in sound."

It *is* similar—and that's weird, because up until this moment, I had forgotten that all the competitors speak alien languages. What are the odds that in the guy—Sol's—language, *Cole*, *coal*, and *Sol* all rhyme? That's not even true for all languages on Earth.

"Are you sure you're not speaking English?" I ask.

His smile falters. "Why? What if I am?"

"Well," I say, and chew my lip in thought. "It could mean we're from parallel universes. Like in sci-fi. Two worlds that are identical, but with tiny differences. Like our eyes."

His grin returns. "Makes you wonder what else is different."

I know he means between our planets, but my mind goes somewhere else entirely and my body prickles in response. It's time to escape this conversation.

"Can you describe the thing in the glitter so I can look for it?" I ask, words tumbling from my mouth.

He blinks. "Yeah, of course. It was long and thin—maybe the size of a spoon—and golden."

"All right. I'll go try to find it." I take a deep breath and tug

the mask down
"You sure?" he asks.
"Yeah."
This is for the best. I've made up my mind.

The dancers dip into the archway one at a time as if in a line dance, and I wait for the right moment to join. It's like timing a jump in a platform game. Finally, I spot a break between a woman with a singing bowl and a man playing a curved horn. The horn makes a warbling sound that clashes with the ring of the bowl and makes my eardrums itchy from the hum. But a space is a space.

Keeping step as well as possible, I join the dance line and find myself inadvertently looping the room, stuck in an oval that dips briefly into the hallway on either side. It gives me time to examine the inlaid metal spiral on the floor, as well as the crystal statues on either side of the archways. They look like amethyst clusters up close, if amethyst clusters were ten feet tall and all held shiny bowl-shaped mirrors.

Those mirrors, I've decided, are the worst feature of the ballroom. Every so often, enough glitter shifts that a whole spotlight beam catches one. It reflects the light back up against the film, causing bursts of pinpoint sparkles with afterimages that linger like fireworks in my vision.

I'm starting to get annoyed.

It's like everything here—the lights, the colors, the droning music, even the laughter of the crowd—is deliberately grating. The star must be eager to experience frustration, because that and a headache are all I'm feeling.

My teeth grind, and I force myself to stare at the glitter, no matter how much it stings. I don't care if I walk right into someone. I don't care if I cause a scene. These people aren't real—they're non-player characters like in a roleplaying game—and I'm finding that shiny spoon thing to make amends to Sol no matter what.

Several seconds later, I spot it. Something larger and shinier than glitter *is* bouncing on the film. Something golden, polished, and shaped like—

"A key!"

I know Sol can't hear me, but I shout it anyway. The key moves with the vibrations of the instruments, just like the glitter all around it. I need to find a way up there somehow, but the film is so high, and I have no ladder. There's a punctured spot in the center of the film, though, where puffs of glitter sprinkle down on the dancers. Maybe I just need to widen that hole.

Someone prods my arm, making me squeal. It's Sol, but before I can point out the key, he's dragging me from my line dance and back to the hall.

"Couldn't you hear me?" he asks. "I've been shouting your name."

"No. Why?"

"I've figured something out."

He takes me to the back of the hall, where we can see more of the ring, and points to the archways on either side.

"Watch the dancers," he says.

One at a time, they appear in the archways, turn around, and head back in, just as I had.

"It's always the same people in the same order," he says. "On both sides of every arch. I went all the way around the ring to check."

I nod. "That's because they're doing line dances, but in big ovals."

"Right. But all together, they're forming a star made of those ovals. Except those."

He points to a handful of people who are dancing in a circle, rather than an oval. They hadn't been noticeable from the inside, where everyone was twirling and weaving together. But from the outside, it looks like they fell out of their oval, and two archways are empty because of it.

"What makes them different?" I wonder aloud.

"For starters," Sol says, "all but three of them have drinks in their hands."

My eyes widen as I recognize their creepy masks. "They're the singers who gave us their cups! I didn't notice they were in a different pattern."

"I don't think they were, originally," he says. "I have a theory. Stay here and watch."

With that, he returns to the beverage cart, fills the three chalices with punch, and marches out onto the dance floor with the nimble bearing of an experienced waiter. When he reaches the three, they collect their drinks, each saying something that may have been thanks. One even gives Sol a dramatic curtsy, which seems a little over-the-top.

I ignore the pang of discomfort I feel when the woman very obviously checks him out, and make a mental note that I'm feeling no urge to taste the crimson punch myself. It's possible our star-stuff bodies don't require food or drinks. If I lose, I'll make the star change that. There's no way I'm living in a magical world without sampling every food I've ever craved.

Sol makes his way back, and the chalice-holders restart their playful dance, this time in an oval.

"Did it work?" he asks.

"They're back in sync with the others. Is that useful?"

"It has to be part of the puzzle. If we disrupt the dancers, it changes their path from an oval to a ring or vice versa. I'm not sure what we're meant to do with that information, though. I only got this far."

I watch the glitter bounce to the thump of the drums, and note where it clumps and where it spreads. "I have an idea, too, but I may need to draw it on paper to explain."

Sol's eyes sparkle in a way I'd never have thought them capable of before. Something about this discovery has lowered his defenses a bit.

"All right," he says. "Let's see it."

I begin.

Seven

As predicted, interrupting the line dancers is more challenging for Sol than me, thanks to my shapeshifting mask. He manages to stop the singing loop again by offering to refill several cups, but the drummers ignore him, and the strings shrug him off. That means I have to sort them out, whether I like it or not.

"Excuse me," I say to a passing drummer in my best impression of flirtation, "but your drum looks so unique. Is it handcrafted?"

The tall man in an insectoid mask smiles at me with bleached teeth and slows to show me the instrument. It has a fancy head with iridescent scales. "Very good eye. I procured this from an estate auction for a fraction of its true value. The poor grieving fellow didn't realize what he had!"

"Baloney!" an older woman behind him shouts, causing him to spin and hold up the line. "It's only plastic, dear, but it sounds just as nice. By which I mean he should have brought a tambourine."

"Like you would know quality if you saw it!" the man retorts before turning on his heel and storming off—effectively restarting the dance.

Good. That was easier than expected.

I shake my hands to relieve my nerves and repeat the act with the strings and singing bowls, interrupting each oval with a relevant query until all the dancers are in concentric circles.

"It's not enough," Sol says with a shake of his head when I catch up with him in the hallway.

He's right. Something about my plan isn't working.

I walk to the concession stand, which I've covered in my stuff, and review the sketches in my notebook. My plan was to get all the revelers as close to the center of the ballroom as possible. If the glitter and key are bouncing to vibrations, it makes sense that more noise would bounce them more—putting stress on the hole in the center of the film.

Unfortunately, the glitter isn't bouncing more. It's just bouncing *differently*.

"I don't suppose you could convince the dancers to toss their instruments at the ceiling?" he asks.

I shake my head. "Trust me, they aren't going to do that, and they'll likely turn on us if we try."

He frowns. "It has to be the vibrations, then. What if we move the drummers to the center? They make the glitter bounce more than anything else."

It's a thought, but I have a feeling it won't work. We've missed something obvious. I rub my temple, which is starting to throb, and observe the glitter for the millionth time. It skitters like startled cockroaches with every heavy beat of the drums, but not in a way that makes me think it will pool in the center or wear at the film.

"Why are there no chairs in the hall?" I complain. "I can't even think straight, I'm so exhausted."

"Are you getting sick again?" He turns his attention back to me. "Take off your mask. Let me see your real face."

I haven't stopped feeling sick this whole time, and he knows it. Still, I do as he asks, and he draws close in the uneven light. Emergency sirens go off in my mind as he steps into my personal bubble.

"You look pale," he says with a tenderness that sends pinpricks of heat across my cheeks. "You should sit down and rest before you pass out."

"Good idea," I mumble, breaking away from him before he notices the flush and thinks I'm feverish. I find a spot against the wall and lower myself to the cool floor. It feels better than I want to admit.

Once again, I expect Sol to puzzle-solve while I recover, and once again, he remains by my side. Though I close my eyes to block out the flashing lights, I can feel his presence and hear him shifting as he plunks down next to me.

I'm not used to having strangers so close, but his presence is comforting. Funny what something as simple as actually talking to another person can do.

"I know I haven't been the best company," I confess, "but I'm glad I ended up with you and not the half-naked fairy."

"Fairy?" He chuckles. "Is that what you call the moth man? I hadn't made that leap, but I can see it."

I rub at my stinging eyes. "I guess I just assumed that's what he was. Maybe I read too many books."

"No such thing."

Does Sol remember reading books, or is he just better at small talk than me? Probably the latter.

"Do you think the emperor finished his trial?" I ask.

"If the trial has something to do with verbal abuse and arrogance, he certainly seems predisposed to that."

Hah! I guess I'm not the only person sizing up the competition. Though, in the case of the emperor, his behavior makes it very easy. I just wish I knew what the rules were. My prior experience with escape rooms has me instinctively collaborating with Sol, but what if I'm meant to be competing with him?

No. That wouldn't work. If we sabotaged each other, we'd spend the whole night moving dancers around. Plus, he's sitting here beside me instead of trying to escape. He must have come to the same conclusion.

"They're probably all finished," I moan. "If Death is right and we're meeting up at the end, I bet they're all sitting around waiting for us."

"Let them wait. Your health is more important."

He's starting to sound like my mom.

"I'm actually feeling a lot better now that I'm not directly in the lights. I think when we moved the dancers around, the beams started hitting the mirrors more."

Sol goes silent, then abruptly stands. "You're right! Stay here a second while I look."

I don't need to be asked twice to remain in dim light and relative quiet. But when he finally returns, the excitement in his voice makes me stumble to my feet.

"That was it!" he exclaims, flailing excitedly toward the ballroom. "The beams are hitting the mirrors more often—and the mirrors are acting like a focus. Guess where they're all aimed?"

My eyes widen. "The hole in the center of the film! It's not a tear. It's a burn!"

"Exactly!"

"So, we just need to get all the beams to the mirrors and let the reflections do the work."

"Right! But how do we shift the glitter around so every mirror gets a beam?"

The past hour of glitter observation falls into place on my mental map, and I rush to the nearest archway to show him. "First, let's get the drummers into the hall. If the sound from out there is quieter in here, maybe the opposite is also true. Maybe without the drums, the glitter will pool instead of bouncing."

"That might work!" He looks genuinely impressed. "But you'll have to do it. None of the drummers will stop for me."

I begrudgingly return to the dance floor, slapping the mask down over my face and feeling its weight like never before. Fortunately, I know my routine and it's easier to do the second time around. I confirm the result when I get back to Sol and give him the rest of my fully formed plan between the booms of circling drums.

"Next we change the order of the rings," I tell him. "We'll do the opposite of what we did before. Singers in the center, horns and bowls in the middle, and strings on the outside ring."

"I guess I'm on singer duty, then," he says, and trots off to rearrange them—presumably with more beverage queries.

I focus on the dance line with horns and bowls, reusing the trick of querying them until they argue about which is better. From there, only the strings remain, but I can already see the glitter shifting. It skitters toward the center, uncovering all but a handful of mirrors. The film bubbles where the lights focus, puffing more glitter through the hole than before—most of which lands in Sol's messy curls. He shakes it out like a wet dog and gives me an enthusiastic thumbs-up.

I grin despite the chaos around us. We're going to get along after all—assuming this trial doesn't conclude with the two of us battling over an exit.

"Is a viola harder to play than a violin?" I ask a dancer after moving closer to an archway.

That earns me a rude hand gesture, but the dancer has to pause their playing to do it, and that has the desired effect. The strings start moving in a ring, and I turn my attention back to Sol.

"Don't stand right in the center!" I shout, gesturing at the film, which is starting to warp.

He squints like he can't hear my words and also gestures to the film, where a sun-like shape of glitter is forming. It's a perfect replica of the fresco after which he's named himself. I'm enjoying his genuine giddiness after he's been closed off and grumpy for so long, but I'm concerned he isn't paying attention to his impending glitter bath.

Ugh. I'm going to have to get him out.

With effort, I duck and weave through the dancers and into the center to drag him away.

"The glitter's about to drop on your head," I explain, far too late.

With all the mirrors exposed to spotlight beams, the thin film suddenly bursts into flame. What I had envisioned as a widening hole pouring glitter onto Sol's head is instead a flash fire that obliterates the film and dumps smoking glitter across the whole ballroom. I shriek, and Sol throws his arms above my head to protect me from the bulk of it.

All at once, the sounds in the ballroom change. Revelers scream and flail as they flee, vanishing into the doorless hallway. As they do, the spotlights abruptly cut out, plunging the room into an eerie darkness lit only by creeping flames along the walls.

Safety lights come on at the edges of the floor, adding a dim yellow glow to the orange, and the most horrible sound of the day comes blasting from seemingly everywhere at once. It is, unmistakably, the hum of bass speakers cranked up way too high.

I hate it.

I slam my hands over my ears, shut my eyes, and bury my face in Sol's shoulder as a chilly breeze whips the glitter around us.

It's possible some of the low moaning is actually coming from my mouth, but I can't hear myself over the punishing bass. I try to become one with Sol's jerkin, which is a lot softer than it looks, and wonder how my perfect plan missed the fact that we were pointing hot lights at thin plastic.

Eventually, the bass stops, the wind dies down, and the room falls silent. I tentatively peel myself from Sol's shoulder and assess our current situation.

The fires are out.

The revelers are gone—to where, I have no idea.

And Sol—absolutely drenched in glitter—stares down at me, brow pinched in concern.

"I'm okay," I fib, and the look on his face says he doesn't believe me.

"That was incredible," he whispers. "I'm sorry you missed it."

I'm not. My heart is still thudding, but not from fear. It's just dawned on me that I'm clinging to Sol—practically hugging a total stranger—for safety. He even has an arm around me, like this is totally natural, and I'm not feeling the urge to squirm away.

It's the least *June* thing I've ever done in my life.

The wise move now would be to say something witty to make this intimate moment more casual before my anxious brain catches up. But the best I can manage is "Thanks."

He's still too close. Too sparkly. If we were in a romance novel, this would be the part where we lean together and share an unexpected kiss.

Of course, this is *my* life, not a romance novel, so he locks his intense gaze with mine and says, "I don't like your face. Can you take it off?"

I flinch. "What?! Oh!"

Mortified, I shove my mask onto my forehead, breaking the illusion in multiple ways and bringing me back to reality. Yep, that's me: a girl so bad at flirting she can repel a guy with no memories while looking like a supermodel. This is exactly the sort of situation for which I require the star's instructions.

Was there something I could have done just then to turn that moment into. . . more?

It doesn't matter. I'm still exhausted and feel like someone has tied weights to my limbs. A nap would really hit the spot right now. Hopefully, the music and light portion of the current trial is over.

"We should find the key," I tell him. "It's going to be harder with the lights out."

"Not really. It hit me in the head."

Sol points down at his feet, where, sure enough, the golden key sits. I scoop it up and turn it over in my hand while he does his best to de-glitter himself. It's futile. Nothing short of a shower is going to remove all the sand-like sparkles.

"You're not going to like this," I say, "but I think the next step is under the glitter."

I brush the tip of my boot through the mess on the floor, revealing the curved metal inlay. As I've suspected for a bit, it's a border where sections of floor meet—sections that together form a spiral pattern with equally spaced lines throughout.

"It looks like stairs," Sol says.

I nod. "I thought so, too. It's like a spiral staircase if you drew it top-down on a sheet of paper."

"Exactly."

He follows my lead, kicking glitter aside and tracing the pattern to the outer edge of the ballroom. When we reach it, he clears a patch to examine a metal plate.

"And there's our keyhole," he declares. "At least that part of the trial was easy."

I cross my arms. "Well, now that you've said that aloud, it'll probably explode or something."

Sol laughs and holds out a hand for the key, which is the antique sort with a heart shape at the end. Because I'm a giant dork, I know that end is called a bow. Funny I can remember things like that and forget the names of people I meet.

I pass the adorable key to Sol, and he slides it into the keyhole. When he twists, it doesn't turn all the way. He scowls and gives it a harder twist, jiggles the key, and twists again. I kneel beside him for a better look.

"Is it the wrong key for the lock?"

He shakes his head. "I don't think so, but it isn't turning all the way. It's like something's blocking it."

"Like a bajillion pounds of glitter?"

He stops twisting. "Yes, exactly like that."

I sit down cross-legged beside him, happy for the chance to rest, even if it's at the expense of our win. "Maybe we can blow it out?"

He shrugs, puffs breaths of air into the keyhole, and tries again. The key doesn't turn. "I don't suppose you have anything in your magic bag that can clean the glitter out?"

I wrinkle my nose. "It's not magic. It's just a bag of stuff I take with me when I travel."

"You take a mask that changes your face when you travel?"

Okay. He has me there.

"The star added that feature. But everything else in the bag seems normal. I'll see if there's something we can use, though."

I shrug the backpack off, unbuckle the top flap, and paw through the contents. Maybe I could poke at the hole with a flosser? That might temporarily un-jam it but wouldn't clear the glitter out.

"Am I the only one who didn't get anything?" Sol asks, probably more harshly than he means to. "Not that I actually want to know what a hanged man would receive."

Is that true?

I try to remember what everyone got. "Meela has stones that eliminate a bad choice. I have a mask that disguises my face—plus a bunch of travel toiletries. I heard the emperor guess that Yvit's empty bag might be able to conjure things, and he got a scepter that might do something. You—"

"Got muddy boots," Sol says.

"Glittery boots," I correct.

He doesn't laugh this time. "If I'm honest, I'm a little envious of your bag. Even toiletries would tell me something about who I am."

My heart sinks. "If it helps, you looked really happy solving the puzzle. Maybe you're into dance or theater."

"It's not that." He picks at the keyhole with a fingernail like stubbornness might dislodge the glitter. "This is going to sound a little weird, but the music made me see colors in my mind. At first, I thought it was part of the puzzle lighting, but the colors were still there when I closed my eyes."

I gasp. "Synesthesia!"

"What's that?"

"It's when pathways between different types of sensations in your brain are connected—like sound and vision. Not a lot of people have it where I'm from."

"Something else the star messed up, then."

I shake my head. "No, it's probably yours. I have something similar called misophonia. I feel emotions when I hear certain sounds. Mostly, it just makes me want to smack people when they chew with their mouths open."

I can tell he's fighting a grin when he says, "I'll do my best not to chew."

"Maybe you're a musician with synesthesia," I propose. "Maybe you wished to be famous. Oh! Maybe that's why you were dressed up! For a concert!"

His eyes narrow as he thinks about it. "No. I think I want something more personal, like you. Something I can feel in my chest but can't find in my head. I want . . . ugh. It's like there's a literal barrier in the way and I can only get tiny glimpses of it."

He squeezes his eyes shut and balls his fists as if willing the memory back into his head. I hold my breath, sure it's on the tip of his tongue, but a split second later he roars and slams his fists against the ground in frustration.

The pain in his expression makes me wonder what he's lost. He could easily be someone like me, heartbroken and seeking clarity, or he could be a spoiled brat, selfishly wishing for even more. Unless he can fight through the memory loss, he'll never know—and neither will I. After coming so close to sharing a kiss, the difference feels more significant.

A strange thought strikes me. "When you say a literal barrier, do you really mean literal? Like, when you close your eyes are you picturing it in your mind?"

He shrugs. "I guess, yeah."

"And it's real? Not imaginary?"

"I don't know how to answer that. It's in my head."

"What does it look like?"

He shrugs again and closes his eyes, pausing a moment before answering. "It's thick enough that I can't see through, but swirling like fog in the wind. Sometimes, there are thin spots when the fog drifts, and— Wait! I can see something behind it. It's the keyhole we just found, but larger and disassembled like an exploded-view diagram. It's big enough I could practically reach in and brush the glitter out with one hand."

I can see the glitter, too. Not in my mind's eye, but on the dance floor, just above the real keyhole. I'm afraid to even breathe as it drifts upward and swirls like the fog in Sol's mind.

"Don't move," I whisper to him.

"What?"

"Keep thinking about the keyhole, and don't move."

Unable to help himself, he opens his eyes. I quickly slide cupped hands beneath the swirl of glitter, but it remains hovering in the air.

"Did I . . .?" he asks.

"I think so. Hold on, I'm gonna grab it."

I raise my hands to catch the glitter, and it turns back into inanimate granules that I easily toss into the rest of the mess. Sol wastes no time fitting the key back in and turning. It makes a satisfying click.

That's when I realize I'm sitting cross-legged on a dance floor that's about to become stairs. The entire spiral drops rapidly downward, thudding into a basement below. Fortunately, I roll away just in time to prevent an embarrassing descent.

Sol offers a hand. "Let's get out of here."

I hesitate for only a moment, then reach out and take it. He tugs me to my feet, then lets go, leaving my empty palm tingling—but not in an unpleasant way.

Despite the glamour and glitter of the ballroom, the sight of the basement at the foot of the stairwell is the most beautiful one I've witnessed yet—a single exit door with no tricks, no keyholes, and no flashing lights. Beside it is a table like the one in the hallway with two paper gift bags set upon it.

"Ready to leave?" Sol asks, picking up the bags and handing me one.

I nod. "Since the moment we arrived."

He gives me a weird look and turns the knob.

Eight

"Yer late again!" Yvit shouts as I stumble onto a rock in outer space.

This asteroid doesn't even pretend to be a planet like the grassy one we started with. It's a chunk of gray slate, and not a very large one. I shudder thinking about how easy it would be to topple off the edge. Would I fall up or down?

"There was no timer for that trial, was there?" I ask.

Yvit doesn't get a chance to respond.

The fairy emperor, resplendent in his crimson regalia, rises from where he sits cross-legged. "Irrelevant. You've missed valuable conversations, and I, for one, lack motivation to repeat them. All in favor of leaving the stragglers in the dark?"

Yvit coughs. "Seems all our roles come with some kinda *perk*. Not everybody's keen on talkin' about theirs. Both of you should have a key as well. Not everyone's keen on sharing those either, but we've established they're not all the same. I miss anything?"

The emperor grunts. "Councilor, I'm disappointed in you."

"Whatever. What'd you two do in there?"

I blink. It was hard enough experiencing the ballroom. I'm not sure how to explain it to others—and I'm still caught up on the concept of *perks*. Is he talking about how each role has different magic, like my mask, or the way Sol manipulated glitter? If so, what does the scepter do? And did he figure out how to pull objects from his bag?

Fortunately, Sol is just behind me and less caught up in his own thoughts. "It was a larger-than-life science experiment. What did you do?"

"Wartime strategy," the emperor says with a wave of his hand as if the trial was boring.

Meela hobbles toward us, hindered by excessive robes. Her yellow eyes are bulging with excitement. "We learned the mystical secrets of nonverbal, interspecies, emotional communication—and took a brief multiple-choice quiz at the end."

Death presses a glove to where their brow might be, if they had a visible brow. "Her perk is annoyingly overpowered. She rattled those stones every time there was a choice, and they eliminated one of the options for her. I had to retake the test *four times* to memorize unscientific rubbish."

Meela clasps a hand to her chest, feigning shock, but Death only rolls their armored shoulders as if daring her to argue their point. She doesn't.

Something crinkles quietly behind me, and I realize Sol is opening his gift bag.

"Excuse me," I say, exiting the conversation.

Careful to keep my back to the others, I open my own bag and remove the gift—a silver key wrapped in star-printed organza. The ribbon on the fabric is easy to tug off, and the key tumbles into my palm. Sol holds his out for me to compare.

"Looks like clubs from a playing card deck," I whisper as he turns his key over.

The two are identical. Both have the same club-shaped bow at the end, the same bit at the other, and the same length. Whatever Yvit meant when he said some were different apparently did not apply to ours. I carefully slip mine into my backpack while Sol slides his into a trouser pocket.

He's changed again.

There's no grin on his face, no sparkle of wonder in his eyes. Rejoining the competitors has reverted him back to the standoffish posture that made me think he was a snob. I wonder what everyone said to him before I arrived that upset him so much. How nasty had they been, that he'd rather be a gargoyle on a wall than stand anywhere near them?

I want to tell him it's okay and he and I are cool at least. I know what it's like to feel unwanted. Unfortunately, he retreats halfway across the asteroid before I can offer any comfort.

It doesn't take me long to figure out why.

"Get anything interesting?" Yvit asks, making me jump and squeak like a mouse.

I open my mouth to let him know it's none of his business what we have. Undoubtedly, the snarky pangolin contributed to whatever abuse Sol suffered. Then again, he did fill us in on all the conversations we missed. I don't know that the others would have.

This is why I always lose board games that require me to suspect other players. I want to give everyone the benefit of the doubt. I should be more careful, though—information could be valuable.

"Well—" I say, but I'm interrupted when the whole asteroid violently shakes.

Golden light erupts from one side like a geyser, and the star-serpent rises above us, twice as bright and much larger than I remember. Its scales shimmer like the spotlight-struck glitter, and its serpentine eyes glare down at us, hazy and white as milk in tea.

When it opens its fanged mouth, a small glowing die tumbles from its tongue and clatters to the asteroid.

"Look who's all grown up!" Yvit snarks, prompting the star to tilt its head in confusion.

"I have not grown," it says, matter-of-fact. "I have rearranged myself."

Yvit crosses his arms. "Never mind. Jokes are wasted on you."

The star's head straightens. "I trust the first trial was challenging enough?"

"For some of us more than others," the emperor mutters.

"Excellent. Consider it your tutorial. The first trial contained no disqualifying mechanism, and every participant received a key. That will not be the case going forward."

"What do you mean disqualifying?" Yvit demands while storming far closer to the star than I would dare to, considering its size.

The star hisses in warning. "As this is primarily a challenge of wits, you must figure things out for yourselves. However, I will clarify this one point. Disqualification is anything that permanently prohibits you from completing the trials."

Yvit scratches his scaly head. "So, each trial from here on out contains a way to lose the whole competition."

The star says nothing in response.

"The keys!" Meela exclaims. "What are they for? Why are they different? What happens if we don't receive one in a trial?"

That's a good question. They must have some significance, or the star wouldn't have noted them. Are they needed to win—or to escape?

The star shows no visible reaction to Meela's outburst. "That, I will not explain. You are all intelligent beings. You will put the pieces together. Are you ready for the next trial?"

The emperor waves a hand. "Get on with it!"

I scowl in his direction. Nobody appointed him our actual

emperor. Unfortunately, the star doesn't share my annoyance.

"Then, begin," it commands, and stares, unmoving, in the annoying fairy's direction.

In addition to whatever insectoid functions the emperor's antennae have, it seems they can also emote. His face remains cold and impassive, stuck in a standoff with the star. Meanwhile, his fuzzy antennae jerk about, betraying his rapid thoughts. He doesn't know what to do next and doesn't want us to know he doesn't know.

As much as I dislike confrontation, my skin itches with the desire to make a fool of the regal jerk. "You're supposed to roll the die," I say.

His head snaps in my direction, and I marvel at how a face so ethereal can become so ugly with a single expression. To his credit, though, he doesn't pretend he knew what to do the entire time. Instead, he marches forward, scoops up the die, and tosses it half-heartedly onto the ground.

Yvit leans forward to see the result. "It's a two!"

The star responds by sucking in a breath and blowing it against the ground. A surprising amount of dust rises, considering the solidity of the rock, and the emperor and Yvit both scurry backward to get out of the range of the twirling blast. As before, the particles rearrange themselves until two perfectly circular doors stand where empty air once was.

"Good luck," the star says before bursting apart and scattering into the lightless sky.

Its remnants turn the empty void into a familiar starry night, and I make a note never to trust the sky again.

"I don't require luck," snarls the emperor. "Shall we choose our doors?"

"Hold on," commands Yvit, who's the only one the emperor listens to. "Let's establish what we're doing first. This is trial two of some number—"

"Nine," I interrupt, pointing to golden numbers on the doors.

"Two of nine," Yvit repeats. "We all got keys in the first one, and they're not all the same. That tells me we're collecting a set."

"Ooh!" Meela cries with a giddy clap. "Collecting is one of my favorite things!"

The pangolin looks her over. "I believe that."

I tug at the sash around my waist, nervous to join in speculation thanks to past experiences with folks like the emperor. The only thing worse than having ideas rejected is having them ignored and later repeated by a dude who gets praised for them like he's a genius.

Maybe aliens are different, though?

Clearing my throat, I ask, "If true, would that mean there's *two* ways we can lose the competition?" I silently kick myself for phrasing the theory as a question in hopes that the others will listen to me. "Getting physically stuck in the trials, or not getting a full set of keys?"

"If true, correct," Death says in their velvety voice. I had almost forgotten they were there.

I frown. "But the star told me chances of failure were low."

The thought that I may have been naïve makes me ill. The snake was so careful with its speech that I took it at face value when it told me I was unlikely to lose. But what if it was speaking in the past tense? What if the current odds of failure are huge?

The thought makes me shudder. My awkward near-flirtation with Sol has reminded me why I'm doing this. I don't want to be alone. I want to love and be loved. I want to win.

The emperor grunts and brushes the crimson cape slung over his muscular shoulders. "Perhaps it's made an exception for us because you *incentivized it*."

I want to argue, even if he has a point, but someone else is quicker than me.

"Back off her!" Sol shouts at the fairy. "None of this is her fault, and you know it. We all knew the risks when we agreed to come here."

Except for him. Does he even know what will happen if he fails? And since when did he rejoin the group?

I feel a little pang of guilt that I hadn't even checked on him. He could have been blown right off the asteroid by the star's puff of magic wind, and no one would have noticed until we picked our doors. Oof.

"Scarecrow," Meela moans, pulling her hands inside her robes as if he might bite her fingers off. "I do not wish to partner with the bad omen. His presence upsets the balance."

"That's not a concern," the fairy says. "You'll be joining the councilor and me. We could use your talents to select our door."

I stare daggers at him. Who made him the boss? And how am I supposed to strategize if I can't get to know my competitors?

Meela's knobby hands pop back out of her sleeves and resume their excited clapping. "Oh! Oh! My first converts to the ways of the Wondrous Grapefruit! And I haven't even been anointed yet!"

She inhales deeply through her pointy nose, closes her eyes, and empties her bag of stones onto the asteroid. With everyone's undivided attention, she drops to a crouch and examines tiny markings carved into the edges.

"We must go through . . . that one."

Everyone turns, following her pointed finger to the leftmost door—after which, everyone tilts their heads. The door on the left is upside-down, based on its illustration. The art depicts a wizard with a staff—or a man with a tall walking stick. It's hard to tell with the image flipped and crudely burned into the cedarwood. I squint to read the card's name: page of wands. I guess that answers that.

Alex always referred to upside down cards as *reversed*. One of the few arguments they ever had with their partner was over the meaning of such a card. Alex thought the meaning was the opposite of the same card upright, and Sudo thought it was the same meaning but blocked or too intense. It probably would never have been a fight if they didn't pull cards before gaming sessions.

The emperor's eyes narrow, but he approaches the door. "Why this one?"

"I do not know. Isn't it wonderful—"

"Yeah, yeah," says Yvit. "Who else is with us?"

"Apparently not me," Sol growls.

Death readjusts their shades. "If not everyone is receiving a key, dividing ourselves into smaller groups may increase our individual chances. I could be wrong, but, for now, I choose the door on the right."

Their logic is sound. I think.

"Same," I say, and I see Sol's lips twitch into a half smile before he catches himself.

"Three and three," Death declares. "Now, what do we have here?"

They lean toward the door on the right, examining the strange scene burned onto its surface. The right door is painted an aqua color that contrasts the orange red of the cedar, and depicts gladiators battling each other with staves similar to the wizard's staff. Five of wands.

"I was also told we wouldn't be physically harmed," I grumble. "Was everything the star told me a lie?"

I imagine having to fight Death—all lean and tall with leather armor—armed with nothing but a walking stick.

It doesn't go well for the me in my mind.

Death's sunglasses shake back and forth. "The star is averse to miscommunication. Lying seems improbable. But it does occasionally struggle with language."

"I don't like it," I say, but suppose the point is moot.

The emperor's self-assembled team has already wrenched their door open, revealing a colorful space beyond that's almost as dazzling as the ballroom had been. Death does the same, tugging our door open and stepping into—a rather nice foyer.

A foyer straight out of my dreams, in fact.

I follow Death, slack-jawed, into the room, which is something I've never witnessed before outside high-budget paranormal movies. Two gorgeous hardwood staircases flank the foyer and curve upward to a balcony. Unlike similar modern spaces, which tend to be marbled, white, and sterile, everything is made of dark, aged wood. In place of electric lighting, real candles sit in chandeliers and sconces, casting a warm glow—and too many shadows.

It's perfect.

There's even a cold breeze in the air that makes the chandelier creak, and a smell like the first foggy night of autumn. It's every kid's Halloween dream, the quintessential haunted house.

My breath catches in my throat as I take it all in, only remembering to inhale when Sol bumps me in passing.

"This is gorgeous," I breathe.

His brows knit. "I thought you hated rich people. Isn't this a rich person's house?"

Ugh, he's right. But it's not like this is a modern mansion built for billionaires. It's probably something old and historic. Which technically makes it even more problematic. Dang it, Sol. Don't ruin this for me.

Death snaps their fingers. "Let's focus on the puzzle, please. This one's timed."

I return to reality like a popped balloon. An ornate grandfather clock stands smack in the middle of the foyer, arms ticking steadily *backward* toward twelve—which is painted with a neon green skull.

There won't be time to enjoy this trial.

Nine

I REFUSE TO get into the creepy wooden box.

It's sitting there behind the clock, rickety door hanging open, revealing the unlit space inside with a single visible wooden bench. I know what Death is going to say before they even finish the instructions. I do not want to get in the creepy wooden box.

"We have to enter the information booth one at a time," they say, summarizing rules from a notecard that was stuck to the back of the grandfather clock. "Someone inside will assign us to a team. Then we each pick a room from which to enter a maze. One team will try to solve the maze before time runs out. One team will try to stop them. The prevailing side gets *two* keys."

We have to get into the box? I'm shocked.

"It sounds like the game needs four players," I say instead of grumbling about the booth. "We only have three. Is this going to work?"

Death replies, "I'm more concerned that this sounds too simple compared to finding emotional resonance with frogs. There has to be a catch."

I nod. The rules are more straightforward than the ballroom puzzle as well, and presented upfront. That's pretty sus.

"I'll go first," Death volunteers.

I am not going to stop them.

They make their way to the wooden booth and hesitate, gloved hand on the door. Without a visible face, it's impossible to tell if they're garnering strength or reacting to something. A moment later, they step inside and shut the wooden door behind them.

Sol leans close to whisper in my ear and my skin prickles. "Is it just me, or is that booth creepy?"

"Why, because it's rickety and dark and probably full of tiny spiders?"

"Or something worse," he offers, "like cockroaches."

"Cockroaches are *not* worse than spiders! That's like comparing earthworms and snakes." I fix him with my sternest look but stop myself from info-dumping everything I know about venom and necrosis. There are some facts you can never un-learn, no matter how much you wish you could.

This, I remind myself, is exactly why I'm incompatible with Jayden. Imagine a romantic camping trip, but I'm bathed in repellant and zipped in a bee suit. I don't get how he can sleep in the woods and not worry about spiders and ticks.

"All right, all right," Sol says with a chuckle, and his playful smile is like a balm for the ache that's rapidly spreading through my chest. I find myself wishing I could keep him laughing for the remainder of the competition. He's pleasant when he's not a sourpuss. Unfortunately, my insect opinions are the height of my current comedy routine.

An awkward silence follows, which is odd, considering the flimsy-looking construction of the information booth. You'd think we would hear every word said inside. Somehow, there's nothing until Death emerges, unharmed by spiders or cockroaches. They gesture for someone else to take a turn, and the lack of webs gives me confidence.

"Which team did you get?" I ask as I step forward. Might as well get this over with.

"It's complicated," Death replies. "Go inside, and you'll understand."

Not ominous at all, then. Yay.

I squeeze into the booth and slump on the bench in front of a cheesy, stagelike curtain that separates me from the other half of the box. The interior smells slightly acidic, as if someone has cleaned it with disinfectant—a fact that does not improve its charm. Despite my concerns, I shut the door, plunging the space into relative darkness, and wait for the so-called information.

Based on the trial's apparent setting and the creepiness of the information booth, I figure I know what to expect. Behind the curtain, there will be a fake psychic, an animatronic from my grandparents' time that's aged poorly in many ways. I can even picture the plastic "crystal ball" with lights that change color to make it glow.

What I do not at all expect to see when the curtain draws back and lights turn on is the grumpy face of a Persian cat.

"A cat?" I blurt, unable to stop myself.

The cat is a pile of multicolored fluff topped with an irritated expression. It glares at me with round yellow eyes that have tiny—yet intense—pupils.

"Rude!" it shouts, but not from the little downturned mouth facing my direction.

The more I look, the odder the cat gets. Instead of one head, it has three, each with little ears of their own and all pointing different directions. The face aimed directly at me has gray coloration and a pinched nose. Its tiny paws rest delicately on a velvet pad as it stares me down.

"Well?" it asks in a huskier voice than I'd ever expect from a fluffy cat. "What question did you have for me?"

I realize the sound isn't coming from its mouth, but rather from a blinking electric collar around the front-facing head's neck. All three heads have their own collars, presumably each with a realistic voice.

"Uh," I stammer, unprepared. "I'm here to find out my team in the trial?"

"That's not a question!" a grumpier head shouts.

"But we understood," the gray one says. "One moment while we assess you."

To my infinite discomfort, each cat head spins round to look me over, as if the necks rotate on an axis. It reminds me a bit of cheap plastic dolls.

After the gray head, there's one with orange fur, a furrowed brow, and a bushy mustache. That's the one that keeps yelling at me. The third is so strange I hold in a squeal at the sight of its round face, wide eyes, and pink tongue. It looks like it's blowing a raspberry.

Fortunately for my composure, the gray one delivers the final verdict.

"Within the maze, there are two hidden gemstones, red as the blood of a fresh meal. It is your job to locate one and carry it to the end of the maze, where you must place it in the right eye of a skull."

"Right!" says the grumpier, mustached head. "Not left. Your partner is responsible for the left!"

The gray head blinks and nods sagely. "Each must place their gem in the correct eye for your team to win the trial."

"Before the time runs out!" the grumpier one adds.

"Yes," the gray-faced one hisses.

I lean closer to the cat. "Wait. So, the third person only has to stop *one* of us, and both of us fail?"

"You only get one question!" the cranky head snaps.

"Only one," the gray one agrees.

"Technically, that was my first one," I remind them. "But fine. Wait. Actually . . . would you have answered any question, even if it wasn't trial related?"

"A question about a question is still a question," the cranky head moans. "This is exhausting. I need a nap."

Crud. I could have just asked it to explain love and circumvented the competition. Though I'm not sure the star knows the answer yet, based on how it handled the ballroom.

Ah, well. The cat is done with me. No wonder Death had been so quick. This was a chat that could have been a text. I lift myself from the hard bench as the heads prattle on with each other, curtain slowly closing before them.

"You just woke from a nap," the gray head admonishes as the curtain brushes its tiny toes.

"Pthhp," replies the round-faced one while the booth once again falls into darkness.

I scrabble to open the door and stumble back into the foyer. Death is already there, arms crossed.

"That took suspiciously long. You, get in, and keep it quick."

Sol shoots Death a nasty look, but steps inside and slams the door shut. I shake off and pace the floor like an over-the-top TV detective.

My partner—whoever that is—and I need to locate the two gems, find the end of the maze, and put the gems in a skull. Our opponent will try to stop us, and if they do, they get two keys. That's an enormous incentive, assuming the keys are needed to win the whole competition. But how exactly will they stop us? A fistfight? Some kind of trap?

Death doesn't have visible eyes, but I can feel them watching me pace. How much do I know about them, really? Almost nothing—not even their name. They're sharp, secretive, and ambitious. I don't even know their age.

Sol emerges from the booth, looking just as confused

as I had been. "Did you also see a three-headed cat?" he asks.

Death snaps their fingers again. "We're timed. Let's get started. Pick your rooms."

I scowl. "Don't we want to share our teams first?"

Both competitors stop to stare as if I said something ridiculous, which is impressive since Death has only sunglasses with which to emote.

"What? What is it?"

Death shakes their head. "The person who got the antagonist role is not going to admit they got it. In fact, they might try extra hard to convince us they *didn't* get that role. For example, by pretending to be naïve and asking us to share our teams."

Oh.

Goose bumps run down my arms and legs, aided by the chilly haunted house breeze. They're right. If I were the antagonist, I would totally claim to be on the other team. That would make the other two distrust each other and keep them from ganging up on me. But I'm *not* the bad one! Is Death implicating me?

"What are you trying to say?!" I snap, hoping my anger registers as genuine so my partner knows I'm telling the truth.

Death only gestures up the stairs. "Pick your room."

Begrudgingly, I follow them to the landing, where six doors open into the hallway. At the first opportunity, I deliberately storm in the opposite direction from the side Death selects, peeking into open doors as I pass.

"*You're* trying too hard to convince *me*," I grumble as I stomp by a tiled bathroom.

The next door is a walk-in closet, which I also pass by in a huff. I glance back just in time to see Sol peek into the bathroom and shrug. He catches my gaze, gives a wave, and steps inside, choosing his room.

I wonder if he's picking randomly or if there's an advantage to starting in a bathroom. Easier to find the maze, maybe?

Meanwhile, my room prospects are improving. Beyond the closet is a bedroom worthy of a princess, if the princess were a goth. The bed has far too many layers of fabric and a canopy with gathered curtains. The wooden floor is covered in ornate rugs in spooky colors. Across from the bed is a vanity with a mirror that must be three feet across, and beside it, another clock ticks backward, reminding me I need to choose.

Fine.

I give in and enter the creepy bedroom, prompting the door to slam shut behind me. It takes several seconds to catch my breath and convince my heart not to thud through my ribs. I'm pretty sure my organs have to stay where they are if I want to win this thing.

"All right, step one," I say to myself as I remove my backpack and tug out my sketchbook. "This is a maze, so I'll need a diagram."

I scribble a small box at the bottom of a page and label it *Goth Bedroom*.

"Step two, find the entrance to the maze."

As any avid reader would, I check the standing wardrobe first. When that fails, I check beneath the bed, behind the dressers, and under the vanity. The mirror is secured to the wall, and I'm not yet ready to smash it in to see if it's secretly an exit, but I realize that option isn't off the table. The star made all this stuff from nothing. I don't have to play by escape room rules.

"If this were a classic mansion escape room," I ponder, "where else would I look?"

I sit in the chair at the vanity and count clichés on my fingers.

"No sconces to tilt. No books to pull from shelves. No random set of scales with different weights. No creepy notes with certain words bolded. No messages scribbled on—"

I jump up.

"The wallpaper."

I quickly run my hands along the walls until I feel an indentation below, then dig my nails beneath the edge of the badly stained wallpaper strip. A half inch of ragged paper tears free.

"Ugh!"

Another tug removes a similar chunk, reminding me of carefully peeling price stickers off used books. Why does nothing ever come up in one piece? More importantly, though, the clock is ticking. I need to stop being delicate.

Sadly, there are no sledgehammers around, but in a vanity drawer, I find a hairbrush, a comb, and a letter opener; the latter of which is unnecessarily sharp.

The wallpaper doesn't see it coming.

With several vicious slashes along the grooves, I carve a rectangle the size of a door. The knob, which turns out to be an inset loop, twists easily, and the door pops open. The maze already has a fork and I need to choose my path carefully, but there's something I have to try first.

Hands trembling, I push up my sleeve and raise the letter opener over my arm. It takes a moment to work up the courage, but I finally exhale and plunge the tip downward, stabbing and dragging it along my skin. I don't actually want to hurt myself, but if I can be injured, I need to know now.

The blade doesn't even leave a scratch.

Ten

I MAY HAVE bitten off more than I can chew with my plan to map the maze in my sketchbook. In my defense, I figured all I had to draw were hallways, branches, and dead ends. I had no idea how many potential clues were going to catch my eye along the way.

Yes, I'm like a dog with a squirrel when it comes to pattern recognition. And yes, it's possible the star knows this and threw in red herrings to trip me up. But there are Halloween bats on the wallpaper, each surrounded by a series of symbols: a teal half circle, a brick-red triangle, and a linked pair of upside-down pumpkin-orange triangles. I'd be a fool not to record that.

Unless it's meant to slow me down.

Which it might be, since the trial is timed, an unknown player is hunting me, and my partner and I will lose our keys if we can't solve the maze fast enough.

I shudder.

Too late now.

The candlelit hallway turns out to be a dead end, but there are three metal levers on the final wall, suggesting a puzzle that needs solving to progress. An etched plaque above them has an eight-word message encoded with clusters of basic shapes similar to the ones around the bats.

"Good news, Star," I whisper to the empty room. "You've been promoted to rubber duck."

Rubber duck is a term I learned in robotics camp. It's when you need to speak a problem aloud to figure out the best solution, but don't really need anyone's input. Like talking to a rubber duck.

"I'm guessing you're hoping I'll wander the halls working out the wallpaper designs to translate this. That would eat up time and maybe run me into my opponent." I grin. "But just because you made the puzzle that way doesn't mean there's only one way to solve it."

In games with three-digit combination padlocks, I often jump ahead of clues by brute-forcing the lock combination— meaning I try every possible number, one at a time, until the lock pops. I can do that here.

"Every lever starts in the top position, and it looks like they only have three positions each, so I'll just—"

I grab the third lever and pull it halfway down. Nothing happens. That's fine, because I didn't expect it to. However, when I pull the same lever to the bottom, a section of the wall slides away. It's exactly enough space for me to fit through— and I find that slightly suspicious.

"Too easy, duck. What are you up to?"

I know the smart thing to do now would be to squeeze through the gap and head on my way. I don't. Unable to help myself, I raise my sketchbook to copy down the plaque, just in case I need it later. The moment my pencil touches the page, the gap in the wall slams shut again with a thunderous boom and a gust of wind that makes the candles in the wall sconces flicker.

I shriek.

My pencil lead snaps.

It takes several seconds of deep breathing to lower my heart rate and regain my dignity.

"Stop doing that!" I whisper, just in case the wall slamming gave away my location. "You already know what it feels like when I'm startled. It's cheap."

Sassing the star feels good, but I know the trap wasn't set to frighten me. It was meant to squish me flat if I got cocky. Grumbling, I click my mechanical pencil twice to produce more lead.

"Fine. We'll do it your way."

It's difficult to shake the mental image of the wall crushing my bones to powder. Even though the star said it wouldn't hurt me, I can't shake the feeling that this trap is one of its "disqualifying mechanisms."

"Bad duck."

I scribble the eight encrypted words—which are really only three, because they repeat—into my notebook and stare at them, hoping a pattern will stand out. Time to let my nerd flag fly.

"Let's assume we're working with a simple alphabetic substitution cipher, and the wallpaper is a clue to decode it. If the symbols on the wall translate to letters, they probably spell the word bat. B. A. T. That's one half circle, one triangle, and a cluster of two upside-down triangles."

I tap my pencil against the page. "Two of three words on the plaque start with *T*. The first is three letters long and ends with the same character the final word starts with. The second is five letters long and ends with two of the same character the final word ends with. So, I'm guessing the words are two, three, and one. Which means, when I read all eight together, it gives me both the positions of the levers and the order to pull them in. That's why brute forcing didn't work."

I quickly reset all the levers to the top position as I had

found them.

"Lever two. Position three." I pull it to the bottom, with no result.

"Lever three. Position two." Again, no result. That's good.

"Lever one. Position three." Nothing.

"And finally, lever two. Position one."

With a swish and satisfying clunk, the wall panel slides back open.

This time, before approaching, I wait and observe the treacherous wall. It's exactly like watching a jump scare video, where you know something will pop up and scream, but you don't know when, so your muscles still clench. When nothing happens for several seconds, I take a deep breath, squeeze my notebook to my chest, and wriggle through the gap in the wall. It's not until I'm safe on the other side that I let myself relax and breathe.

I did it!

There's a new wallpaper on this side with a picture of a grinning witch and a continuation of the colorful symbols, suggesting the clues will be needed again. Maybe it's adrenaline from surviving the trap, or maybe it's the thrill of discovery, but I can't help showing off.

"This is the alphabet boiled down to basic shapes," I tell the star-slash-rubber-duck, "and the number of a shape in a cluster is its relative position in the alphabet."

The goofball grin I give the star slides off my face a moment later. Alex's taunting echoes in my mind, judging Jyden's taste in hobbies and asking what I see in him. The same could be asked in reverse. What would he ever see in me?

My shoulders sag. "How do I get someone to like me if I don't feel . . . likeable? I'm proud of myself for solving this, but there's no one to share it with. All the guys I know think puzzles are boring. They want to watch videos and play games."

Except, that isn't the whole truth. I *have* met someone who would enjoy this puzzle, and I can already picture his brightening smile as he works his way through the same maze. The thought makes my imagination wander to impossible futures on foreign worlds, so I shake it off, huff, and glare at the ceiling.

"If you saw me thinking that, no you didn't."

Speaking of the other contestants, all this stalling is putting my partner at risk. I need to finish writing down the alphabet and add the lever puzzle to my sketchbook.

"Or," I consider as a melancholy sound from far away tickles my ears, "I could follow the music."

I'm definitely going to follow the music.

And finish the alphabet along the way.

I have complex feelings about this maze.

"Okay, I'll give it to you, that's pretty good," I tell the star as I follow the sound.

The spooky music is warped and lilting like an old-timey song that's playing in reverse. It's certainly more evocative than the droning noise in the ballroom trial. I like the chill it sends down my spine and the goose bumps that rise on my arms and legs.

This is the type of scary I enjoy—which tells me the star is trying to experience every emotion, not just the bad ones. Hopefully, that means it's done with jump scares.

With a laugh, I picture the snake with a sketchbook, furiously scribbling down my reactions while I scribble down its ciphers. I really hope it doesn't conclude that my interests are standard for every human.

"Upside-down tea party," I mutter as I doodle a box on the map in my sketchbook to represent the room I discover.

It's the best description I can think of. Like the bedroom,

the new room has a grandfather clock and a massive mirror on one wall. That's where the similarities end.

I can picture the room as it once was, before everything faded and the ceiling crumbled, covering the floor with dust and plaster.

No. That's not right.

It may be more correct to say the floor crumbled, covering the ceiling. It's hard to tell when the room is upside-down and I'm standing on the wrong side. Either way, what once was a sewing room, with antique machines and mannequins, is now a dusty, decaying hazard.

Time and nature have done away with everything but empty cups and plates, but it's easy to envision the tea party that once took place on the table above me. Sometime after its abandonment, someone had moved four mannequin heads with absurdly long necks into each of the chairs—all facing the door and weirding me out.

I can envision the party, pre-heads, not because of my sleuthing skills, but because I can see it on the other side of the mirror.

There, like some kind of twisted reflection, is the same room, but right-side up. Tiny cakes sit on pristine plates, teacups brim with steaming tea, and dozens of candles brighten the space, spilling their light into my own. I cautiously creep along the ceiling, avoiding the burnt-out chandelier that dangles upward toward the table. When I reach the mirror, I peer in.

The other room must be a clue to escape mine, since there isn't much I can deduce on this side, as most everything above my head has decayed. Sadly, the right-side-up room also has only one visible door. I suppose it would have been far too easy to look in and spot where the star hid the exit.

I scan my side, which is dusty, barren, and smells like a shirt that's been left in a dresser, and compare it to the room in the mirror like I'm doing a spot-the-differences puzzle. On that side, bolts of patterned fabric are set out on racks and pinned to mannequins. The fabric itself has colorful stripes, and the colors are immediately familiar.

"Another point to June for taking notes."

Each bolt has repeating stripes with the same colors as the wallpaper shapes, and in between each repeating pattern is an illustration of a gemstone. A smug grin spreads across my face as I lift my sketchbook and translate what I see. The stripes become letters on my page, values changing depending on thickness rather than cluster, and I read the result when I have it deciphered.

"As above, so below."

Sure, I guess. That describes this entire room. But how does that help me find the gemstone?

Sudden movement catches my eye, and I flatten myself beside the mirror, cringing as spiderwebs catch on my sleeve. A figure steps into the mirrored room.

Sol.

I watch his face as he takes it all in. At this point, I'm 80 percent certain the one with the antagonist role is Death, seeing as they tried to cast doubt upon me. Better safe than sorry, though. Sol slowly scans the room, taking in every detail. It's not the wild look of a predator hunting for an opponent to thwart. He's having the same reaction I had.

Cautiously, I step away from the wall and into the room where he can see me. He doesn't react to me at all, and instead starts searching through the racks of fabric.

"Sol!" I say, waving a bit, just in case the mirror is soundproof.

He turns on a heel and walks toward me, and for a moment I assume my waving worked. Then he searches the mirror's frame, tugging on the edges like it might come free.

He can't see or hear me.

I lean away as his face draws close to the glass and he presses his palm flat against it. The romantic in me wants to set my hand to his—especially since he still looks as gorgeous as he did when we briefly embraced in the ballroom—but it feels invasive to watch him from this distance when he's not aware that I can see him. Shamefully, I know if our places were reversed, I'd be making goofy faces and muttering to the star. Meanwhile, he looks relatively composed, save for some worry lines beneath his curls.

I should be worried, too. Time is ticking away, I don't have a gem, and the person I'm pretty sure is my partner is visible and unreachable. This is like a real-life horror movie. He thinks he's alone, but I'm right here—literally a foot away—and there's nothing I can do to get his attention. I'm a ghost.

This is so cool.

And bad.

Like a caged animal, he circles his room, growing increasingly frustrated, until he finally collapses in a chair, legs splayed and head tilted back. A small part of me is a little annoyed that he hasn't noticed the fabric print, but without a sketchbook he could reference, what would he do with that information?

About as much as I'm doing now.

I really should give him privacy and take up the search in my own creepy room. After all, I've been standing here so long, the music has entered an annoying loop, only playing the last seconds of the song. Still, I can't make myself look away as he stares at the ceiling and lets out a cry that could be laughter or could be sobs.

It's a good thing that I keep watching.

Sol leaps to his feet, climbs onto his chair, and hops up

onto the tea party table, knocking over cups and spilling the tea. He reaches up, grips the chandelier, and gives it a violent yank. Plaster rains onto his head.

"As above, so below," I whisper.

I examine my copy of the chandelier, which also dangles, though up instead of down. There's nothing remarkable about it, other than the fact that it's the only object in the entire room that I can reach. Which, in hindsight, is a massive clue.

The shattered molding around it was likely star-shaped before it fell apart. Its counterpart on Sol's side is more conspicuous and painted gold.

How did I miss that? How did he spot it?

His chandelier and the molding around it crash to the table at his feet, and as they do, a knotted rope drops down from the resulting hole in the ceiling. He wastes no time climbing up. Clearly, he's more fit than I am.

Well, I guess it's my turn to try. I gingerly cross the crumbling ceiling and grab my fragile-looking chandelier, twisting and tugging on the chain. My version is far less secure, and the tiniest tug sends the whole thing flying, leaving me pinwheeling by a hole in the ground.

There's no knotted rope.

No ladder.

No light.

Just a dark hole from which a breeze blows, carrying with it an odd floral scent. It's my least favorite fragrance again: lavender.

"Don't think I haven't noticed you're doing that on purpose," I tell the star, giving it my nastiest glare.

I don't like this, but down is my only option, and Death could catch up at any moment. I sit, dangle my legs over the side, take a deep breath, and push off.

Eleven

In the seconds between utter weightlessness and the impact of my butt on the slide, I realize how humiliated I'll be if the hole is a disqualifying drop. Imagine losing the entire competition not because of some elaborate puzzle, but because I jumped into a bottomless pit without even considering the danger.

Thankfully, luck is on my side for once, and though the slide itself bangs my elbows, I land in a half-full laundry basket.

"I should have dropped something in here first," I realize before lifting my head from the basket and freezing in alarm at what I see.

The laundry room is pre-ransacked. Someone has been in it before me, and that someone was likely not Sol. Pulse accelerating, I scan the walls for exits, finding only one: a crude tunnel that must have been hidden behind a cabinet before someone dragged the large cabinet aside. Whoever did so left gouges on the wall.

This is bad.

It also answers a question that's been rattling around my brain since we started. If it's true we can't hurt one another, how would Death stop us from finishing the maze?

Answer: They'd find the gemstones first.

That's even worse, because now I don't know if I should avoid the tunnel so Death doesn't find me, or run in to stop them and take back the gem.

"Ach!" a high-pitched voice shrieks from nowhere, almost making me scream myself. "Another one!"

"Oh, you've got to be joking!" a second voice says in an odd accent that I can't quite place.

My head swivels, but I see nothing around me except mountains of unfolded laundry. Is there a camera somewhere? A speaker system? Surely the house is too old for that.

"We won't let your lot cause us mischief again!"

"Yah! Fool me once, or however that goes."

"We may be small, but we've got sharp teeth!"

Small?

I scan the laundry piles again, paying closer attention to the contents. Sure enough, several objects I had initially thought to be faux fur are, in fact, animals. They're the size of cats, with red-brown bodies, panda-like faces, and fluffy tails.

They're cute, but I don't want to get bit.

I attempt a swift exit from the laundry basket, which results in an undignified face-plant. When I lift my head again, three of the creatures are within arm's reach.

"Are you giant squirrels," I ask them as I pick myself up off the floor, "or red pandas with fluffy tails?"

"Not sure," the closest one says. It's wearing overalls, like a mechanic. "Could be squirrels. We weren't given our species. We were given names, though. Mine's Jeffrey!"

". . . Jeffrey," I repeat.

"Aye."

"You look like a squirrel to me. What do you mean you weren't *given* your species?"

Another squirrel, wearing a peach sweater, replies, "We

know what we need to know, given what we are. Not that any of us really are what we are, you know?"

"Right," I say, though it takes me another few seconds to untangle the meaning. "Because you're made of star stuff."

"Who isn't?"

I don't have time for philosophical debate with giant squirrels, though I'm curious how they're all so chill about the fact that they're non-player characters. Like the rooms before, the laundry room has a large round clock nailed to one wall. Time is precious. The squirrels are a distraction.

"The person who was in here before me," I ask, pointing to the shifted cabinet, "did they happen to leave through that door?"

"Aye, and look what they did to our wall!" Jefferey complains.

The long-winded one in the peach sweater adds, "Awful shame, that. We weren't given anything to repair our walls. Just the laundry. Mind you, it's very good laundry. Lots of trinkets left in the pockets, and all the pockets we want—as long as we keep washing and folding. Which was fine, until your lot came and—"

"Were there any gems in the pockets?" I interrupt.

The bitey one glares. "Our trinkets are none of your business!"

Oof. The squirrels are obviously touchy about their stuff. They're probably like guards in a roleplaying game, simple beings created with a single mission to stop the player getting from what they want. Which tells me the gem must be here—or was here, before Death found it.

I change my tactic. "Did the other person arrive the same way I did? Through the chute?"

"Oh no," says Jeffrey. "They came through *our* door."

"Which is where?"

"Beneath the piles, I'm afraid."

The third squirrel, whom I recognize by voice as the one who had threatened to bite me earlier, snaps, "And we just got those piles sorted by size, so you'd better not be thinking of touching them!"

"But—" I begin, still unsure if I should chase Death or run away from them.

"That's final!" it shouts. "We had everything in perfect order, then the other one came and messed it all up! They unfolded our laundry, went through our pockets, and tossed our trinkets before ruining our wall!"

"Aye! We're lucky they didn't find our stash!" Jeffrey added.

"Stash?" I ask.

"Stash?" Jeffrey squeaks.

If Death went through the pockets of every item in the laundry, as it certainly looks like they did, what are the chances they were unsuccessful in locating the gemstone before they left?

"You said the other person didn't find your stash."

"I did?" Jeffrey asks.

"You did. What's in it?"

". . . Nuts?"

I get to my feet, towering over the squirrels. "I need to see what you have. It's very important. There's something I'm supposed to be looking for."

"Not a chance!" shouts the bitey one again. "They're our trinkets! We earned them!"

Fair.

"What if I offer a trade?"

This piques the interest of the long-winded squirrel, who draws closer and asks, "A trade for what?"

I consider the contents of my backpack. If I offer something to the squirrels, it has to be of value to them, but nonessential for the remainder of the trials.

"Ah! What about an electric toothbrush?" I dig around in my backpack and produce my travel brush, which is battery operated and bubble-gum pink—like a mature person would have. "I'll even throw in the toothpaste with it."

The long-winded one wrinkles its furry snout. "What's an electric toothbrush?"

"You turn it on," I explain, pressing the button to make it hum, "and use it to clean plaque from your teeth. It keeps them from rotting out of your head."

"Bah!" says the bitey squirrel. "The star won't keep us around long enough to worry about rotting teeth. We probably won't even have these bodies for the next competition."

The one with the sweater clicks its claws together. "Actually, the cat told me she's been a cat for seven or eight competitions. I'd hate to stay around that long without any teeth. What if I need to bite something?"

"Oh, I love biting things," Jeffrey moans.

The bitey one sighs, not really needing to give its opinion on the joy of biting. "Fine. It's a deal. You give us the brush, and you can have one thing from our stash. *If* you can find it."

"Okay. Deal."

How hard could it be? I scan the room again, taking into account the fact that Death searched all the clothes. That doesn't leave a whole lot of other places.

"Is it in the cabinet?" I ask.

". . . No?" squeaks Jeffrey.

The bitey one sighs again.

Jeffrey's reaction is all the proof I need, though a nagging voice inside my head tells me Death would have searched the cabinet before leaving. It only has six large compartments, each with a cartoonish painting on the front to illustrate what's kept inside.

The door with a teal bottle of bleach contains teal bottles

of bleach. The one with a brick-red pincushion contains pins, needles, and assorted clips. The one with a gray clothes iron on the front contains an old-fashioned iron and board.

I open all the doors, confirming my suspicions, and shake the plum-colored boxes of detergent, which are so pungent they make me sneeze. Nothing seems like it's hiding a gemstone.

Unless . . .

I close the doors and re-examine the cabinet, to the sound of hushed bickering from the squirrels. Brick-red. Olive. Teal. Mustard. These are all the same colors I noticed on the wallpaper and the striped fabric in the upside-down room. Without shapes, I can't make letters of them, but what if they're not meant to be letters?

Retrieving my sketchbook, I do my best to add the laundry room to my map. I hadn't anticipated multiple floors, so it's connected by a dotted line. When done, I go back to my alphabet and note the first time each color appears.

"I've got it!" I say, to more whispers from the squirrels. "It's the numerical order that the colors appear in."

First, I open the pincushion door, then teal, plum, olive, mustard, and gray. Something inside goes pop, and the entire bottom panel of the cabinet falls off. Behind it is a long drawer, filled to the brim with pocketable treasure, just as the squirrels had accidentally confessed. Intermingled with bobby pins and thimbles is a small fortune in gold coins, twinkling jewelry, and pocket watches. I run a hand through the contents—under the squirrels' tiny scrutiny—and pluck out a gorgeous circle-cut garnet.

"This is it," I whisper.

Death didn't get it. I can still win.

"A rock?" Jeffrey asks as if scandalized. "When there's a perfectly good pine cone right there?"

"Yep."

But that introduces a new problem. If I have the gemstone, that means Death is somewhere through the tunnel, still looking to stop me. I need to get out another way, and fast, because the clock is almost halfway to twelve.

"Do you know which pile of laundry is in front of the other door?" I ask.

All three squirrels look at each other, and Jeffrey reluctantly answers for them. "Aye, but we're not shifting the pile again. You'll have to help us fold."

I glance nervously at the clock. "What if I don't have time?"

The bitey one glares. "Then we'll follow you through the rest of the house and gnaw your ankles like angry beavers!"

Jeffrey looks at the bitey one, unsure.

I pull a face. "You can't hurt me, can you? The star said I wouldn't be physically harmed."

"Try us and find out," it barks.

I grumble and glance at the clock again. This really is like a roleplaying mission, down to the time-wasting chores, but I've got to get out of here. I look down at my still open bag.

"Let me tell you about dental floss."

Twelve

All mirrors are suspicious. Even the tiniest one gives me a chill, knowing anyone could be watching me through it. Unfortunately, the uncomfortably narrow hallway I'm in has several on every side, displayed as if they're cute family photos.

My mind returns to the image of Sol standing alone in front of the glass with his hand pressed flat against it. I imagine someone doing that now—touching one of the mirrors in the hall from the other side while I walk past—and the thought makes me stop to ponder.

Why *was* Sol touching the glass? It's not like he could have learned anything by setting his palm against the surface.

Or could he?

I approach the nearest mirror and gingerly raise a finger toward it until I tap the glass. The reflected fingernail touches mine.

"Oh. You are clever," I whisper.

Sol wasn't being romantic or defeatist. He was checking the depth of his reflection. Old two-way mirrors are coated with a reflective surface on the victim's side, where most normal mirrors have the reflective coating on the back of the glass. No gap between my finger and the reflection means the one in front of me is likely two-way.

Another chill runs down my arms, and I hurry down this latest hall, hoping to reach a stairwell to a subbasement floor with fewer mirrors. The maze has taken me several stories down, which has ruined my ability to properly map it. Thankfully, I've figured out how to navigate without looking at my sketchbook at all.

Using the color-number key I devised in the laundry room, I can read the order of each new hallway based on the paint and wallpaper.

"As above," I mutter, "so below. And below. And below."

I'm starting to sound like a conspiracy nut explaining why rainbows will lead me to Bigfoot, but I'm 90 percent certain I'm right. When I hit a branch again, one hall will have a lower number, and the other one will be higher. Lower numbers always lead to dead ends. So, if I pick a higher number every time, in theory, I'll go straight to the end.

I hope.

Unfortunately, when I finally reach a stairwell down to a subbasement floor, the air wafting up from it is rank.

"Gross. The odors are getting old, duck."

I was okay with the foggy-night scent, but this basement stinks of must and mold. As I descend, I realize the floor is unfinished, flooring replaced with damp, splintered concrete, and the paint is peeling from slimy stone walls—which are blessedly free of mirrors. I wouldn't be shocked to go down another floor and find myself in a stalactite-filled cavern.

The paint colors do not disappoint, however. At the next branch, one corridor is teal and mustard. The other one is gray and red. I take the gray-and-red one because sixty-one is a higher number than twenty-five, which increases my odds of spotting Bigfoot. Just kidding. The ability to follow the maze by color without fear of spies behind mirrors frees my mind for more strategic thoughts, like breaking down how the trials function.

"Why have a haunted house with squirrels instead of ghosts?" I whisper. "Can you only create things that are real? Or is there an emotion you were trying to trigger by putting silly creatures in a spooky setting?"

I toe a large crack in the moist concrete. It reminds me of my mother's assumption about why the Victorian never sold. Structural damage, she always said. Cracks in the foundation are expensive to fix, especially in a historic house.

"And why are the squirrels so calm about the fact that they're fake and you'll disassemble them at the end? Doesn't that scare them?"

Another branch, and a slight drop in temperature. I run my hands over my tunic sleeves, wishing I still had my sweater.

"Come to think of it, if everything is star stuff here, what makes me more authentic than them? My experiences? The way I'm assembled? If I'm stuck here forever, will I always be me, or will I become a figment of your imagination?"

I once again compare the competition to one of my role-playing games, having no better frame of reference.

"No. There must be something about player characters that makes us different from NPCs. A soul? An independent mind that will always think differently than yours?"

But the squirrels seemed so self-aware and . . . squirrely.

I pass another branch, spot another crack, and it's big enough to tear my attention away. When I look down, my eyebrows shoot up.

No wonder the basement's getting chilly. The cracks in the floor lead to outer space.

I get dizzy staring down at the night sky, and shudder at the thought of falling. It seems the cracks are disqualifying traps, getting larger as I bumble along talking NPC theory with a duck. Understanding how the trials work is important—both for my survival and for my future should I lose—but I need to pay more attention to the ground.

Two more turns and branches go by while I force myself to watch the floor. My eyes burn from lack of blinking as I try to discern cracks from shadows, but I keep pressing forward—until suddenly I can't.

"That's not fair," I moan.

The gap in front of me is so wide, I'll practically have to long jump to make it, and I'm no athlete. For a moment, I question the color-coded logic that led me down this particular path. It's tempting to turn back, but I know I'm right. With luck, this jump is like the final boss before I reach the end of the game: challenging, but necessary to win.

After several deep breaths, I step back, run, and leap across the starry chasm. It's not enough. I feel my toe clip the edge and slip before my stomach strikes concrete, making me cry out despite a lack of pain. My arms scrabble for something—anything—to grab onto and pull myself forward.

Someone else grabs ahold of me first.

Initially, all I can think about is getting up and away from the disqualifying void. Leaning heavily on my savior's strength, I pull my dangling legs from the gap. Gasping, my head swimming with panic, I look up to see who rescued me. A worry-lined face with dark eyes stares back, just as terrified as I am.

It's Sol.

Still gulping in ragged breaths, I wobble to my feet and throw my arms around him, squeezing like he's a teddy bear. "Thank you!"

Gently, he shrugs out of the hug. "June."

I frown, afraid I crossed a line by hugging him without asking first. I don't even know why I did it. Spontaneous stress response, maybe? It wasn't meant to be inappropriate.

"I know you have a gemstone," he says. "And I'm going to need you to throw it in the pit."

My spirit detaches from my body and spirals into the crack behind me, sucking the warmth from my flesh as it goes. "Why?"

"You know why."

"No. Death practically confessed."

I try to push past him into the hall—to put some distance between me and the crack—but he moves his body to block my path. I'm trapped. Sol is forcing me to fail the trial, after everything I've been through. All that puzzle solving for nothing.

No!

If I fail the trial, I don't get a key. If I don't get a key, I might not escape—and I've seen enough of the Star's handiwork to know a magical world built for my enjoyment will not be enjoyable at all. I'll be alone. Forever. Or worse—trapped in a house with imaginary squirrels who think folding laundry is peak entertainment.

"You wouldn't," I say, calling his bluff.

He's a good person deep down, even when he looks like a pretentious twerp. I saw the warm side of him in the ballroom. He protected me from burning glitter and took care of me when I felt sick. I feel sick now.

Sol looks away. "I'm sorry. I can't remember what I wagered, and that makes me afraid to lose."

"You know what *I* wagered!" I snap at him. "You want that to happen to me?"

"No!" His chest heaves with a frustrated breath. "I get two keys if I win. I'll give one to you. I promise. We can be a team."

A team where one partner forces the other to forfeit at the edge of a chasm? Yeah, right. I try to shove past him again, this time shouldering him hard in the chest. He doesn't budge.

"How do you expect me to trust you?" I demand. It's not like he trusts *me* enough to offer his deal without trapping me by a void first.

His face pales. "What? You know me."

"Do I? How can I know you when you don't know yourself?"

Sol jerks back as if struck, but keeps my way blocked. He sounds like he's coaxing a terrified puppy as he slowly explains his reasoning to me. "I've been searching the barrier of fog in my mind for memories of what happened before I got here. It's a struggle, like the fog is fighting back. But I feel dread when I try to find my deal. Maybe I gambled away my life."

I shake my head. "You're too smart for that."

"What if I'm not? Or what if I did something that made it seem worth it? Please—"

"*Get away from her!*" Death bellows, voice echoing down the hall.

Sol spins, attention falling from me just enough for me to squeeze by his shoulder. Death charges, armored fists already clenched as if eager to pound Sol straight through a wall. There's no time to properly react. I flatten myself against the stone as Sol launches like a cat across the crack. Death is faster and reaches the crack in a split second, leaping in pursuit.

Time feels like it slows as I witness Sol's perk for the second time.

Without looking back, he swings an arm toward the wall, which responds to his will like the glitter in the keyhole. Fist-sized stones tear free from its surface as easily as dust blown from a shelf and propel themselves in Death's direction. There's no time for Death to react. The stones strike them in the chest while they're midway through their leap, knocking them backward and into the crack. There's no other sound as they plummet downward.

I'm unable to breathe, watching in horror as Death's writhing form grows smaller and smaller. When I can no longer bear to watch, I meet Sol's gaze across the crack. His eyes are wide.

"I didn't mean to," he says, stumbling backward. "I didn't. I wouldn't."

But he *had*.

I run. Forget the maze. Forget the patterns. Forget placing gemstones in the eyes of a skull. None of that matters, because the trial is *over*. We lost, and even worse than that, Death has been disqualified. Whatever they wagered, that's now their fate, and Sol was the one to seal it. Why didn't I listen to the others?

Thankfully, the concrete floor is solid, but I keep my gaze on the ground anyway, suspicious of everything and everyone. The maze turns and branches, and I pick random directions, not even bothering to check the colors. What's the point if I can't win? What's the point if I have no friends in this place and everyone is likely to betray me?

I slow.

Is that what I'm really running from? Not Sol as a physical threat, but the realization that I've been naive in thinking I could form alliances? I assumed Sol would treat me like I treat him, and I'd feel awful in his position after everything we went through in the ballroom. But he's just following the rules of the trial and playing to win. Everyone is—even me.

I stop at a fork in the maze that, for all I know, I've passed three times. Somewhere nearby, I can hear Sol's footsteps—or the ominous oncoming steps of some horror roaming the maze to finish me off. Figures. The star won't let me ride out the timer and walk away. It wants emotions. Good thing I'm too miserable to care. The closer the steps get, the less human they sound. I swear they have the same pattern as—

A skeletal horse crashes up through the concrete like a zombie rising from a grave, and unlike when I encountered the star, my mouth remembers how to scream. I scream, the horse screams, and someone atop it shouts, "Yeah, let's let everyone know where we are. That seems like an excellent plan."

Then everything is okay again.

"Apparently, I have a horse," Death says, dismounting from the awful thing.

The skele-horse crumbles into hundreds of bones, which turn to dust and blow away.

"Had a horse," Death corrects.

I gape. "You're okay! But I saw you fall!"

Death's floating sunglasses nod. "It's more or less what I hoped the role would be when I selected the card. I assume you still have your gemstone?"

Without waiting for an answer, they pick a direction and set out, leaving me chasing behind.

"That's the wrong way," I call, and they turn. "Pumpkin is a higher number than mustard."

I hope they know what I'm talking about, because that sounds pretty weird out of context.

"Ah. Is that how the colors work? I knew they had significance, but couldn't work it out myself."

I blink. "How have you been finding your way?"

They tap what I assume is the side of their head. "Superior recall. Mostly mnemonic devices."

"Oh." I hurry to catch up. "So, if you get disqualified, that horse will always carry you back to safety?"

"That appears to be the case."

"Wow. And you thought Meela's stones were overpowered."

They stop at the next branch. "Still do. Thus far, the star has placed more emphasis on chance than logic. A perk that bypasses the worst outcomes of chance sets the owner up for success. Whereas my own perk has a limited application. Imagine having Meela's stones in this maze. Hmm. Well. I suppose you don't have to, since you worked it out faster than I."

I flush a little at the compliment and quickly point down one of the halls. They stride in that direction.

"I get it, I guess," I say, "but the star gave me a bag of my own junk."

"Has it come in handy?"

My nose scrunches up. "Well, sort of. But only because I thought of ways to use it. I'm not certain the trials *needed* my stuff."

Death turns a corner. "Perhaps the fool's perk is not in the bag itself, but manifests in the ways the items come in handy."

"Huh?"

"Never mind, it's just a thought. Like I said, the star seems enamored with chance—likely because organic creatures become frustrated when things are out of their . . . Hmm."

I look ahead and immediately understand the abrupt silence. A long corridor stretches before us, terminating in a solid wall. Unlike other dead ends in the maze, this one has a replica of the grandfather clock and an ornate marble table, upon which rests a skeletal cat. Unfortunately, Sol also sits by the table, arms wrapped around his knees. His spooky eyes are wide with shock.

"You're back!" he says, leaping to his feet.

Death gestures for me to get behind them and slides into a fighting posture. "Don't speak to us," they say. "Don't move a muscle. I will use our remaining five minutes to drag you back to that hole and pitch you in if you make me."

"I wouldn't—"

"I said don't speak!"

Sol shuts his mouth and lowers his head, waiting silently as Death leads me to the table. I glance over at him as I pass, noting how he gnaws his lip, and my stomach drops. He was only playing by the rules—but Death is right. Time is running out. We can't take chances.

"Right eye," I mutter, and dig the gemstone from my bag.

The gem slides awkwardly into the hollow of the feline skeleton's eye socket. Death shifts a tasset at their hip and pulls a matching stone from their pocket, placing it in the opposite eye. A three-toned howl echoes around the maze, and the skeletal cat stands to paw at a button that must have been hidden beneath its skull.

The floor disintegrates beneath us.

At first, I assume something has gone wrong. The darkness brings back memories of the empty void between the cracks. Then I feel the familiar sensation of my butt striking a metal plate, and I slide into a boiler room with a single exit on one side. Beside the door is a fortune telling booth, the kind I had imagined the cat's cabinet would be, with a plastic wizard, crystal ball, and a flickering sign that reads, *One fortune each.*

Death wastes no time approaching the thing and pulling a slot-machine-style handle. Gears grind, and a tinny laugh pours out of ancient speakers before a slot opens, revealing a rectangular cardboard box. Death grabs it and gestures for me to do the same.

The fortunes are the keys. We won.

I grip the handle, which has the same sticky texture as old plastic toys in my grandmother's basement, and give it a pull. Again, the wizard laughs, the lights flicker, and the slot opens. I snatch up the box, noting its familiar weight and size.

"Come on," Death says, shoving open the door.

Bright sunlight spills through.

Thirteen

Sol is already waiting outside when I step through the door and into the blessed, skin-warming sun. Likely, the trial booted him out while Death and I were gathering keys. I don't really want to look at him right now, but our eyes meet accidentally before I have a chance to turn away. One pointed cough from Death banishes whatever intention Sol has, and he flinches away without a word.

I know I have nothing to feel guilty for, but my gut twists anyway.

"A moment," Death says, and strolls into the shadows beside what appears to be a grass-roofed cottage.

Where is this place, anyway?

This new asteroid—assuming the same chunk of rock isn't changing shape after every trial—is nothing like the otherworldly ones before. It's a span of cozy farmland with rolling green hills, the scent of cut grass, and moss-covered buildings. It could easily be a location on Earth, if not for the bright sun and midnight sky.

Beside the cottage, Death fumbles with their cardboard box, discards it, and slips a hand in their pocket. Whatever key they got, it didn't interest them much, because they spent no time examining it. I hurriedly open my own box and, turning my back to Sol just in case, slide my key out of the cardboard.

My shoulders slump.

To confirm my suspicions, I pop open my backpack and dig out the key from the first trial. The two club keys are identical in every way, just like the one Sol got from the ballroom. All that effort, and it's possible I'm still falling behind, assuming I need a set.

"Is there a problem?" Death asks, making me jump and drop both keys back into my bag.

When had they returned from the shadows?

"Uh," I stammer, and search my brain for a sufficient fib to excuse my reaction. "I got the same key twice."

Really, brain? That's the best you could do?

"Interesting."

I zip up my bag before it, or my big mouth, give away any more. "You didn't?"

"No."

My brow furrows. Getting too close to Sol had burned me, and Death seems the sort to hold secrets close. But maybe there's information we can trade.

"Do yours have playing card suits on the ends?" I ask, unsure if I'm making a mistake.

There appear to be a lot of similarities between our planets—or universes, magical realms, or whatever—but also many differences. If my key is meant to be a clover, not a club, that changes my strategy. On the flip side, if it's meant to be a club and Earth is the only planet with those suits, I might be giving away an advantage.

Death falls silent, likely also evaluating risk. "Yes. But I'm unsure if we're collecting a set of four—meaning, one key per card suit—or if there are keys with matching suits and different bits."

So, our planets do have the same cards. That knowledge

strengthens my theory but also confirms that I'm behind if we're trying to collect one key of each suit. Crud. I factor in that Sol also has a club, and try to do some mental calculations. "So far, the bits on the duplicates have matched. So, with only seven trials left, it has to be a set of four we're collecting. The star said disqualification is rare—"

"That hasn't been my experience."

"I know, but the math doesn't work for more, right? If there are nine trials and not everyone gets a key every time, the number must be less than nine. Factoring in the duplicates, it has to be even smaller than that. Four makes sense."

"You're still operating under the assumption that most of us are going to escape."

I'm not, really. I'm just trying to be hopeful—a perspective that Death doesn't seem to share. Thankfully, shouts interrupt the conversation, and the second group pours out of a thatched cottage doorway. They're already mid-argument.

"I don't see what the problem is," the fairy emperor snaps. "You won the thing, didn't you?!"

Meela spits. "Your behavior has robbed us all of the opportunity to understand the universe beyond our short and shallow existence! We may never have such a chance again with the damage being done to the balance! The Wondrous Grapefruit—"

"I've been robbed of a key, which is far worse! Don't you agree, Councilor?"

"Have we defined *the balance*?" Yvit stumbles through the doorway behind Meela. "If I'm gonna be evaluated on this metric, I should know what it is."

Meela shoots out a hand from beneath her robes and points one dark, knobby finger toward the pangolin. I can't help noticing that she has four fingers and a thumb, but her middle finger is thin and long.

The finger wavers, then drops to her side. "You at least tried. The Wondrous Grapefruit is pleased with your efforts."

Yvit grunts. "Thanks. That clears up a lot."

With a dramatic flourish, the hierophant whips a bottle of sand from within her robes, uncorks it, and pours it into her palm. A silver key drops out with the sand. Yvit follows her lead, attempting to be discreet, but his fingers are thicker and less dexterous.

"Great Grapefruit," Meela whines, staring at her key. "Another copy of the three-leaf clover. If you had only obeyed the rules—"

The emperor's eyes flash with rage. "I'm not singing for free, I'm not holding your hands, and I'm not giving anybody here my real name!"

That's the second time he's refused to give his name. Rationally, I know he's an alien, not a fairy, but I *really* want to believe. Surviving a competition with the fae is even more impressive than with aliens.

Meela flaps her robed arms. "We can't just call you *The Emperor*!"

The emperor snorts. "And why not?"

"It takes too long to say! What if you're in danger and we must call quickly?"

"Then shorten it."

Yvit snickers. "Emp. Empy. Emperoony!"

The emperor glares and ruffles his wings. "Emperoony is just as long."

"Yeah, but it's way more fun to say."

Death clears their throat and steps forward. "What have you been calling me?"

"Death," answers Meela without hesitation.

"Death," confirms Yvit.

"Same," I confess.

They cross their arms, consider it, and say, "Fitting. It'll do."

The emperor throws his hands into the air, and, much to my shock, takes off in flight. Apparently, the mothlike wings on his back are not simply decorative. Unfurled, they more than double his size and appear to depict blobby skulls on each side rather than eyes like I thought. He flutters to the top of the cottage, sits where no one can speak to him, and pulls his scepter from his robes.

Meela ignores him and reaches toward Yvit. "Did you also get a second clover—"

"No," Yvit snaps, turning away. "I got something else."

I count keys in my head. Between me, Sol, Meela, and Yvit, there are now at least six club keys in play. We must be collecting a set of four. Nothing else makes any sense.

"Are you all aware there's a floating die over there?" the fairy calls from atop the thatched cottage.

He points with his scepter, and everyone turns to look at an unassuming well. Above it hovers a six-sided die that must be at least a foot across. The roleplaying nerd in me squeals with delight at the patina on the oxidized cube.

"The star too busy to see us this time?" Yvit snarks. "Got other places to be?"

Meela charges toward the die, making excited squeaking sounds, but upon nearing it, discovers she's too short. She bounces up and down in a sad attempt to claw at the die without falling into the well.

"Move aside," the fairy commands, swooping past the others to scoop up the die and hold it aloft.

"Now, hold on," Yvit says as he runs toward the fairy. His legs are much shorter than his torso, making it harder for him to catch up. "Nobody appointed you our actual leader."

Finally. Someone had to say it.

The fairy raises a perfect brow. "I thought it was implied in the role I chose."

"It was not."

Death groans. "It doesn't matter. Roll the die."

The fairy smugly obliges, and the die tumbles to the earth before rolling several times and coming to a stop. I'm disappointed it didn't hit the grass with a satisfying thud and stick in the soil. It must be hollow on the inside.

"Four," Meela reads. "But what might it—"

The ground shakes, and four pits open up in the grass, each as wide as I am tall, and each with a shiny, translucent surface. I creep toward the nearest one, noting the colors and patterns on the film. They remind me of holographic stickers.

Based on the orientation of a stone slab with the carved words *three of nine*, I know the first three images are reversed.

The closest one to where I stand has a picture of a clumsy juggler and is labeled the two of pentacles. The second has a flying creature with a handful of worshippers below it. It claims to be judgement, but I don't see how the picture relates to judgement at all. The third upside-down image shows cute children with cups of flowers and seems to be the best option of the four. I don't know what the six of cups signifies, but children and flowers can't be that bad.

The only one that's right side up has a terrifying image of a horned beast. The devil. I don't have to know much about tarot to suspect that one is going to be trouble.

Meela grabs her bag and dumps her stones, despite what appears to be an obvious choice.

"Not that one," she says, pointing to the one with the flying creature—which surprises me. I expected her to point to the beast.

Without a word, Sol moves toward the judgement pit and stands there, head bowed. I dig my nails into my palms to stop myself from joining him again. What if it's another competition where only one of us can get a key? What is he willing to do to win?

As if reading my thoughts, Death steps in front of me. "I wouldn't do that, if I were you. Personally, I choose the two of pentacles. You're welcome to join me if you want."

I narrow my eyes at them, suspicious. "What makes you more trustworthy than him?"

"Nothing, but I feel safe with *you* because you don't have the capacity to lie."

My face heats. "That's not true!"

I'm pretty sure just saying that aloud is proof. Denying that I can't lie, if I couldn't, would be a lie. So, I can. Ugh. These puzzles are getting to me.

"I choose the one with children," Meela declares, surprising no one.

"Enh, I'm gonna go with that one, too," says Yvit.

The emperor looks as if he's been slapped. "Councilor! I thought we had an agreement to exclusively pair with each other!"

"Yeah, well. I trust kids more than monsters. Sorry."

"Then you haven't met many children," the emperor snaps.

He holds his regal head high and strides to the devil pit, unafraid.

"Do we jump?" Death asks, examining the ground. "I don't see any doors."

I suck in a breath. "Can I hold your arm? Just in case it's a mistake and I need your . . . bravery?"

See? I can lie. That was a good one.

Death gives an unimpressed grunt but links our arms anyway. They're strong, in a firm-handshake way, but not as rough as their armor makes them look. I can't help myself and shoot one final glance toward Sol just in time to see him drop into his pit. He doesn't even jump—just steps in.

Death's arm jerks mine toward our own pit, and I'm tugged forward, ready or not.

I fall.

And fall.

While clinging to Death.

Fourteen

When characters in children's tales crawl into magical holes in the ground, they often experience a slow tumble or graceful float toward the bottom. The star does not concern itself with that, as it has the benefit of teleportation and our bodies are invulnerable. There's a flicker of light as we fall through space, as if we're passing through some kind of membrane, after which we violently impact the ground.

Death gets to their feet faster than I can, apparently unfazed by the collision. "Talk about childhood nostalgia," they say.

There's nothing nostalgic about the third trial unless Death grew up atop a pinball machine built by a roller coaster engineer obsessed with astrology. The surface directly beneath our feet is an impossibly large sheet of glass—how thick it is, I don't want to know. It's the cover of a pinball cabinet for giants, complete with rails and tunnels I could probably ride through on a mining cart. A complex mechanical system inside supports far too many moving parts.

"This isn't nostalgic for me," I admit. "The closest thing we have is way smaller."

That's a massive understatement. The machine is larger than a football field.

Death shrugs. "Ours also, but I know this game. Do you?"

I'm not sure how to answer the question. Have I played pinball before? Sure. Every trampoline park has one in a corner. Do I know the actual rules or gameplay? No. In the past, I slapped buttons, lost some balls, and someone stepped up to *show me how it's done*—without teaching anything. Something about pinball attracts that sort of person.

Hopefully Death isn't one of them.

I shake my head. Better to let them assume I don't know the game and surprise them later than make them think I know what I'm doing and embarrass myself by messing up. Speaking of which, I should probably look around.

We're standing next to the score display, above point-labeled buttons painted with stars. The controls are a couple hundred yards downhill, housed within the cabinet itself. I suspect the star dropped us where we are to force us to learn the mechanics as we walk. It's more helpful for me than for Death, but they examine the machine, nonetheless.

"Looks like a competitive trial," they say as if that fact is not obvious. "Good thing your friend isn't here with us. Imagine what his 'perk' would do to this glass."

I try not to look beneath my feet or think too hard about falling through. I'm still not sure how Sol's perk works—or how it applies to the hanged man—but surely there are smarter uses within a massive pinball game than breaking the glass. Death is just bitter.

"His name is Sol," I say instead of what I'm thinking, which is that I feel guilty for leaving him behind without giving him a chance to apologize.

"He has a name now?" Death asks, intrigued. "When did that happen?"

I stare down at the glass, not wanting to meet their nonexistent gaze. Below me, I can see a curved metal track with a switch like I might see on a railroad. That's new.

"In the first trial. He remembered his real name was short, so we picked a short nickname for him."

Death's glasses turn toward me, and I try not to flinch. "He never had a real name. He's not a person."

"Why do you keep saying that?" My voice has more venom than intended. "It's cruel."

Death chuckles and continues their stroll down the glass, checking out the game, same as I am. "First, I don't have to be nice to someone who tried to eject me into space. Second, you were not present when he appeared. By the time you arrived, he could speak and think. Before that, he was empty, like a statue. He didn't talk. He didn't react. He's a *prop*, not a person."

Something about their word choice makes my jaw clench, and I realize I'm getting angry. That's surprising, since I'm typically conflict averse.

"I'm not questioning what you witnessed," I say, refusing to let my rage steer my words. "But I've spoken to the star's creations. The squirrels in the laundry room had names and jobs. They knew the star created them. You have to admit, Sol isn't like them. It's possible his brain was scrambled, like he said."

"Counterpoint," Death replies. "You spoke to the squirrels. That proves you're predisposed to personifying the creations."

"What?"

"You want to believe the boy is real, therefore he's real to you—even if he isn't."

I chew my lip and turn away, fighting all the nasty things I want to say. I don't know if I'll need Death's help—or mercy—as this trial plays out, so I don't want to pick a fight. Instead, I focus on an intersection of tracks where two pinballs might collide. It reminds me of the tracks for toy car playsets.

"I just care about people," I say finally. "You should, too.

Why hurt Sol on the slim chance that you're right, when it hurts no one to listen to him?"

"Again, he hurt *me*."

I huff. "Not really, though. You're fine."

"Because of my perk, not any action of his."

"Sure," I admit, "but I don't think he meant to hurt you."

"It doesn't matter what he meant. This is his purpose. He's part of the trials."

"You don't know that!"

I clamp a hand over my mouth, realizing how loudly I just shouted. Why am I getting so defensive? I don't entirely trust Sol myself. Fortunately, Death seems amused, not upset.

"Ah, young love," they say with a chuckle, "so dramatic."

My face goes hot, and I give up on restraint. "It's not love! It's compassion. I literally just met the guy."

"So, you're not a believer in love at first sight? Or just where it concerns the boy?"

"Neither!" I snap, but the question strikes a nerve.

This is Alex and Jayden all over again.

How am I supposed to know my own feelings when everyone keeps redefining love? Is it instant, based on looks, or only real if you're compatible? "You have to know someone well to fall in love, yeah?"

"Are you asking me or telling me?"

There's no smirk on Death's face, because they have no face to smirk. Still, I can *feel* the expression in the air, like ripples above a hot summer street. They're mocking me in the way old people do, smug in the certainty that they have knowledge someone younger could not possibly have learned. Hating myself for it, I take the bait.

"Why? Have you experienced love at first sight?"

Death laughs again, but eventually answers. "From a very young age, I was obsessed with my career—determined I could save my dying world if I fully committed to my work. Love was a frivolity. Something I could not afford. Putting a single person above everything else was contrary to my entire being."

"Right, so—"

"Appearance? Mannerisms? Those were self-categorization. A way to ensure colleagues addressed me properly without time consuming questions. Not once did attractiveness factor in."

"I get it, but—"

"Did I fall in love anyway? Absolutely. And do I ever regret my disciplined ability to resist indulgence in that moment? Every minute of every day since we parted. I could have put effort into my looks while I still had the chance. I could have said . . . well. It's pointless now."

I balk. "Every day? Why didn't you reach back out or try to meet somebody new and move on?"

"Hah! There's no one on my planet who would ever love me—or even speak to me as you do right now. Why do you think I hide my face?"

"Hah! There's no one on my planet who would ever love me—or even speak to me as you do right now. Why do you think I hide my face?"

My brow involuntarily rises. I thought Death was naturally invisible, not deliberately so. To think they accused *me* of being dramatic.

Then again, I'd be lying if I said I'd never wished to be invisible. I can think of plenty of times where looking or acting differently made me a target. But Death has the kind of attitude that makes odd behavior cool. It makes me wonder how other people really see me.

This is a distraction, I realize. If I'm focused on Death, I'm not focused on the game—and they already have an advantage.

A pattern is starting to emerge below: two paths intertwining and occasionally crossing. Through those paths, at random intervals, are odd mechanics. Some divert tracks away from a hazard. Others switch from rails to ramps, offering choice at the expense of control.

I should let the conversation drop. Death is steering me, like the tracks below, messing with my head to make me fail. But there's one thing I can't resist asking. "Is that what you wished for, then? To be loved?"

This time, Death's laughter sets my teeth on edge.

"That would be asking too much, even for the star. No. I wished for a shot at redemption."

My stomach goes queasy in the way it always does when I think about really, truly bad people. The kind that, even if you believe in forgiveness, could never entirely make up for their crimes.

"Why? What did you do?"

Death takes their time answering—or, perhaps, like me, they're half distracted by the trial.

"I'm unsure how similar our home worlds are, but my planet is at constant war. Every few months, one faction obliterates another. It's a countdown to the end of the world."

"That sounds somewhat familiar," I admit.

"On top of that, resources are running out. But instead of joining forces to find a solution, we're fighting to rule the last scraps of land that haven't been rendered uninhabitable."

"That also sounds familiar," I mumble, doing my best to look, listen, and walk without messing up all three at once.

"I was personally unaffected, raised in a relatively safe location and given the resources necessary to become a microbiologist. Perhaps the greatest in history."

"So, no ego, then."

"It's the truth. I am also the greatest fool in history, because

I thought my discoveries could be used to bring peace and never questioned why I was sheltered."

Distracted, my foot slips on the glass, but I catch myself and ask, "What did you discover?"

"I had a theory that a microorganism commonly found on invisible fruit could be tricked into safely inhabiting skin."

They make air quotes when they say *invisible fruit*, which somewhat gives away the punchline. I prepare my yuck face in advance.

"As I see you've guessed, it was a success. Taking a harmless daily supplement and transplanting the swarm-minded, color-changing organisms resulted in active camouflage—a symbiotic relationship that renders one functionally invisible."

Yuck face activated. "You're invisible because you're covered in bacteria?"

"As are you."

"Eugh!"

"Welcome to microbiology. My dream was to use the technology to sabotage weapons and hide peace keepers. I later discovered that my lab and education had been paid for with funding accepted by my parents. The local faction owned anything I made and had been monitoring my developments."

I whisper, "Oh no," and stare down at the glass, avoiding their germy, invisible eyes.

"Not only did the faction repurpose my work for military espionage, they fumbled it and alerted other factions. Because of me, armies claimed 'invisible soldiers' as justification for civilian deaths—including their own dissenting people. The concept of civilian protections evaporated overnight, and my name was attached to the event."

In a desperate attempt to think about anything other than the horrors of war, I examine a mechanized spring below that might send a ball flying if properly triggered. The trial is so complicated, and I'm way out of my depth. Meanwhile, Death is literally brilliant, experienced, motivated, and knows the game. Maybe the snarky fairy was right, and the trials are deliberately stacked against me.

"You couldn't have known what would happen," I mutter for lack of anything comforting to say. There's no script on Earth to help with this one.

"I could have predicted it easily," they retort. "I never asked how I had fruit for my research while the world battled for potable water. Besides, someone suffering that kind of loss doesn't care if you *meant* to cause their pain. Intentions don't bring families back to life."

I can't even put myself in their shoes, as I've never messed up on a global scale. But I vividly remember all the times I've hurt people by mistake, and I replay those mistakes in my dreams. If Death suffers the same guilt, times however many people, it's a wonder they can even function at all.

Still, I have to wonder what redemption means to them. If their ego led to catastrophe, what makes them think a second chance won't turn out the same way? Some folks do more good by disappearing than seeking forgiveness from their victims.

"Stairs ahead," they say, gesturing to two gaps in the glass that resemble subway entrances. "Looks like we're meant to split up here."

Is it weird that I'm more frightened by the idea of going it alone than accompanying someone named Death who just confessed to literal war crimes?

Unfortunately, they're correct. I reluctantly nod in agreement and make my way to the stairwell on my left. The stairs are smooth glass with no safety features like handrails or textured steps. Because of that, I spend most of the descent paying careful attention to my feet, and do not look up to assess my surroundings until safely inside the cabinet.

"What?!" I blurt when I take in the controls.

This is not an Earthen pinball game with a couple grimy plastic buttons and a sticker warning not to tilt the machine. There are baseball-sized buttons, switches, levers, pedals, plates, wheels, and cranks—and no explanation for any of them. In fact, the closest thing to instructions is a placard explaining the winning team is the first to score three points in the game. That winner will again receive two keys, while the loser—let's face it, that's me—receives none.

"You look nervous," Death's voice purrs, and it takes me a moment to spot their glasses at a porthole-like window along the partition.

"I told you. I've never played this before."

"And I've never played a game this large before. You may have me beat for agility here. I'm not as young and spry as I look."

I huff. "Beat how? I don't even know the rules."

"Hmm." Death considers it. "Then how about a deal? I'll teach you if you explain your wish."

"What, really?"

"You're the only one I haven't figured out. The politician and emperor are likely power hungry. Meela Cast-Stones seeks enlightenment. And you know my feelings on the one you call Sol. So, what does June get if she wins, and why?"

"It's private," I say out of habit.

"All right, suit yourself. Let's get started."

"Wait."

There's no way to save face and win. I grit my teeth and approach the window.

"Promise you won't laugh, and I'll tell you."

Death's glasses nod. "You have my word."

"You asked for it," I say—and tell them everything.

Fifteen

I'M GOING TO collapse.

My body aches. My brain aches. My breathing sounds like a snoring cat. Turns out, despite their imperviousness and lack of need for nourishment, these reconstructed-star-stuff bodies can be worn ragged, just like our real ones. As I dash from a switch to a wheel and yank it down, I thank the star that I can't bruise myself. If I could, I'd be pink and purple all over.

Half a football field away, a Y-shaped track spins around in a circle. Shortly after, a glowing blue pinball the size of a tire crosses over, heading for a star-painted bumper. It's my ball—and this time I'm ready.

It took a while for Death's instructions to click, because words like *gyroscope* and *differential*—in the context of a pinball game—make no sense without trial and error. I suspect it was Death's strategy to give me just enough info to roll the ball around but not enough to actually win. That makes what I'm about to do satisfying.

I watch the pinball, anticipating an electric *ding* when it impacts the star-painted bumper. When it does, a matching star will light up on a constellation on my side of the scoreboard, and Death will learn that I'm a quick study.

But, of course, this is my life, so that's not what happens.

To my dismay, instead of a satisfying ding, I hear a pained grunt from the other side of the partition, after which a spring-loaded block pops out and slams my pinball completely off the track.

"Not fair!" I scream while scampering for a button that will save it from vanishing into a hole.

Understanding how the game works is one thing. Playing it well is another entirely. It's taxing every part of me to keep an eye on my blue pinball, plus the track, plus everything I have to control to get the ball where it needs to go—all while watching Death's orange ball and paying attention to the ways I can thwart it.

Speaking of which.

I spot Death's orange pinball bouncing around between a series of thin pegs and decide it's a good time for revenge. Fueled by spite, I dash forward and fling out my palm, smacking a button that slams a door shut in front of the pegs and opens another farther away.

"Nice!" Death calls, but they swiftly recover and redirect their pinball onto a curved slide.

I whimper, completely deflated by how long it's taking me to set up every win and how quickly Death can halt my progress. With everything combined, it's too much: the lights, the sounds, the sweaty heat inside the cabinet, two pinballs to track at all times, too many controls to think about, and everything super far apart. I'm exhausted, and worse, Death's not stressed at all. So much for the advantage of agility.

I exhale as my pinball comes round again and push a button that sends it back where I need it. With Death distracted rerouting their pinball, mine crosses the Y-track again and flies toward the bumper for the second time. The exact same block pops out to strike it, and this time, I'm not fast enough.

Sad electronic music plays, and the empty stars on the

scoreboard flicker. Neither of us has filled a constellation to get a single point on the scoreboard yet. It will take *forever* to get three. My skin feels like it's swarming with ants, I'm so agitated by this game.

"Gah!" I scream, and slam my fists into the wheel.

It doesn't hurt, but that also makes it less cathartic. More music chimes, and a new pinball appears, waiting for me to pull the launcher that will send it out into the game. Instead, I sit down right where I am and bury my face in my arms.

I'm not going to cry. I refuse. I may scream or stomp or flail my arms, but I will not let this thing make me cry.

"What are you doing?" Death asks between breaths.

"I need a moment," I manage to say before all the words catch in my throat.

Death won't understand, anyway. They're the sort who finds this kind of game *fun*. Meanwhile, my hands are trembling and my nerves feel like exposed wires. There's nothing fun about repeating the same tiring steps over and over just to go back to zero every time.

Death's orange ball pings around again, and a fifth star lights up on their constellation. Annoying electronic fanfare plays, and they maneuver the pinball for another star.

"At least try," they suggest while doing something that drops their ball from a ramp to a tube. "You're half my age, and I'm covered in armor. You could win this one by attrition."

That may be their way of encouraging me, but it's making me furious instead. Why try when twenty minutes of effort got me zero stars—which we each need ten of to earn one point out of three? It's infinitely easier to give up the game and hope the next trial is less annoying.

"You need to get up and play if we're going to make it out of here," they command.

Their pinball twirls around the tube and stops, held at an angle by a flipper.

"Forget me. Just finish the trial," I call back.

"No, I mean—ugh."

They let go of whatever button they're holding, and the pinball drops. It bounces back and forth between a couple slingshots before falling into a trough and exiting play. The sad song chimes, and all their stars go out.

Why?

Death approaches the window in the partition and leans against it, catching their breath. "Time to come clean. I . . . was wrong. This isn't a competitive game. There's no way to win with only half the controls."

I look up at them. "Half?"

Death sighs. "This game is normally played in turns with one person controlling both sides. You currently have me blocked from scoring."

I shake my head. How is that possible when they already filled out multiple stars?

"I'd hoped," they explain, "we could outwit each other—trick each other into opening passages. But the truth is far more sinister."

"How so?" I ask while shaking out my limbs to calm myself down and stop trembling.

"The star wants us to decide who wins."

"Like, we just pick someone and that's who wins?"

They rub a spot where their temple might be. "We'll still have to play, of course, but together—once we decide who gets the keys."

"But," I say, struggling to my feet. "There's two keys. So, the winner can share."

"Do you trust me to claim both and split them fairly afterward? Or do you expect me to trust you to do the same when lover-boy is out there waiting?"

A strange icy feeling makes its way down my arms, even as heat radiates from my body. In my mind's eye, I'm back in the maze with Sol as he begs me to betray Death and share his keys.

"You can trust me," I say. "I've protected you before."

"And I you," Death counters. "But this is different, is it not? Too easy to back out after we've won."

Death makes it sound like this is a standoff, but moments before, I was willing to give up. I trust them—probably more than they trust themself—and know they'll do what they think is right. Too bad *right* to them might mean betraying me for the chance to save countless lives on their world.

From their perspective, what's my wish compared to that?

"I'll help you win, and you split the keys," I decide. "And don't think I haven't realized you made me tell you my wish when you knew you had to teach me anyway."

"I had to know what you were playing for."

"So you'd feel better about stabbing me in the back?"

Death holds their tongue and makes their way to the controls on their side of the cabinet. I do the same and wait for them to launch their ball. Jarring electronic music plays again.

"Give the wheel half a clockwise turn, and press the round button," Death shouts over the clatter of the enormous pinball rocking around the track.

I do as they say, and with effort on their part, the pinball circumvents my favorite bumper and collides with a similar bumper above. Festive music plays, and the first of ten stars on their constellation lights up.

"Switch down, lever up," they command while running from one side of their wall to another.

"The switch is already down!" I shout back.

"Leave it down. Grab the lever. Quick!"

I do, and an entire section of track spins, diverting Death's pinball down into a tunnel rather than up to a spiraling rail. It impacts a trigger beneath a painted star, and another light illuminates on Death's constellation.

"Have you got this whole game memorized?" I ask.

"The game itself, yes. This specific machine, no. Stomp the pedal on my command."

I jog to what looks like a guitar pedal on the ground and raise one foot over it, waiting for their word.

"Now!" they shout, and I slam my foot down. It feels kind of cool.

A metal bar swings like a baseball bat, propelling the pinball into a cluster of pegs, where it pings around until more stars light up.

"So, you want a cheat sheet for love," Death says unprompted while the pinball flies through a spinner that triggers a light show. "It's an interesting wish. Most people would have asked for true love outright, if not the affections of a specific person."

I pause to catch my breath and wipe sweat from my forehead. There is no way I'm explaining Jayden to them, but I can defend my reasoning without bringing his name up. "Of course I didn't wish for a specific person. If you're not compatible enough with someone, would you really be happy with them? I figured I could learn what I'm looking for and then find the right person myself."

"There should be a round knob on your side. Twist it to the left."

I do, not even glancing up to see the result. Happy music plays, and I wait for the next instruction.

"You're analytical, like me," they say. "You try to rationalize emotions. But here's the thing: Love isn't rational. It makes you care about things you've never cared about before. You make decisions that affect you for years—or your lifetime—without a thought to the consequences. Love changes you, and not always for the better."

They punctuate the last statement with a roar of effort and the clank of a thrown lever. Festive music chimes again, twice in a row. I look up to see only three stars left before the constellation completes.

"You're saying love would change my perspective on things?" I ask. "Like, I might suddenly decide I enjoy camping? I'm not convinced."

"Spin the wheel a full turn counterclockwise, and if you have a wooden handle on a chain, tug that down."

I do have a wooden handle on a chain, which I have hesitated to touch until now because I thought it was the flusher from an antique toilet. Thankfully, it's only a symbolic flusher. The pinball enters a funnel-like circle and triggers another star as it slips through the bottom.

"I think that was supposed to be a black hole," Death says with what sounds like actual amusement. I'm glad someone is having fun.

"What did love physically feel like to you?" I ask, realizing what they're doing. They're trying to give me answers to my wish, assuming we'll both escape, but they'll win. "My mom says it's like butterflies in your stomach, but my best friend says that's just a cliché. How can you tell real love from a crush, or a crush from an intense interest?"

"I don't know. I've never had a crush."

"Never? Not once?"

"Switch up, lever down."

"Right."

I huff back over to the wall and toggle both.

"I'll take it from here," Death says as another round of

music plays. "And no. I didn't have butterflies. I didn't even realize I was in love. Do you recall how glorious it feels when pain lets up for the first time? Love was like that moment for me, a brief period in my life where all the suffering in the world couldn't reach me. There was no kissing or touching or romantic language, just the act of being together. We *were* . . . then we weren't, and the pain returned."

They fall silent, save for quiet huffs as they jump between controls on their side. The orange ball travels in an arc around the machine, eventually impacting the same bumper I had tried—and failed—to hit several times. Their constellation fully lights, then flashes while an overture plays. The song seems inappropriate after their confession, but at the end, their score changes from zero to one, and their resulting sigh is relief, not sorrow.

"You mind if we do the rest without chatting?" they ask, leaning against the window.

I nod. "I didn't mean to bring up your past."

"It's not that," they say. "It's difficult to exercise in costume armor and carry on a conversation."

"Oh. Right."

"Anyway." They vanish from the window and shout back, "One full clockwise turn of the wheel when you're ready."

"Again?" I reply.

Nonetheless, I turn the wheel.

Sixteen

As I plummet through the exit door—another holographic hole in the ground—it dawns on me that I've become the pinball. Every time I fall into a pit, it signifies the end of a round. It's cute, except for the impact at the end.

"Ooh! There you are! Just the one of you, then?" Meela asks while scurrying toward me.

It's a wonder the hierophant doesn't trip on her robes as she scampers around in far too many layers. Good thing there's nothing else to stumble on—at all. We're on a pale rectangle in space, with no other objects visible, save for two faintly glowing moons.

"No," I say as I get to my feet. "Death should be here any minute."

As if on cue, Death drops from above, landing in a superhero crouch. They straighten, nod to Meela and Yvit, and gesture for me to step aside with them.

"As we agreed," they whisper, tossing me a colorful capsule that looks like it came from a claw machine.

Eagerly, I pop it open and tug out the plastic-wrapped item inside. It's a golden key with a diamond-shaped bow. Finally, something other than a club!

Death sighs, holding up one with a spade. "A duplicate

with the same bit, as you said."

"Oh! I don't have a spade," I say, fighting to hold in my excitement. This is exactly why I need allies. If the purpose is to get a set of four, we can exchange to fill out our sets! "Do you need a club? I have two. We could trade."

Meela squeaks, and I jump. I'd forgotten that she was so close. "Are the clovers the ones you call clubs? If so, I also have two of those!"

The hierophant's hands slide inside her robes and re-emerge with three keys: two clubs and a spade.

"Yes," Death says hesitantly, "but you clearly don't need my spade."

Meela shrugs. "The Wondrous Grapefruit speaks to us in mysterious ways, and it's our job to listen. A slight tickle of the tongue, a subtle itch behind the ear—any of these could be a message. I tell you, I *do* need the spade, but I cannot explain the reasons for this."

"I got two diamonds," interrupts Yvit while waddling closer to join the conversation.

Somehow, he's found a tie. It doesn't work with his old-fashioned tunic, but he seems more comfortable wearing it.

Death holds their key out to him. "Deal."

Yvit greedily snatches up the spade and tosses Death his extra key. I'm disappointed and irritated, but also a little curious. Does Death already have a club, or are they making strategic trades knowing clubs will be easier to trade for? From what I know of them, it's the second—and that gives me an idea.

As Meela fusses in Yvit's direction, I step back and slip my sketchbook from my bag. On a fresh page I write:

June: 2 Clubs, 1 Diamond
Meela: 2 Clubs, 1 Spade
Death: 1 Spade, 1 Diamond, 1 Heart?

Yvit: 1 Spade, 1 Diamond, 1 Unknown

Even without looking up, I can feel Death's gaze upon me. "Smart," they say.

Anything additional they might have added is immediately drowned out by shrieks of rage from someone tumbling out of the sky. The emperor flits like a moth in a tantrum, flailing and shouting at someone not present.

"That goes double for you, you ugly bag of blisters, and your unsightly orphaned children, as well!"

He carries on shrieking until his feet touch the rectangle that serves as the ground in our current location. I hadn't really noticed before, but faint shapes are painted on the surface.

"Orphaned children?" Yvit asks. "I thought you were fighting a monster."

"A financial monster!" the emperor snaps back while tugging his regalia around him like a blanket. "The star put me in charge of a key factory, and I assumed it was an easy win. I'm a successful businessman in my realm, to say the least. But the workers were owed excessive wages—with benefits, even—and the materials weren't cheap. At best, using honest practices and fulfilling all existing orders, I'd have wound up with a single key for myself."

Yvit scratches his cheek with a thick claw. "That's weird. Ours was a finger-painting session."

"Not *just* painting, no!" Meela objects. "We surrendered our minds and flowed with nature! We let go of the stressors of the past and opened ourselves to the joys of the future!"

"I do have a lot of past to let go of."

"I'm not finished!" the emperor shouts. "One of the overpaid slugs had the audacity to call out sick—and expected me to pay him for it! I would have had to operate the machine myself, which is unacceptable. So, of course, I fired him, and five other slugs with him. If any jerk could do the labor, why should I pay them so much to do it? Reallocating those funds for metal and hiring less expensive labor, I could have minted all four keys and completed the set in a single trial."

"I see where this is going," I whisper.

Yvit catches my eye and nods.

"Apparently," the emperor continues, "that was reason to burn my factory down. I barely made it to the door before the roof collapsed."

"Where do the orphans come in?" Yvit demands.

The answer seems obvious, so I stop listening and turn my attention back to my sketchbook.

Emperor: 1 Unknown
Sol:

Where is Sol?

"That's why you sabotage your competition," the emperor explains to Yvit. "Buy up all the resources, cheapen your production, and bribe shipping companies. Make it impossible for them to distribute or compete with your prices. Then offer their customers convenience. Sheep will do anything for convenience. You can make up in subtle markups and cheap materials what you've lost in overhead—like boiling a frog in water."

"Again," Yvit says, "what does that have to do with kids?"

"Once you're the only provider of essential goods and no one can afford to compete with you, you can charge whatever premium you like. The cost of living increases. People get desperate. Desperate people take jobs for less money, and leaders agree to tweak regulations so families can supplement their incomes."

Yvit crosses his arms. "You tried to hire the orphans, didn't you? Where I come from, you'd be locked up."

"That's why you buy the politicians and judges."

I lean closer to Meela and whisper, "What's wrong with

that guy?"

"Ooh, he's very proud of himself," Meela declares at normal volume. "Claims he's the second wealthiest person on his planet. Of course, he's wished to become the first. In my modest opinion, that's an unfortunate goal. It will only move him further from spiritual peace."

My brow furrows. "Yikes. What did he wager?"

The emperor swoops closer, thanks to Meela's indiscretion. His crimson regalia looks even more ridiculous up close, but I must admit, it's better than hot pants. Why the second wealthiest man on a planet would run around half-nude was baffling to me. Perhaps it's a cultural thing—or the star caught him midway through an evening swim.

"If I fail to escape this awful place, my workforce will successfully unionize," he informs me with a perfectly straight face.

"That's all?" I ask.

He sets a dramatic hand to his chest. "All? Do you realize how much money I'll lose in delays while I fire and re-hire every position?"

"Ew," I say. "That's gross."

"Tell me about it," he replies, misunderstanding my response.

Yvit shakes his head. "So, what's next? I don't see a die to roll."

The emperor swings his head around, causing his antennae to bob. "Indeed. Where is that ugly space snake? I have some choice words for it."

"Where's Sol?" I ask.

The emperor pulls a face. "Who?"

Meela clicks her tongue. "You know who she means. Only one competitor is absent."

"The hanged man," he says with a snarl. "Perhaps he was

reabsorbed into the star."

A knot forms in my stomach. More likely, he fell through a hole to outer space or got trapped underneath a pile of rubble. There's no one with him, and he was so upset. Anything could have happened to him. I should have at least said something nice to smooth things over before we left.

"Never fear. He's on his way," Meela says, patting my sleeve. "For better or worse."

"How do you know that?" Yvit asks. "Some kind of premonition?"

Meela closes her yellow eyes and shakes her head. "The next trial would have started otherwise."

"Eh. That's a good point."

As if to prove it, a light flashes above, and Sol tumbles down, landing in a heap. His face is flushed, his hair is disheveled, and his eyes dart wildly until he spots Death. In his hand, he grips a crumpled envelope.

"I'm so sorry," he says, stumbling toward Death. "What I did was wrong. I want you to have this."

When he holds up the envelope, I already know what's inside. Unlike the emperor, he won his trial. Death's spine straightens, and their hand curls into a fist. For a moment, I expect them to haul off and strike him. But the moment passes, and they shake their head.

"No need. I'm fine, and I . . . forgive you."

Their sunglasses tilt in my direction as if daring me to say a word. I don't.

Sol's eyes widen. "Really? Thank you. That means a lot."

"Don't make too much of it. I have my reasons."

Their reasons, I suspect, have much to do with their own desire for forgiveness, and little to do with compassion for Sol. Even knowing that, I'm a little suspicious that they didn't take a free key. What do they know that I don't?

The emperor twirls a hand. "So very touching. Where's the die? Where are the doors?"

Sol ignores him and approaches me. His hands are clutched together so tight his fingertips are turning red.

"June," he says before his breath catches.

I don't make him say the rest. Apologies make me uncomfortable, so I give him a reassuring smile. "I'm glad you're okay. I was worried."

He returns the smile, only just. "I'm not *that* helpless." The smile fades. "I tried the trick you taught me again—the one where I search the fog in my mind for memories—and didn't like what I found."

The emperor interrupts with a flail. "Come on! We're all here. Get a move on, star!"

"Perhaps he must first observe his key?" Meela suggests.

Sol groans at the interruption, tears the envelope dramatically, and shoves the key into a pocket without pausing to examine it. It's only because of where I'm standing that I manage to catch a glimpse of the bow. Another spade. How many does that make?

I need to write this stuff down to remember it, but Death doesn't. They have a superior memory. That's right! They know how many keys are in play and must be convinced that we're collecting one each of the four suits. With so many clubs, they turned down Sol's key because they're confident they can trade for one later. Which means they *must* have a heart.

Meanwhile, Sol didn't bother to look at his key before offering it up. The judgement trial must have lived up to its name.

"Now?!" the emperor shouts.

The star replies not with an appearance, but with a thunderclap so loud I jump and scream despite myself. Half the competitors glare at me as if I did it to be dramatic. Their attitudes change when something falls from the sky and strikes Yvit directly on the snout, making him jump and yelp as well. More small objects tumble from above, and most of us cover our heads with our arms. Only Death is chill enough to hold out a hand and catch a falling object in their palm. When they do, the painful rain ceases.

"They're numbered tokens," Death explains, while holding up what looks like a gold doubloon. "I grabbed number six."

"That's what the star came up with?" the emperor scoffs. "The number of doors is based on the token? If you'd told us, we could have selected a better number."

Yvit picks a token up from the ground, bites it, and spits as if he expected it to be chocolate. "You'll live. You got to pick all the other doors. Give someone else a turn."

"Untrue. No one rolled for the first set."

The rectangle beneath us trembles, and dozens of identical rectangular shapes flutter out from beneath one edge. They twirl in the colorless sky, and I finally recognize the pattern on the ground.

Meela beats me to the punch. "We're on a deck of cards!" she squeals.

Somehow, I managed to miss the fact that the rectangle beneath us is a cardstock box. The enormous cards that spill from inside sound like crackling fireworks as they shuffle. They're a strange mix of mismatched suits and styles, most of which are unfamiliar. Two at a time, they're dealt in our direction, shrinking and assembling into six house-of-cards style stairwells that I assume we'll soon have to climb.

Every card is the size of a cafeteria table, and every stair is made up of two cards side by side. This doesn't thrill me after the pinball trial. Hopefully, it isn't a race.

"Everyone for themselves?" the emperor asks, as if two people would want to share a stairwell when chances are there's only one key per route.

Before anyone can respond—or in Yvit's case, snark—another six cards are dealt from the shuffle and float into the distance beyond the forming stairwells. Those six appear to be tarot card doors, but not all of them are legible from far away.

There are some easy-to-spot repeats, such as the death card stairwell near Death. Sadly, the one atop the nearest stairwell is not as recognizable. It's an upside-down person surrounded by swords. I want to say there are eight of them, but that's just a guess at this distance.

While everyone is distracted by the cards, Sol moves next to me and sheepishly waves in the exact way I might if I were nervous.

"You didn't let me apologize," he whispers.

There's not a ton of privacy on a floating deck of cards.

"You don't have to," I whisper back. I've never had the energy to hold a grudge, and I get the impression he's punishing himself more that I could punish him.

"Yes, I do. I made you feel unsafe. I'm sorry."

My heart does a little flip. He may not like what he found in the last trial, but it must have done him a lot of good.

"Also," he says, "I need you to know that I wouldn't have pushed you. I thought about blocking you until time ran out, but I'd never hurt anyone here on purpose. I almost wish I fell in the pit instead of Death."

I scowl. "That's not funny. Death is fine. I'm fine. Everything turned out okay, and I really am glad you're safe."

He looks at the ground. "Thanks."

Our whispers are interrupted by shouts from the emperor, who's growing visibly impatient. "If you're going to take this long setting up, why not come out and speak to us? I have feedback I wish to share!"

Meela flails her knobby fingers, flinging the arms of her

robes around. "Your discomfort is the reason the star's drawing this out. If you want it to stop, you should calm yourself."

That's surprisingly decent advice. Either the hierophant is wiser than she looks, or this is her one moment of clarity, like how a stopped clock is right twice a day. As if to double down on the temporary wisdom, she whips out her bag and rolls her stones.

Death does not wait to see what she rolls. They claim the stairwell that leads to the death door before anyone else gets a chance. By now, I'm convinced they're a genius, so I take their lead and claim the stairwell nearest me, prompting a dirty look from Meela. She finishes her roll, huffs, and claims a stairwell on the opposite side.

"Let's get this over with!" the emperor declares. "I'm ready to win."

He marches toward a stairwell that leads to a door which, like mine, appears to be reversed. On it, there's wealthy looking person surrounded by nine pentacles. The emperor scowls at the first card-pair step as if making a choice between the two cards, then steps nonchalantly onto the rightmost one.

It dissolves into nothingness beneath his feet.

Seventeen

I GASP, EXPECTING the emperor to fall into the void and drift away like Death had—and for a moment, that's exactly what happens. Once he registers what's occurred, he deploys his wings and flutters back up to the cards, surprise morphing into indifference.

"Seems you forgot I could fly!" he bellows into the night.

I wouldn't taunt the star if I were him.

"Seems you forgot this is a trial, not a race," Yvit snarks. "Why didn't you solve the problem first?"

Problem? I squint at the emperor's stairs and note that there are questions printed on them.

"Because I don't have to," the emperor retorts, turning to flutter up the playing card staircase.

"That's not fair," I cry, watching him drift past the obstacle course.

"That's life!" he calls back. "Some of us are born better!"

Strong words from a gilded turd. How did he even hear me from there?

"I believe this is another multiple-choice test," Meela says, crouching at her stairwell and reading something on the first step. "Mine has questions from the entrance exam for the Order of the Wondrous Grapefruit. I, of course, know all the answers. But just in case…"

Her long, knobby fingers retreat into her robes and return with the bag of stones. She pours them out and lowers her face until her long nose nearly brushes against them.

"That one," she declares, and gathers them up before leaping onto the leftmost card.

The card beside it disintegrates, and I let out a nervous breath. This is worse than the basement floor in the mansion maze. Every move is potentially disqualifying, and worse, I chose my stairwell at random, while Death likely read their questions first. Ugh. Why didn't I notice the text? I'm just as bad as the emperor.

Dreading what I'll find, I read the question scrawled on the near edge of my first step. Or, rather, I read what I think will be a question, based on Meela's declaration. Mine isn't so simple. It's a phrase with missing gaps in the words, like a half-finished children's game of hangman. I glance over at Sol on the stairwell next to mine and wonder if this one was meant for him. Some kind of morbid humor from the star?

I compare the phrase with two illustrations printed on the cards that make up the first stair. It seems I'm meant to figure out the phrase and step onto to the card with an illustration that best matches whatever it says. It's impossible to guess based on the images alone.

"Mine's arithmetic," Yvit calls to us. "I'm not taking any chances."

He reaches into the magician's bag at his hip, which I'd all but forgotten about, and retrieves an oversized calculator. I gawk. It makes sense that a magician can pull items from an empty bag, but it hadn't crossed my mind that he could pull *any* item. I wonder if there are limitations on the number of times he can do it per trial, or what he's allowed to pull. Surely, if the bag was infinite and boundless, he'd have all four keys and an escape hatch.

I would.

His stubby fingers and thick nails move surprisingly quickly on the calculator. Without a word, he hops to the card on his right and pauses to read the next stair. His fingers tap out the problem on that one before the card beside him fades away.

"Mine's math, too," Sol says.

Calculator-free, he jumps to his first card, and I crane my neck to see what he solved. It's a math problem, like he said, but not one that makes any sense to me. There are symbols and letters I've never seen represented in any of my textbooks.

"Is that advanced physics or something?" I ask.

He pauses and stares at the next question as if he hadn't thought about it. "Maybe."

For the first time since the ballroom, he looks pleased with himself. I guess the star finally cut him a break and gave him a challenge he can win. He leaps to the next stair with a spring in his step, gives me a goofy grin, and takes a bow like he's performed a magic trick.

Is he trying to impress me with his house-of-cards math skills?

I mean, it *is* impressive that he can do in his head what would take me hours with an app. It makes me wonder what kind of world he came from. But why show off for my benefit? Why not head straight for the— Wait. No!

Is he . . . *flirting*?

I honestly can't tell. Why am I so bad at this?

Over my shoulder, I hear Death chuckle—though if it's at their own challenge or my situation, I'm unsure. They nimbly leap from one card to the next, taking little time to read. I know why; there's nothing for them to fear. I suppose, though, they're putting on a show to hide their perk as long as possible.

"Best of luck!" the emperor calls in a sickeningly sweet sing-song voice before vanishing through the open door at the top of his untouched staircase.

I grumble and check out the remaining doors. Meela's is justice again, but right side up this time. Yvit's is a king with pentacles. Sol's, disconcertingly, is the star, but reversed, whatever that means. I'm sure I'll figure out the tarot cards just in time for the competition to end.

"What's yours?" Sol asks, and it takes me a moment to realize he's asking about my questions, not my door.

"They're not math problems, they're phrases," I say. "This one's missing all its vowels."

The explanation escapes my mouth before my brain even catches up. I guess some part of my subconscious was solving the problem while the others distracted me. The missing letters are vowels, and even without them, I can read the phrase. It says, *Hitch your wagon to a star.*

"It's an idiom."

I own multiple idiom books, because—according to my mother—I got angry as a kid if anyone used one without explaining the etymology. I can picture my young self stubbornly arguing that my math homework is not a piece of cake.

Examining the stair cards before me, I note that one depicts a sleeping kitten, and the other a child with a little wagon. I jump to the wagon card, and the kitten dissolves.

"You're doing great!" Sol says.

I'm starting to think he's being patronizing, not flirting, seeing as this is my first stair. My brow furrows. Sol is several cards ahead, Death is halfway to the end of their staircase, and Yvit isn't too far behind them. The only thing slowing Meela down is the time it takes her to clear up her stones. I am, in fact, not doing great.

I try to focus on my next question, but the star has changed the parameters, and it's not a hangman puzzle anymore. The four-word phrase now consists of numbers instead of letters—assuming it's a phrase. There has to be some overarching theme. Is it still an idiom?

For some reason, knowing Sol is watching makes it harder for me to focus. It's the same mild panic I feel when teachers ask me to speak in class. The fear of peer judgement for a wrong answer overrides my ability to reason.

Of course, a wrong answer on this quiz means disqualification, not embarrassment. I'd never see Sol's reaction to my failure. I'd never see him—or anyone—again.

That snaps me out of it.

I briefly consider the pros and cons of trying to jump so I straddle both cards, but I haven't had the greatest luck with jumping, and the star could easily disintegrate both. It's fine. The solution is coming to me. I'm pretty sure all I have to do is swap the numbers for their position in the alphabet, just like I did with the colors in the maze. Easy.

"Thank your lu—"

That's enough. One of the cards has a four-leaf clover, and I jump to it. *Thank your lucky stars.*

These aren't just idioms. They're star idioms! How many of those can there be?

Someone shouts something that sounds like "Cabbage!" Probably a mistranslation.

I turn my head just in time to see Death plummet through a dissolved card and into the inky blackness below. Meela and Yvit understandably panic, then panic even more when Death bursts back upward, riding on the back of a skeletal horse.

"Blazing mongoose!" Yvit shouts—and I hope that one wasn't mistranslated. "What is that?!"

"It appears to be some kind of equine," Meela replies. "Though I fear it has seen better days."

"Better days?! It has no skin! Hey, Death! How does your bum stay on there?"

Sol whistles to get my attention.

"You have to keep going," he encourages.

Right.

My next stair has a two-word phrase, this time in English, but with scrambled letters. It likely would be simple to sort out if my inner peace wasn't destroyed by Death's tumble.

"Why did everyone but me get easy questions?" I wonder aloud.

"Clearly, not everyone," Sol replies, gesturing toward Death's horse.

His reassuring smile should be comforting. Instead, it has the opposite effect, and I realize—I want to impress him, too. I want to be the one two cards ahead, putting on a show and dancing around.

I'm the one who wants to flirt.

Like clockwork, every one of my brain cells that isn't focused on solving puzzles urges me to check him out. It's like the mere suggestion that he might like me has moved him from the *Acquaintances* box to a sad, neglected one labeled *Maybe?*

I refuse to give in to the urge, mostly because this is not the place, but also because our time here is short. If he's not into me and I make things weird, I might start to freeze up like I do with Jayden. That could cost me the competition. Then again, if he is into me, I might have a real ally after all.

Like a boxer preparing for a fight, I shake my hands and roll my shoulders to help me refocus on the stairs. The second word in the two-letter phrase looks like an anagram for *star*. Seeing as the illustrations are a twinkling night sky and a glittering shoe, I take my chances and jump to the sky card. Shining star makes more sense than sneaker star, after all, and the anagram looks correct.

"See? You've got this!" Sol says, and jumps to his next card as well.

How long had he stood there waiting for me after solving his equation?

Movement in the distance catches my eye, and I watch Death depart through their tarot card exit without even a glance back at us. I need to pick up the pace.

The next phrase may be an anagram again, but scrambled across the whole phrase this time, based on the breakdown of vowels and consonants. I have a new trick, though, now that I know they're all star-based idioms. There's a two-letter word in the second position, and I think I know which idiom fits.

"Stars in your eyes," I say, jumping to a stair card that depicts literal stars in someone's eyes.

The card beside me fades away.

"Whoa!" Sol says, "That was quick."

My cheeks warm, and I'm torn between revealing my hack or letting him think I'm brilliant. I'm leaning toward brilliant. In the end, Yvit and Meela steal my thunder by calling farewells and leaving the trial. It's just me and Sol here now.

"Mine are getting a little tougher," he admits. "But I think I can handle it. How are you holding up?"

How *am* I holding up?

I'm standing on the edge of a playing card, hovering in outer space, faced with an incomprehensible phrase—the deciphering of which will determine if I fall and become the property of a star. And all I can think about is saving face in front of a guy I barely know. I'm just peachy, thank you very much.

"I'm good," I fib. Nobody really wants to hear the truth when they ask me how I'm doing.

The next step is another two-word phrase, possibly scrambled and encoded. But there are only so many two-word star idioms. Both words are four letters, so it's something-star, or star-something. How hard could it be? The illustrations on the stairs are a singer with a microphone and a dragon curled up on a pile of gold.

"Rock star," I guess, and leap for the singer.

It's not until my toe impacts the card and its surface dissolves beneath my boot that I realize *gold star* also fits the pattern. It's too late. The stair-card vanishes, and a shriek escapes my lungs as I plummet, heart flying into my throat. My vision swims while I drop, feet first, into nothingness.

It's done.

I'll never see my parents again. Never text Alex terrible dad jokes in the middle of the night. Never join another roleplaying game or share my silly fan art online. Worst of all—no one will know where I went. I didn't even leave a note behind.

Something pale whizzes through my peripheral vision before I slam into a solid object and collapse in an undignified lump. My hand brushes a picture of a dragon—the idiom card I should have chosen—and I jerk my head up to see Sol above. Wide-eyed, he stares down at me, one hand extended in my direction. Slowly, his expression shifts, elation spreading across his face.

"It worked!" he exclaims before pulling his arm back.

Jittering, the dragon card rises up, as if I had chosen correctly all along. My heart leaps like a rabbit chased by a dog. Sol used his perk to move the cards and save me!

In a sad attempt to be flirty, I make a shaky heart with my hands, and his grin widens even more. Then, as if a switch has flipped, it falls. His whole expression goes blank, and he collapses like a rag doll onto his card.

"Sol!" I scream, even as my card shakes and golden dust clouds my vision.

The looming form of the serpent-star—larger than I've

ever seen it before—materializes in the darkness above me.

"That was not supposed to happen," it says.

Sol's lifeless eyes stare out into space.

Eighteen

"What did you do to him?!" I scream.

The serpent's head casually turns to Sol, then back to me. Its two-toned voice makes me shiver when it answers. "The flesh? I've done nothing to it, yet. I must decide what to do with you first."

I scramble to my feet, hot with rage that dulls my fear, for better or for worse. "Is he dead? Did you kill him?"

"I repeat, I did not damage the flesh, but you should have lost, and that is a problem. It was not my intention for the game to alter here—and yet, I did not give you rules. Environmental manipulation has become a core facet of gameplay, despite my efforts to restrict its use. Perhaps I must accept this outcome as a failure of my own calculations."

What is it talking about? Is Sol not supposed to be able to move objects? Isn't that the perk the star gave him?

"Stop calling him flesh," I hiss. "He's a person. And if he's not dead, what's happened to him?"

The star's semitransparent head bristles, giving the illusion of sunlight reflecting from thousands of holographic scales. "I acknowledge your confusion, and it is, again, of my own creation. This competitor did not originate on a foreign planet, as you did. The flesh was formed when you declined my invitation and was hastily repurposed when you changed your mind. I believe my feelings on the matter are similar to the emotion you refer to as regret. I should have anticipated your indecision and delayed the creation of your replacement."

The words feel like ice water thrown in my face. All the heat and rage saps away, leaving unbearable hollowness. Sol is my replacement? A fake Earth human? The others had been right all along. But only two minutes before, his eyes had shone with pride in his accomplishments. He believes he's real. This is unethical.

"If you made him, you can fix him," I snap.

"Fix? Explain."

I puff my chest up as if I have the power to demand anything of a serpent made of stars. "I get that he came from your imagination, but he has real feelings. You gave him a life. And then you unmade him for breaking some rule that none of us knew about in the first place. That's unfair."

It really is. Maybe the star put the barrier of fog in Sol's head to stop him from accessing his abilities, but Sol doesn't know that. He's innocent!

The star shakes its head and sprouts arms and wings, looking more like a dragon than a snake. With one clawed hand, it brushes at the cards in Sol's staircase, dashing them to dust. I flinch, and the rage cooled by shock boils anew. Erasing Sol's exit is like severing his lifeline. Is the star torturing me on purpose?

"Stop, please," I beg.

The star pauses. "Why?"

Is it giving me a chance to argue for Sol's life, or is it really unsure why I would care? For that matter, why *do* I care so much? If it's true that Sol is a fake character invented by an interstellar storyteller to take my place—why does it matter what happens to him? Would I fight so hard to save a character in a tabletop roleplaying game?

Probably, yes. Yes, I would.

Death had been right about that, too. Sol is real to me, even if he's not. Maybe that's why the star is toying with me. Maybe it's savoring my anguish.

Disgusting.

"You can't do this to him," I insist. "It's not his fault *or* mine that he altered your game. It's yours, for making him that way. Intended or not, he's part of your trial and has been from the very beginning. So, bring him back, right now."

The star narrows its pale eyes at me in a way that would make me shrink away if I were not standing on a flimsy scrap of cardstock.

"I cannot," it says. "I must determine how this trial ends so the other competitors can progress."

"You can bring him back and *then* decide."

"That would significantly complicate the decision."

The star raises its golden tail—a shimmering, semi-transparent appendage with glowing bones that make me think of necromancy—and uses it to dash the cards on my side. For a moment, my rage falters, replaced by a twinge of panic.

Does the star intend to trap me here on the premise that Sol's perk is cheating? Is that even allowed in the deal we struck? Or is this just another ruse intended to stimulate my emotions? If the latter, the star is in for disappointment if it thinks I'm new to bullying.

"I could make this simple and jump," I offer.

The star pauses. "Why would you do that?"

That's a good question. What am I doing? My heart is thudding so hard I can barely hear my own thoughts, but I'm pretty sure they're screaming *shut up*.

"You want me disqualified so you can keep me," I say far more calmly than I expect. "I want Sol back. So, bring him back, exactly as he was, with a real chance to escape this place, and I'll voluntarily end this trial. No need for a complicated decision."

If I were speaking to anyone else, I might try to hide my shaking hands. But that's moot with the star, who can feel what I feel. *Enjoy all the trembling, snake.* With luck, my terror and uncertainty will only make it more eager to agree.

The star's body coils, and it asks a question I'm entirely unprepared for. "How long?"

"What?"

"How long after you end the trial would you have me honor this agreement?"

In every trickster story ever, the best part is the bit where the trickster exploits some loophole the hero did not specify. For example, if the hero wishes for wealth, they might find themselves crushed under a mountain of cash. The star is doing the opposite, giving me a chance to close a loophole.

Suspicious.

I remind myself of what Death told me: The star is averse to miscommunication. It values clarity and precision. If it's so very precise, however, how did its own creation surprise it? Is Sol's perk a side effect of hasty assembly, as the star would have me believe, or proof that he's a real person struggling against the will of his creator?

It has to be the second. I need it to be.

"Forever," I demand, and the star recoils. Remembering its tendency for literal thinking, I add, "For the rest of his natural lifetime."

The star says nothing.

It does nothing.

The pale gaze remains trained on me, unblinking, as if someone hit a pause button.

Then, with a flick of its reptile chin, it turns its head away.

"I decline."

"No!" I cry. "You can't!"

But the star is finished with the failed bargain. It erases what remains of the house of cards, and with a mighty beating of its wings, kicks up a sandy wind that moves Sol's card close to mine. The sand whirls around us, abrasive against my skin, and forms a wooden door with a copper knob—a door with no imagery on it.

"You are correct," the star says. "The miscalculation was mine. You are free to continue the competition."

"What about Sol?" I ask, gesturing to where he now lies at my feet. "You can't leave him like this. Please, reconsider my deal."

The star hisses, showing off its skeletal fangs and flicking its tongue to taste the air. In one swoop, it soars above my head and dives back down beneath my card, dissolving until I can't tell snake from stars.

Everything falls completely silent.

It's too quiet to bear.

Sol still isn't breathing, and I'm not sure I can move him. Can I really just leave his body there? I'm not strong enough to drag him from trial to trial begging the star to save his life—and I already know what the others will say.

Biting back tears I refuse to shed even if no human is present to judge me, I crouch and set a hand against his cheek. There's no reaction. His glassy eyes stare into space as if admiring the universe. I want to scream. I want to destroy something. I want to hurt the star for what it's done.

"I will not let you have this," I declare through clenched teeth. "I will not give you the satisfaction of feeling another emotion from me, no matter how long I'm here."

I don't know if I can realistically pull that off, but I sure can threaten it, and I plan to try. Breath held, I stand and reach for the doorknob. If it's grief the star hopes to feel right now—too bad. It gets nothing. Not a single thing.

"Satisfaction of what?" Sol's confused voice asks, shattering my fragile calm. "What are you talking about?"

That's all it takes to destroy my resolve. I gape like a kid in a haunted house, unable to form a coherent response while he stands and quirks an eyebrow at me. Surprisingly, he's not weak or groggy, like I would expect from someone who was unconscious. It's as if the star has switched him back on, just as casually as I flip a light switch.

"I thought you were dead," I confessed. "I almost left you behind."

A part of me desperately wants to hug him, but everything is weirder now, and my skin prickles at the thought. Sol is both positively fake and more real than he's ever been. There's no villainous personality lurking behind fog that will emerge when his memory returns. I've known him since the day he was born.

Which is today.

I'm gonna stop thinking about that.

"Why would I be dead?" he asks. "What happened to the cards?"

Oh, crud. I'm going to have to tell him.

"Um." I scootch closer awkwardly and tentatively reach for his hand in a way I hope is comforting and not creepy.

Somehow, knowing he's made of star stuff does not change the realness of the touch. I don't drop his hand when he steps to my card and stares at me inquisitively.

"What?" he asks. "What's going on?"

"I wish I didn't have to tell you this," I say, "but you collapsed, and the star appeared and said—"

"I'm not a real person, am I?" he interrupts.

That was not the response I expected. I nod, afraid he's

about to panic, but he appears to relax instead, as if I've confirmed what he already knew.

"In the last trial, when I searched the barrier, I found things. Things that frightened me. The more I pushed the fog away, the more I realized my own past wasn't there."

"I'm sorry."

He looks down at our clasped hands and runs his thumb along my skin. "What do you want me to do?"

My brow furrows. What's that supposed to mean? He's alive and apparently still competing. We keep going.

"We're gonna get you out," I say. "Don't worry. I don't think the star will try to stop you again."

Sol's face twists into an unreadable expression. "Out where? I don't have a home to return to."

"Then you should come to Earth. It's not the most friendly planet for strangers, but it's better than turning into stardust."

"I don't know if it works that way. You think I can choose a home to return to?"

I squeeze his hand. "I don't know, either, but I'll argue for it. The star said competitors can escape, and you are a competitor."

He squeezes back, then drops my hand and frowns at the door.

"I'm not sure why you're being so kind, but the others won't see things the way you do."

"Then we won't tell them," I insist. "They weren't here to see it. They don't have to know."

He ponders it. "Okay. I'll keep going. But you need to think about this more. Make sure you want to bring a bad luck charm like me along for the rest of the trials."

"Don't say—" I begin, but he lifts a hand to stop me.

"I'm not fishing for compliments. You don't know how the star is going to respond to my presence going forward."

I feel the chill of outer space again, but I can't imagine

sending him away. Nobody deserves that. Not even a non-player character.

"Let's go," I say with a confidence I don't feel. "The emperor must be having a tantrum by now."

That made Sol smile a little. "Let him whine. But yeah. Let's get out of here."

I nod and turn the doorknob.

ineteen

Flashing lights assault my eyes, not the twinkling starlight I'm accustomed to, but strings of round, blinking bulbs with incandescent filaments. The scent of buttered popcorn wafts toward me as I watch strange creatures dart back and forth across the grass between large tents.

The carnival creatures aren't human, but they aren't recognizable as animals either. Standing two feet tall at most, they have gray faces with puffy cheeks and wide-set eyes that bulge in their sockets, like pugs with humanoid faces. They're the first beings I've looked at, other than the star, and thought, *Yep. That's an alien.*

Since the start of the competition, I've suspected the six—or, rather, five—of us were taken from very similar worlds so the star could build trials we'd recognize. This circus, with its dizzying patterns and gravity-defying decorations, screams *Yvit* to me for some reason. At least, I feel like he's the only one of us who might have encountered the little gray beings.

It also looks like a failed attempt to pacify competitors while they waited around for us.

"There you are!" the emperor shouts from above. He flutters downward from the tallest tent, where he must have perched for a better view. "What took you so long? Did you have to count on your fingers?"

My eyes narrow. It's not like he has room to talk. He failed the only card he stepped on.

Death rounds a corner, takes in our appearance, and asks a couple more pointed questions. "One door? And no keys?"

Ugh. They would notice that right away.

I suck in a breath and brush messy strands of blue hair out of my eyes while searching my stressed-out brain for an excuse. As I do, the others catch wind of our arrival and emerge from various tents. I can do this, though. I can fib to save Sol.

"We got in trouble," I explain. It's technically the truth. The best kind of fib, in my opinion. "Sol tried to help me, and the star didn't like that. It, uh, it made us a new door. I guess without keys."

Seems everyone who made it to their doors got a key, and we, apparently, missed out. I had guessed as much when I saw the new door, but saying it aloud hits me harder. Not only am I out another key, I missed my chance to see everyone else's.

"It's never cared about cheating before," the emperor says. "I hope this isn't a trend."

Death lowers their prescription shades in a gesture I recognize from my parents. They know I'm holding something back, but for some reason, they choose to remain silent. I suppose I should feel grateful for that. Instead, I feel small and chastised.

"Meela Cast-Stones," they ask without turning, "are you still interested in a trade?"

I frown. Had they been waiting to see what key I got before deciding who to trade with?

The horned, marsupial hierophant gathers up her robes and excitedly approaches. "Indeed! I now have two duplicates! You have your choice of either clubs or spades!"

"The clubs, please. For my diamond."

Ouch.

It's fine, I tell myself. Even if I had more keys to trade, I don't need another diamond. Sol, on the other hand . . . he could use one. Maybe Death knows that and they're sending a message, punishing me for dishonesty. It's not the end of the world, though. There are five more trials, so Sol has plenty of time to find another—if star doesn't stop him.

As stealthily as I can with everyone watching, I pull my sketchbook from my bag and open to the page with recorded keys.

June: 2 Clubs, 1 Diamond
Meela: 1 Club, 2 Spades, 1 Diamond
Death: 1 Club, 1 Spade, 1 Diamond, 1 Heart?
Yvit: 1 Spade, 1 Diamond, 2 Unknown
Emperor: 2 Unknown
Sol: 1 Club, 1 Spade

Is that it? Only four trials in, and Death likely has a full set. Perhaps the star was telling the truth and it really is uncommon to fail. But like Death once said, that's not been my experience.

"What do you have there?" the emperor asks, drawing uncomfortably close to me. "Some kind of record? Are you keeping tabs on us?"

I clutch the sketchbook close to my chest. "You have your perk, and I have mine."

"Is it a spellbook?" Yvit asks.

"No, just a normal sketchbook."

He sniffs. "My condolences."

I hope that was a subtle mistranslation and not his way of telling me I'm doomed.

"You have no idea what my perk is, do you?" the emperor asks with a sneer.

Between the royal regalia, fuzzy antennae, and bedazzled

bun, he looks like the villain from a superhero series. I can vividly picture his mwa-ha-ha pose as he hatches a plan against his archnemesis: Pants-wearing Man. Or something like that. For all I know, his perk is the ability to sap flavor from brand-name cereal.

"Observe!"

I blink. I wasn't expecting him to *tell* me. His ego must overpower his common sense.

Another gray creature scurries from a tent, a wild-looking one in a sequined suit. The emperor whips his scepter from his sleeve and aims it at the innocent thing.

"Dance!" he commands.

The creature drops its popcorn, spilling colorful kernels across the grass, and pirouettes like a ballerina. The emperor raises the scepter, and the creature stops, momentarily confused. Realizing what must have happened, it runs for its life, popcorn forgotten. I frown.

"Sadly, it's only effective if the subjects remain within eyesight. Seems to work on all the star's little beasties, though."

I share a nervous glance with Sol.

"Please tell me you didn't use it on the orphans," Yvit says in a mildly threatening tone.

The emperor sets his hands on his hips. "Are you still hung up on those sticky children?"

"Children are sticky. That's their natural state!"

"Everyone, quiet!" Meela shouts. She crouches and sets a long ear to the ground, making tiny humming sounds as she listens. "Something has further upset the balance. A new mood courses through the very atoms of the soil. Perhaps one learned from our own misbehavior. It would behoove us all to listen more to our host and less to the smacking of our gums."

"Did she just tell me to shut up?" Yvit asks.

"Shh," Death says. "She's right. Something feels off. The

hairs on my arms are standing on end."

"How can you tell?" the emperor asks while curiously eyeing Death's black armor.

"I'm invisible, not incorporeal."

"How dull."

"Hold on tight, everyone!" Meela cries.

The ground shakes.

Where I come from, earthquakes are rare and mild when they do occur. They feel like a tractor trailer driving impossibly close to my bedroom window. The current situation is similar. It's less like the star shaking the asteroid and more like coordinated footsteps—and there's a good reason for that.

"The tents are moving," Sol points out, stepping closer to the rest of the party.

Death edges away from him but agrees. "They're surrounding us."

Sure enough, the patterned tents have lifted several inches off the ground, exposing the leather boots and calves of the little gray creatures—hundreds of them. The alien creatures in carnival garb have hoisted the tents from the inside and are dragging them into a circle around us.

"Maybe you shouldn't have made that thing dance," Yvit says, noticing the tiny feet.

"Or maybe this is the setup for the next trial," the emperor shoots back. He's probably aiming for nonchalance, but an edge of uncertainty bleeds through his voice. "It's about time, is it not?"

"I fear we can trust nothing we have come to know," Meela moans. "The balance. Oh! What could have done this?"

Despite the lack of visible eyes, I can feel Death's glare on me. Do they think all this drama is somehow my fault? It's hard to read the star's emotions, seeing as it's a snake made of sparkles, but it did seem a little irate. Still, isn't Meela always like this? It's not like the nonsensical raving is new.

The emperor is also unconvinced. "And you know this balance is upset because, what? A grapefruit has tuned you in to the star's—"

"Greetings!"

Everyone jumps at the sudden appearance of a creature in a top hat with a neon green parrot. The gray alien has a tiny tuxedo with curved tails that make it look like a penguin. If this were a normal circus, I'd say it's the ringleader.

"I hope you've enjoyed the entertainment and refreshments! It's now time for the games to begin!"

"I didn't get any refreshments," I mutter.

To be honest, I'm not hungry and haven't even thought of basic needs for hours. Missing out on carnival snacks is still disappointing, though. I wonder if they had shaved ice or cotton candy. Does a sci-fi circus make funnel cakes?

"First," the tiny ringleader shouts, "you must choose the number of games!"

The only way to describe what happens next is to say—a tent approaches. Its sides roll up so we can peer inside, and I can't help but grin at what I see.

It's one of those games where you toss a table tennis ball onto a bunch of jars and try to get it to land inside one. Every jar on the table is a different size and shape, some physically impossible, and at least one with no opening. All of them are numbered between one and six.

"There are balls to throw on all sides of the table," the ringleader declares. "When the first ball lands inside a jar, the number on the jar will be the number of games. You may wish to deliberate now and determine what number you're aiming for."

"No need for deliberation," the emperor declares as he marches to the table and picks up a ball. "This is a game of chance, not pure skill. I, for one, am not fooled by your ruse."

"Disagree," Death says, even as the emperor tosses the ball and it pings off a jar. "It may be worthwhile to strategize. For example, it seems we get more keys overall with a greater number of doors."

"But more chances for disqualification without a partner to watch our backs!" Meela whines. She and Death approach the table to play.

"I just want to play toss," Yvit says, and I have to admit I feel the same.

All of us join the carnival game, even Sol, who hasn't said a word since arrival.

"Six is the optimal number," Death argues. Their ball nearly enters a twisted vase, but swirls around the lip and flies off the table.

"How about one?" Yvit says. "We haven't done a trial together yet."

"Oh no. I'm unsure," Meela moans.

I like the idea of company, but every ball I throw wedges itself between the jars. It's a good thing the supply seems infinite. I could probably manage to wedge more between jars than there are spaces in which to wedge them.

"How about two?" Meela suggests.

"It doesn't matter!" the emperor snaps.

"Three!" declares the ringleader. "The number of games shall be three!"

Everyone stops their bickering and searches the table to see who won. The ball in the jar marked three is directly in front of Sol. Our eyes meet, and in that moment, I know it wasn't chance or skill.

He smiles.

I nervously look away. This is just a strategy he's chosen. Nothing personal. So, why are my prickling nerves reacting like he's asked me out in front of everyone—including Death, who knows what Sol can do. We'll probably pay for that perk use later.

As the ringleader speaks, it produces a baton and points it at three very different tents. "We have three exciting games for you tonight! Each can award *one* competitor a key." As it gestures toward each, the tiny feet shuffle and the tents turn around to reveal entrances.

The first, an unusually tall tent with stripes in alternating saffron and ochre, has a simple rectangular flap at the front through which nothing inside is visible. Beside the flap is a tiny clown—or rather, a creature dressed as a child might describe one. It balances in a perfect handstand atop a pentacle-like hoop.

I'm guessing the creature is acting out the page of pentacles reversed, but the trial itself has a fancier name.

"The Tower of Self-doubt!" the ringleader names it. "Do you believe in yourself enough to reach the top before your partner? Beware! If you try to fool yourself, you may wind up plummeting to your doom!"

A squat burgundy tent with a domed roof turns next, revealing a rolled flap with golden tassels. Inside, a creature with a long staff juggles seven pentacle rings with one hand. Near it is a table set out with cards and a rather unamused-looking dealer.

"The Long Con!" the ringleader announces. "Can you best your partner in a game of deception? The winner walks away with everything but their dignity!"

I suspect I know who will jump at that chance, but I hold my tongue so I don't influence anyone. The final tent turns: a black-and-white cube with sharp angles and an oval mirror. The mirror reflects our party in black and white with only one noticeable difference: a creature holding a walking stick hovers upside down above our heads.

I glance up, just to be sure it's not there—it isn't—then return my gaze to the mirror. The walking-stick creature moves deeper into the tent, like an amusement park pepper's ghost illusion.

Am I the only one who's noticed there's no tent flap on this one?

The ringleader clears its throat. "Last but not least: The Mirror Room! A test of bravery and imagination. Beware who you partner with, as their bravery may not equal yours! Now, it's time to pair up and—"

"Yes, yes, we've got it," the emperor interrupts. "Hierophant. Do your thing."

Meela produces her bag of stones and dumps them once again upon the ground. It takes her almost no time to examine them and point at the black-and-white tent.

"That one is to be avoided."

"Right," Sol says, and makes his way directly to the tent.

He's likely doubled down on the idea that he deserves the toughest trial now that he's learned his origin, but I'd like to continue partnering with him without always taking the eliminated trial. After this one, I'll do the choosing.

As if in a race to prove my earlier presumptions right, Yvit and the emperor dart for the red tent. Between a career politician and a heartless billionaire, the winner of that trial is anyone's guess. Death and Meela competing for self-confidence presents a more interesting challenge. Both of them speak with authority, but Death's self-loathing might get in their way.

"How do we get inside?" Sol asks while searching for an entrance to the tent.

"It's the mirror room," explains the ringleader, as if that's enough to answer the question.

Sol groans the same way Alex does when I tell them a terrible dad joke, and sticks his arm into the mirror. Or, rather, he sticks his arm through the hole in the tent that I assumed was a mirror.

Apparently, the walking stick creature suspended from the ceiling is not a pepper's ghost illusion. It is, in fact, a tightrope walker. The illusion is the room itself, which is coated in a black-and-white material I can only compare to electronic ink. What I had taken for a reflection had been moving images on every surface at the perfect angles to resemble one.

Sol's arm is now breaking the illusion.

"You can have the key when we find it," he offers.

I shake my head. "If you need it, it's yours. We're a team."

"Are we? You didn't seem interested in the idea when I suggested it before."

That's not fair.

When he'd suggested it, he was blocking my path until I forfeited or ran out of time—not that the rules gave him many other options. Had he expected me to eagerly comply and split his keys with him at the end? Other than losing Death's trust forever, what would have happened if I'd agreed? Would it have been us against everyone? Would that have changed anything?

I mean, other than the possibility of us growing closer with every trial.

My heart quickens at the thought, and I mentally order it to stop. One, he hasn't explicitly expressed any romantic interest in me. Two, I've only known him a few hours and might only know him a few more. Three, I need to rescue him, and alienating the other . . . aliens . . . will not help. Staying in everyone's good graces will come in handy when it's time for trades.

Oh, crud. He's waiting for a reply. What were we talking

about? Being a team?

"Yes," I confirm. "We're *are*."

Technically, I remind myself, he's a fake person created to replace me by a star that doesn't know human emotions. Based on what I learned from the squirrels, it's likely he doesn't know what flirting *is*—just like he didn't know how music felt—and I'm reading too much into a smile. Yeah. That's it.

"All right, then, partner," Sol says. "Let's get in there and be brave."

He steps inside.

Twenty

The optical illusions in the mirror room are disappointingly mundane. Compared to a maze full of color puzzles or a pinball machine you can walk inside, the grayscale images shifting on the walls of the empty cube feel like a cheap trick. It reminds me of franchised art museums designed to suck money out of tourists.

"I don't get it," I complain. "What's the goal of this trial?"

"A test of bravery and imagination wasn't enough explanation?" Sol asks with a silly expression that thankfully makes it clear he's not mocking me. "Let's just look for a way out. Maybe all the lines are disguising a door."

Above us, the tightrope creature clears its throat and speaks in a tiny, childlike voice. "Would you leave before claiming that key?"

Key? What key? All I see are white walls, black patterns, and the alien creature—who is not so much walking upside down as dangling from a patterned tightrope. Even that illusion is cheap, it seems, which is unnerving for the work of an alien that otherwise disregards the laws of physics. The normalcy of the room is strange.

"I don't see a key," Sol says, as if reading my mind, "but it might be blending in with the walls."

"Maybe look a little closer," the creature suggests.

I glance up to glare at the thing and am surprised to find it's disappeared. Even the tightrope has vanished from the ceiling—that, or the rope and creature both have changed patterns to blend in with their surroundings.

"A little closer," Sol repeats, followed by a louder "Oh!"

He points to a far wall, where a key hangs from a nail. It had not been there two seconds ago, which isn't exactly fair to us. I open my mouth to say as much, and two other keys appear beside it. Three rapidly become six, six become uncountable, and soon every wall of the cube is covered in shadowy trial keys.

I groan. "Okay. You take one wall, I'll take another, and we'll try to find the key with our hands instead of our eyes."

"Makes sense."

Sol gets to work brushing a wall with his palm, and I move to the opposite side. The surface is surprisingly smooth—more like vellum over drywall than a tent—which makes it all the more surprising when my hand bumps into something squishy.

"I've got something," I say, but Sol doesn't reply.

I run my fingers over the soft lump, then recoil when it responds in kind. Is there someone standing right in front of me and blending in perfectly with the wall?

"Truth or dare?" a cheery voice asks.

I search for the source and see no one. "What?"

A feminine face made of light and shadow appears on the wall in front of me. It doesn't look like a person in hiding. It looks like an old newspaper photo. "Truth or dare?"

Details emerge as more of the girl's body appears on the wall like spreading ink. Her white hair hangs in perfect ringlets, falling across exposed shoulders and a strappy top that is far too revealing. Her lips are black with dots of white that make me think of glossy lipstick.

Like Sol when we first met, she's stunning—in an artificial way. My breath catches when she bats false lashes.

"No thanks," I mumble while backing up. "I don't like that game."

There are two flavors of truth or dare. The first is a game played with close friends, where you confess experiences you've never had and occasionally drink a spoonful of hot sauce. The second is a game played at parties, where all the questions lead to breakups and every dare involves body parts. I don't like to be in the room for those, much less participate.

Three more girls appear beside the first, none of whom I recognize, though all of them feel vaguely familiar. It reminds me of the way some people in dreams are recognizable even if you can't see their faces.

"You have to play," a girl in a pleated skirt whines. "Everyone's playing. Just pick one! Truth or dare?"

"Fine," I say, assuming the game counts as the *bravery* part of the trial. "Truth."

Yes, I know truth is the coward's answer, since dares are designed to cause suffering. It's not the wisest choice for a trial of bravery and imagination, but I'm not picking dare until I know what the girls are capable of. The four of them titter as if excited to hear my secrets, and one leans forward to ask me the question. She has freckles and cute glasses—which I'm a little jealous of. "What's the worst thing you've ever done?"

I freeze. The question is too vague. Worst to whom? To me? The law? Someone else?

I instinctively grab for sweater sleeves I don't have anymore. "What do you mean?"

The illusion of the glasses girl shifts so it looks like she's leaning even closer. "I mean the *worst*. Tell us something you'd never confess to anyone. We want all the juicy details."

That's a lot of things.

My head spins as my memory volunteers one mortifying incident after another. The time my dad caught me drawing adult-themed fan art. Faking illness to get out of class enough that a doctor diagnosed me with something. Laughing along with class bullies out of fear they might otherwise turn on me. But which one?

Not only am I terrible at lying, I struggle to truthfully answer vague questions. Does she want the most embarrassing thing? The most harmful? The one that's cost me the most friends? My instinct is to blurt them all out just in case the star is reading my mind and will do something awful to us if I lie. But I really don't want to confess everything I've ever done if I don't have to.

Not with Sol standing right there.

And besides, the way the girls are looking at me is so judgmental I'm terrified to speak. It makes me want to hedge what I say to avoid torment, like a bullied child. Why couldn't the bravery trial be a physical fight, or mountain climbing?

Actually—scratch that. I'm afraid of heights, too.

"Uh." My skin prickles as a spider crawls across the girl's glasses. I just have to pick a story and tell it. I can do this. "One time, an ex-friend from camp talked me into going to a birthday party for a guy she had a huge crush on. It wasn't my kind of party, so I sat on the edge of a chair in a corner. The birthday guy came over to ask if I wanted to help him pick out a board game, and like a fool, I followed him to his room.

"When I realized he wasn't interested in games, I panicked and blurted that I was only at his party because my friend was into him. I don't know what I was thinking. She saw us leaving his room together, assumed the worst, and overreacted. He told her what I said—without context or correcting her—and let her know he didn't find her attractive. Probably to get back at me for bruising his ego. She hasn't spoken to me since."

Ugh. That was rough to confess. The guilt alone makes my face burn.

. . . and still, it feels like the wrong answer. Not malicious enough. Not embarrassing enough.

All four girls darken in mood and shadow, their images taking over the whole wall and making me feel the size of a cricket. They seem to push forward from the surface as well, glaring down at me and speaking over each other. I spot more spiders on their clothes and take another half-step back.

"The star can see your thoughts, and so can we," snarls the one with the pleated skirt. "We know that wasn't the worst thing you've done."

"You can't lie to us," glasses girl adds.

The white-haired one twirls her ringlets, and spiders drop to the floor by her feet. "We already know the answer. If you don't tell *us*, we'll tell everyone."

Okay, this is getting worse. My helpful brain is serving up things I did wrong all the way back to preschool. Are they talking about illegal things, like breaking into the old Vic, or morally dubious things, like enjoying old shows that are objectively sexist?

"Who is everyone?" I ask, with a tentative glance toward Sol. "You mean the other competitors?"

"I mean *everyone*," she says. "We'll put your shame out in public where your whole planet can see it, and we'll make sure the gossip cycle stays fresh so you can never escape your past."

The spiders crawl toward my shoes, but I barely acknowledge them. No matter how hard I try, I can't figure out what the girls want to hear. What *is* the worst thing I've done? Something from my childhood that I can't remember? Something I didn't even know was wrong because I'm bad at reading people?

I reflexively stomp a spider by my foot. Instead of crunching, it crawls away, unaffected.

The girl with glasses grins. "Getting warmer. You'd be surprised how an innocent misstep can turn a whole mob against you. Random losers will crawl out of the shadows to criticize you for attention."

I would not be surprised by any of that, as someone who survived junior high. My stomach turns at the thought of it.

"But first," she says, "we'll tell that boy you're smitten with. He'll never look at you the same again."

Huh. They must not be able to read my mind as well as they claim they can, or they'd have picked a better target. "Nice try, but I'm only in this competition because Jayden makes fun of me already. I don't care what he thinks anymore."

All four girls glance at each other, and it takes me a moment to realize why. It's not because I thwarted them with logic. It's because I assumed they were talking about Jayden. The girls were expecting . . . Oh no.

I spin to see Sol standing alone, one palm against a wall, with another version of himself staring back. The reflection is instantly recognizable as the person the star referred to as flesh, a gaunt Sol with jaw hanging open and glassy eyes staring into space.

The girls behind me fly into a rage.

"Don't you turn your back on us! We haven't finished truth or dare!"

I ignore them, but they keep taunting me.

"The hanged man doesn't really care about you. He doesn't have feelings of his own."

The white-haired girl's voice grates on my nerves. "Next competition, he'll be my boyfriend. We'll do things you couldn't imagine, and he'll enjoy every second of it."

"The star can make him love anyone it wants," the one with glasses chimes in. "It can do *anything* it wants with him."

My nails dig into my palms so hard they'd draw blood if that were possible. The girls are trying to get under my skin by implying Sol is just some toy, but it won't work. They're wrong, and they're lying. This is part of the trial.

"Is this what I look like to you?" Sol asks, so quietly I almost miss it.

I swat the teasing voices away and hurry to his side of the room. When I do, I can feel the girls' spell break. It seems ignoring them was the bravery I needed, not some perfect response to their game.

"No," I tell him. "These illusions are trying to mess with our heads."

Sol leans closer to the reflection, and it responds with jerky movements like a fancy marionette. "Then why do I feel like this is the real me? Why am I afraid the others are right and there's nothing deeper than the role the star gave me?"

"Because that's what the mirror room is. It's reflecting our fears back at us. But I'm here now. I can help you break the spell."

As I speak, a black-and-white copy of me appears beside the empty Sol. Like his reflection, mine's from a different time. It's the version of me who stood on a rooftop in a baggy sweater and a narwhal shirt, staring wide-eyed up at the sky with my bangs whipping around my forehead.

"It's okay," I say, leaning a shoulder against his so he can feel my presence beside him. Reflection-June does the same, but the empty Sol is unresponsive. "You'll learn who you are over time. We all do. Remember, this is your first day alive. You can be literally anyone you want."

He nods, then shakes his head. "You spoke to the star. Why did it want to stop me? Am I dangerous? Do you think my perk will break your world if I escape and try to flee there?"

I want to respond that he can manipulate the star's world because he's part of it, and he's not a part of Earth, so Earth is safe. Then I remember the star was able to deconstruct my real body. It's not a thought I want to linger on. I squeeze his arm and watch my colorless reflection do the same.

"Let's talk about who you want to be," I suggest. "Apparently, not a famous pop star."

The real Sol cracks a smile and shakes his head. His reflection, annoyed by my interference, sprouts three extra eyes on its forehead and widens its mouth to reveal serpent-like fangs.

Sol flinches, and I remind myself that, as exaggerated as they are, these are his innermost fears. The giggling girls preyed on my social anxiety, but poor Sol is afraid of himself—and apparently worries he's dangerous.

He rubs at his forehead as if confirming by touch that extra eyes haven't sprouted. It seems unnecessary. I'm pretty sure I could tell if I had extra eyes without poking my fingers into them. The worry is understandable, though. He's an imaginary creation of the same alien who made the wall. Who knows what the star can do to him.

"I don't understand what it's showing me," he whispers. "Can the star change me however it wants? Could it make me attack you to prevent your escape?"

I shake my head. "The images on the walls lie. Ignoring them is the only way to beat them. What's your favorite color?"

It's a cheap question, and I know it. My whole life, adults have asked the question, as if children are born with a preference. I love them all in their own context. I guess that's why I'm an artist.

Sol looks as confused as I always felt, but answers the question anyway. "Blue."

"Light blue? Like the sky?"

"Darker. Like the ocean."

Sol must be imagining one now, because the room is altering along with his thoughts. Salty sea breeze tickles my nose, and I swear I can hear faint waves in the distance.

"Are you doing that," I ask, "or the room?"

Sol stares at his distorted reflection for far too long before responding. "What if there's no difference between me and the room?"

"Okay, now you're getting a little—"

"We're the same thing, right? Me and the room? Just *stuff* the star came up with for fun. Where does the room end and I begin?"

I think I'm starting to lose him, and I'm a little concerned about how this might go. I do my best to bring him back. "Sol. You're a person. Not stuff."

The sound of waves draws nearer still, loud as if crashing against a beach. Mirror-Sol, meanwhile, eats up the drama, toothy grin widening on its face.

"You know I'm not," the real Sol says. He can't stop staring at the wall. "Any minute, I could become a monster or turn to sand and wash away. The star can do whatever it wants. You think I didn't hear what those girls said?"

I flush from my toes to the top of my head and imagine dissolving into sand myself. I don't want to think about what he's heard. I need to pull him back for both of us now.

"By that logic," I argue, "so could I. This body is just a replica, right? I'm technically made of star stuff, too."

His breathing slows. "It's not the same."

"Have you heard of the Ship of Theseus? How much of me can the star replace before I become something else?"

That's a stressful thought for me, too, but it appears to calm Sol significantly. It seems he has a hard time applying the same fears to my body that he applies to his. I suppose

I find it flattering that he doesn't think I'll become a monster.

The room does not find it flattering. The room is downright *furious*. Mirror-Sol silently shrieks, casting jarring patterns across the wall, and proceeds to shred the clothes from its chest with black claws that drip with ichor. More eyes sprout along its stomach, bulging and swiveling in their sockets. A gaping maw opens in its abdomen.

The real Sol whimpers and drops my hand. Desperate, as if he can feel the change, he tears at the buckles on his starry jerkin, rips it open, and tugs up his shirt. I have no time to avert my eyes, and find myself navel-gazing with him.

It turns out, there's a reason his jerkin is flattering, and it has nothing to do with tailoring. The star apparently knows a thing or two about how to assemble a decent-looking human. What I do *not* see on his torso are eyes. What I do see makes me bite my lip.

"Oooo!" the girls behind me sing. "We saw that. We're telling everyone!"

"Go away!" I snap.

Fortunately, for me—if not for poor Sol—he's still focused on his stomach. He watches his chest move with calming breaths, lowers his shirt, and buckles the jerkin.

"Sorry, I don't know what I thought I'd see."

His voice seems clearer, and I know why. "Don't look back at the wall. Look at yourself, or at me, but not at the wall. It messes with your head if you give it attention."

He nods and focuses on my face. "Got it."

"Okay, now that I have you: You're real, even though the star made you. I think that's what upset it so much. You changed the game in ways it didn't intend, and it almost disqualified us for it. That's how real you are. You're not going to turn into anything you don't want to."

That may be incorrect, but I want to believe it. Also, it was the right thing to say.

If anyone had asked me before that moment if it's hard to tell when ink-black eyes show emotion, I would have guessed it was—and, it turns out, I would have been wrong. Sol looks so happy he might cry . . . until he glances past my shoulder.

"Don't turn around," he whispers.

I can hear the tittering of the truth-or-dare girls but know not to look back. "Just ignore them. They're trying to humiliate me, but if I don't care, they'll go away."

"I don't think—" he says, but snaps his mouth shut.

"Don't think what?"

Sol's brows knit, and he reaches for me. "I don't think the mirror room likes what you're doing."

I can't help it. I turn to look, anticipating something awful, like embarrassing videos of my awkward childhood. That's when the whole room tilts on its side, and Sol and I slide toward the wall behind me.

Twenty-One

The first thought I have when the floor tips forward is that it must be another mirror room illusion. It's not that the room is physically turning, but rather a twist of the lines and shadows I've come to associate with the borders. When I teeter, I have a moment of annoyance, assuming the effect has messed with my balance.

It's not until the room continues to tilt and I physically slide into the far wall that I'm forced to admit something has gone wrong.

"Hold on to me," Sol says, pulling me close.

My first thought this time is *Yes, please*. To be clear—I do not say this aloud. In fact, I'm mortified by my reaction and wind up wrapping an arm around him like I would an uncle in a reunion photo.

I don't know why my thoughts are suddenly so racy. It's not like I haven't seen torsos before. The girls' taunting must have led me down this path, making me feel like I have competition when I've barely determined if I want to flirt. I hate it. The only thing worse than manipulation is knowing it's happening but not how to stop it.

Sol is more composed than I am. He kicks the wall and spins us around so we're not sliding headfirst toward the ceiling—which has changed from a boring tent top to a massive image of one of Sol's eyes.

That's creepy, especially as we slide toward it, but the real fright is the starry expanse visible in the sclera and pupil. Something tells me if we fall into the eye, we'll keep falling. I don't know if this is part of the trial or if Sol's perk has broken the room, but it doesn't feel like illusion anymore. I tighten my grip around his shoulders.

"I'm inching us toward the corner where there's still room to stand," he says, but the mirror room reacts to his words and the eye expands to fill the whole surface. It's now a huge empty square with an iris around the center.

"Maybe we shouldn't tell it our plans," I moan.

Not only is the eye eclipsing the ceiling, but that ceiling is rapidly becoming the floor as the angle of the wall we're sliding on steepens. I wish I could say that I've all but forgotten the truth-or-dare girls in the circumstances, but I can still hear them tittering away.

"I don't think she's going to tell us," they whisper.

"She has to! We dared her. That's not fair!"

"We should punish her. We should punish them both."

Sol's muscles tense like a cat preparing to pounce. "Hold on as tight as you can. I have an idea."

I don't know what else he thinks I can do. Sliding and clinging are all I have left. I hold on for dear life as he launches himself from the side of the wall and toward the center of the eye. The move is not so much a dive as a flop, though he manages to travel a foot or so forward as we tilt toward the starry void. The pale ring of the massive iris rushes toward us, and Sol reaches out to grab it.

A flash of white light disorients me as his hand strikes the iris and thousands of angular paper seagulls soar out from underneath. Gull calls and fluttering wings assault my senses as my shoulder hits the ceiling. It feels like solid ground. The spaces between the gull wings expand, exposing hundreds of black paper fish between them, and the resulting pattern makes me dizzy.

"Gonna be sick again," I warn Sol.

"I'll stabilize it."

What does that mean?

I close my eyes but can still see the flashes of black and white. "You can control the room?"

"I think so, yeah."

The fluttering of wings turns to crashing waves and settles into the hiss of surf.

Sol taps my arm to let me know it's safe. "All good."

I open one eye and lift my head. We're on a grayscale island in the middle of the sea, with no boundaries or walls in sight. Tiny crabs scuttle around the sand, and lizards dart between flattened reeds.

"How did you do this?" I ask as I sit up.

He grins and lifts himself with a grunt, running his fingers over the sand. "I altered the trial in unintended ways, like you said. To be specific, I made it show us dreams instead of fears."

"Is this your dream, or mine?"

"I'm not sure."

I stand and make my way to the water. Toeing it produces a tiny ripple, but I can feel nothing against my boot. The grayscale water is solid and flat, just an image.

"Realistic, isn't it?" Sol asks.

He joins me at the shoreline, and I note his reflection as it appears in the rippling water. Unlike before, it's not the switched-off version of Sol under the star's control. It's bright eyed, cheery, and full of life—more human and joyous than he's ever appeared. The reflection even wears swimming trunks with grinning cartoon stars on them.

"Oh," I say as an image of me appears beside his, also smiling. "They look happy."

"Well, they made it to the beach. I'd be happy, too."

My reflection grabs onto mirror-Sol's arm, and I sigh. I guess it was too much to hope that the room would stop taunting me after the change. Whether it's trained on our nightmares or our dreams, its purpose is still to mess with us. Even knowing this, though, I can't look away as my reflection rests her head on Sol's arm and gives it an embarrassing nuzzle. The real Sol jerks away and turns around, looking as awkward as I feel.

"We should search for the key," he says too quickly, like someone waking from a daydream just in time to answer a teacher's question. "The room is still trying to distract us."

No kidding.

With great difficulty, I tear my gaze away and glance around the ocean-like room. "How do we find it without getting sucked into the illusions again?"

"We keep checking in with each other," he suggests. "If one of us goes silent, the other intervenes."

"I guess."

That's fine, except for the part where the walls can, at any moment, humiliate me, pulling scenes from deep within my subconscious. I can't wait for Sol to check on me and discover the wall has drawn fan art of us smooching beside a sandcastle or something.

Bracing myself with a calming breath, I set a foot onto the water's surface. It's as solid as the floor had been before, so I cross the ocean until I bump a wall.

"I made it!" Sol calls. "Checking this side."

"Me too!" I call back as if we're really across an ocean and not on the other side of a room.

Motorized boats splash through the water on my wall, and families dot a distant shore that appears from nowhere and grows ever closer. I remind myself that nothing is moving, and rapidly swipe my hands across the surface before it has a chance to distract me.

The sound of laughter reaches my ears, and moments later, I find myself watching an illusion of a seaside vacation with my family. The star must have reached deep for this one.

"Another wave! Get ready, June!" my father shouts.

Mirror-me giggles, but the sound is tiny and high-pitched.

Leaning close, I notice my father looks younger. His dark hair doesn't have a speck of silver. My mom's suit is high-waisted and brightly patterned, a look she hasn't sported in years. Moments later, a wave crashes against them, and my parents lift a tiny me over it, all three of them laughing and splashing. It's been ages since we took a family vacation. Money and time have been in short supply, and if I'm honest, I've enjoyed the solitude. Now I wonder if we ever will again.

It's only when I feel my eyes dampen and hurry to stop the impending tears that I realize I haven't been checking in with Sol. That gives me a decent excuse to turn my back on the vacation scene and dab at my eyes.

Oddly, Sol's wall hasn't zoomed in on a scene to tug at his heartstrings, as mine had. It's pulled back to show the ocean from above, with diving dolphins and schools of fish visible in the top-down view. From there, it continues to retreat into the sky until the earth is spinning beneath Sol's hands, half in sunlight and the rest in darkness sprinkled with electric lights.

"I don't think it looks like that from space," I say, accidentally startling him. "I mean, all the photos I've seen show the unlit half in complete darkness."

"It does," he mumbles as if half awake. "Your world is bright and noisy—and surrounded by trash."

I snort. "Those are satellites, I hope. Is this knowledge the star gave you?"

He nods, then shakes his head. "It's getting easier for me to search the memories beyond the fog. I think this one belongs to the star itself. Your planet is so aggressive and messy, it's like catnip to the curious star. But through all that noise, it heard *your* voice. Why do you think it came to you?"

As soon as he asks, he gives the wall a broad swipe, reminding me I should be doing the same. Shamefully, I slink back to my side of the room, but try to focus on the conversation.

"I think the star chose me because of my wish."

"What do you mean?"

I brush my hands across the wall. It's smooth and unsurprising, making me wonder if I'd imagined the girls' fingers touching mine, or if it was the circus creature all along.

"Well, according to Death, most folks would have wished for love, not a cheat sheet to understand it. But I don't want some magic snake to come down from the sky and hand me a boyfriend. I want to meet someone and fall in love. That's the most exciting part of dating . . . and the scariest."

There's a pause in the conversation, and I turn to see Sol looking back at me with his lips parted. He glances away as if thinking better of whatever he might have been about to say.

"So, the star thought it found a like mind," he says instead. "I wonder if it still believes it."

I chuckle, and the family scene beneath my hands gives way to another sunny beach. It seems like the wall is never-ending, which makes it even more surprising when my knuckles bump into a corner. The scene on the wall changes at the bend to one of children flying kites. I used to love flying kites.

"After everything we've done to break the trials, it's probably rethinking its bargain to keep me."

"I doubt it." He frowns. "The star wants you to respond in ways it can't predict."

"Oh. Right."

Sol brightens his tone, noticing my growing discomfort. "Forget the star. Look at this beach! It's wild. I can't wait to see a real one."

That gets a genuine grin from me. "When we make it out, I'll save up my commission money and take you on a vacation. Promise."

"Sounds great!" He seems excited, but his smile falls. "I'll need to get a job, too. Or go to school. How do you even—"

"Hold on. Don't move."

Something thin and white has caught my eye. When I was standing alone in the corner, it had looked like a string from a child's kite, but with Sol influencing his half of the wall, it stands out as separate from the illusion.

The tightrope. I forgot we were on the roof!

I reach up and grab it before it has a chance to blend back in with the rest of the scene, then drag my hands along it until I find a knot. Tied there is a familiar shape: small, thin, and cool to the touch.

"I found the key!" I have time to shout before the room twirls again and I pitch toward the floor, gripping the tightrope and key like a lifeline.

Sol cries out, the tightrope snaps, and I find myself tumbling to the ground beside him inside an empty, white-walled cube. Quickly, lest the room change its mind, I tug the knot loose and slide the key free. A mirror appears on the far wall, reflecting our image—and a confused Yvit.

"It's a spade," I tell Sol, feigning enthusiasm for the key, though all I want to do is get out of the room.

"Four more chances to reach the sea," he mumbles as he follows me to the mirror door.

The odds aren't in our favor.

Twenty-Two

Every word from the emperor oozes condescension. "I must say, I'm surprised you didn't put up more of a fight. You're a formidable strategist, considering your age."

He's delivered four underhanded compliments to Yvit in the two minutes since Sol and I arrived, an impressive number of complisults for a single conversation. Good thing Yvit is a scaly bag of snark.

"You know what they say. You hit a hundred rotations 'round Alpha Four, and the evil just flows right out of you. Next thing you know, you're all upset about old people stuff, like abusing orphans."

"Oh, for the last time," the emperor moans with a dramatic eye roll. "The sticky brats are fine. They didn't even make it to the factory before the angry mob set it on fire."

I am so done with the bickering. The latest lobby is a muddy clearing in the middle of a gloomy forest. It must be sometime in the late fall, as the trees are barren and the grass is brown. Every bush and weed in the area looks trampled, and the trees are creaking without any wind. None of it helps my pre-frazzled nerves.

"What was your trial about, anyway?" I ask in a desperate attempt to change the subject.

The emperor waves a hand. "A long con. You wouldn't understand. You're just a child."

"Basically, a race to the bottom," Yvit adds. "Turns out, there are layers even lower than that."

"Which reminds me," the emperor says, pulling something from his pocket.

Sol moves closer to me, something he rarely does around the others. He's laser focused on the emperor's pocket, as if the guy might draw a weapon. I suspect the only thing that spares the fairy from an unexpected Sol attack is the fact that his mouth is faster than his hands.

"You, girl. Are you still keeping notes on us?" He whips something from his pocket and points it toward me. Another silver spade key. "I'll show you the keys I have if you let me read the page."

Sol's exhale of relief is loud enough to make me nudge him with a boot. I don't need his protection from the fairy. Old jerks in robes don't stress me out as much as attractive jerks my age. I mean, as long as they're not real judges.

I unbuckle my backpack. "You first."

The emperor grunts but complies, opening his palm to show me a second spade and a silver club. I frown. A trade with him won't help either of us. Still, he kept his side of the bargain, so I open the notebook and show him the page.

There's some unimpressed humming before he asks, "Only Death has a heart? Are you certain?"

I nod. "As far as I can tell. Unless Yvit has one and isn't sharing."

"Naw," Yvit confirms, again revealing information without asking for a trade. "I've got a club, a spade, and two diamonds."

The emperor perks up. "Diamonds, you say? I could use one of those, and everyone else worth trading with has one already. No harm in swapping, right?"

My eyes widen. Sol could also use a diamond! He might not have anything to trade, but *I* do. I could trade my spare club and give the diamond to Sol to catch him up. Except, I'm far too slow.

"Yeah, why not. Give me the spade," Yvit says.

Before I can form a counteroffer, the men exchange keys, and the chance is gone.

Yvit scrunches up his nose. "So, what's the deal with the keys? It's pretty clear we're each collecting a set, and Death hasn't automatically won, even though they've got all four."

"I assume we need them to escape," the emperor replies, twirling his new diamond key.

"Then what's the winning condition?"

Against my better judgement, I answer. The pangolin has shared a lot with me, and I haven't done much in return. "The star told me the first to escape will win. I take that to mean we all need a full set of keys to avoid losing what we wagered, but at some point, we'll have to compete or race to get our wish."

"Then why does it make us wait for everyone to catch up at the end of every trial?" Yvit asks. "Wouldn't it be more competitive if we had to race each other the whole time?"

The emperor answers this one. "For the same reason it makes us roll a die. The point is not to race to the end. It's to interact and . . . feel things. Take this as an opportunity to gather data and sabotage opponents."

He doesn't look at Sol when he says it, but he twirls the golden key in our direction. I narrow my eyes and kick myself for showing him the book.

Moments later, Death and Meela stumble out of their tent, looking more bedraggled than we did.

"You very nearly had it," Meela says.

It comes across a little patronizing, the Meela version of

the emperor's taunting. In her hand is the unmistakable shape of a diamond key, which makes my heart leap. That's Meela's second diamond, and now everyone has one but Sol.

"No," Death replies modestly, as if they didn't notice her jab. "I set my goal too high. I never would have completed it in time."

Meela tuts. "True, yes, yes. We must set reasonable goals for ourselves. To do otherwise only sets us up for letting ourselves down later, I'm afraid."

"You don't know the half of it," they grumble.

I wave to interrupt them. "Hey, Meela! Do you think we could swap my extra club for your diamond? Everyone but Sol already has one."

Meela pauses, and her little lemur face contorts.

"Don't," Sol whispers. "You need that key."

I glare. "For what? Everyone else has one."

"What if someone gets a second heart? That key could be your ticket out of here."

"Or it could be yours."

Meela interrupts. "I've decided no. The Wondrous Grapefruit has sent me a message in the form of an itch on the pad of my foot, and I'm afraid it's telling me to avoid this bargain. Nothing to do with the scarecrow, of course."

I'm pretty sure that message came from Meela's bum, not the sole of her foot, but I'm too deflated to argue with her. Nobody wants to help Sol—even Sol. I give my mechanical pencil a click and correct the status of the keys in my sketchbook.

> *June: 2 Clubs, 1 Spade, 1 Diamond*
> *Meela: 1 Club, 2 Spades, 2 Diamonds*
> *Death: 1 Club, 1 Spade, 1 Diamond, 1 Heart?*
> *Yvit: 1 Club, 2 Spades, 1 Diamond*
> *Emperor: 1 Club, 1 Spade, 1 Diamond*

Sol: 1 Club, 1 Spade

Four trials left of nine, and only one heart key so far. Unless the drop rate dramatically increases, there's no chance all of us will make it out.

The emperor cups his hands around his mouth and shouts at the twinkling sky. "Get a move on, star! We've all seen our keys!"

A painfully high-pitched voice responds, "Step right up!"

The emperor jumps so high, I'm amazed he doesn't flutter off, but he manages to whip his scepter from his sleeve and aim it at the source of the noise. "Why are you still here?"

"Step right up!" the ringleader repeats. "I've always wanted to say that."

"Are we back in the same location?" I ask, looking around at the empty woods as if tents might pop from them at any moment. "That's never happened before."

The ringleader shrugs, as does the bird on its top hat. "Beats me! The star hasn't shown up to give us new instructions, either. But we can make do with what we have. Maybe it'll show after the next one."

Meela approaches the little creature, which is the only thing shorter than her thus far, save the squirrels in the mansion maze. "Does the star communicate its desires through physical sensations or telepathic mood?"

"Neither. It's pretty direct."

She presses her hands to her cheeks as if surprised. "Is it not unnerving to speak directly to one's creator?"

"No, ma'am. We enjoy the conversations. It has some interesting perspectives."

"How bizarre. I think I would collapse in fright if the Wondrous Grapefruit used words to speak. That is, assuming my humble body did not disintegrate in its presence."

"What exactly is—" I begin, but the emperor cuts me off

in his impatience.

"Show us the way to the trials, little fellow. I have a good feeling about this one."

"First, we must—" the ringleader begins, but the emperor waves his scepter at it, silencing the words instantly.

"Just pretend we've already rolled a die. The number is . . . two. Get going."

"Hey!" Yvit protests. "You can't do that."

"Wrong. That's precisely what I can do. Otherwise, what's the point of this perk?"

The ringleader blinks and snaps its fingers, summoning yet more tiny creatures, all struggling to carry heavy objects. One group hoists a massive prize wheel that clicks between prizes with every step. The other carries four wooden poles, which they assemble into the vague shape of a doorway by standing on each other's shoulders. I wonder how long they can hold the top pole in place before the whole thing collapses.

I struggle to remember my tarot cards, all but thumping my forehead like a cartoon, and eventually the answers come to me. There is a wheel of fortune card, and that must be what the prize wheel represents. The other is the four of wands. I have no idea which is better.

"Welcome to trial six of nine!" the ringleader announces. "Before you, there are two paths. Each path will be awarded a single key! It's up to you how you divide your party."

"Hmm," Death says, crossing their arms. "I still say odds are better for us if we split ourselves evenly."

An idea strikes me. "Meela, would you come with Sol and I this time? I'd like a chance to talk to you."

The emperor pulls a nasty face as if attempting to dislodge a fly from his teeth. Meela, surprisingly, seems excited.

"Ooh! A chance to talk, just us girls?" She hesitates and glances at Sol. "And the scarecrow, of course."

I inhale and nod. There'll be time to change Meela's mind in the trial without the influence of the others—I hope. Even without looking their direction, I can see Death shaking their head. I don't care. I don't need their permission.

"Allow me to cast my stones!" Meela says. She produces her bag, dumps the stones on the ground, and spends a moment examining them. "We should avoid the wheel."

"Now, wait a minute," Yvit protests. "Just because she has the stones doesn't mean she gets her pick of the doors. Right? Maybe we shouldn't use our perks outside the trials. It's a slippery slope to using them against each other."

I give him my sharpest glare. Funny how he had no problem with the stones while the results were benefitting him.

The emperor approaches the wheel, examining the prize options on it. "In my experience, the stones lead her to the paths most opportunistic for her—not all of us. Our odds may be better with the wheel."

"In my experience, the stones lead her to trials that don't disqualify us," Yvit counters.

"Oh, don't be a baby. Let's go."

Death follows the bickering duo to the wheel, which the emperor is picking and poking at. "You have to spin it," they explain.

The emperor straightens and snaps, "I know that!"

With a dramatic flourish, he grabs the edge of the wheel and yanks down. The colorful prize sections with their cartoonish text blend together into a blurry circle while the wheel rapidly clacks. I fully expect the thing to slow with a *click-click-click* and settle on a prize. Instead, it accelerates until the wheel itself resembles an empty white doorway.

Good thing I don't have to use that portal. With my track record, I'd crash into it like a cartoon walking into a painted tunnel. Then again, my doorway is made of sticks held aloft by circus performers. I suppose there is no perfect option.

"I'm not going first," Yvit declares, likely imaging the same outcome.

Death chuckles and steps into the portal—thankfully without incident.

"We should go as well," Meela says while making her way to the pole holders.

The ones on the bottom lower their pole a bit to assist with her robe-laden hobble. Despite no visible portal to speak of, she vanishes as she crosses through the door. Sol follows, and I hustle to keep up.

The last thing I hear as I cross the fake doorway is the emperor telling Yvit, "After you."

Twenty-Three

The house, if one can call it that, is extraordinarily pastel, not the cute colors of children's toys, but unnerving shades of minty green, bubble-gum pink, and butter yellow. The kitchen, where the three of us enter, is oddly homogenous in appearance, with everything painted matching colors, from cabinets to counters, to floor tiles. It also has an unfamiliar odor, like metal and varnish, but dustier.

Every horizontal surface is covered in wooden shipping crates of the sort I might smash in a video game. I'm fighting the inclination to smash them. Unless I'm supposed to, in which case—woohoo!

My assumption is that the house is meant to reflect something in Meela's world, based entirely on the height of the counters, which end slightly above my knees. I keep the assumption to myself, because it feels a little rude.

Meela's assumption is "An alien home! Something from your planet, perhaps?"

"This isn't exactly like my world, either," I tell her, barely containing a smile.

Though the space is unmistakably a kitchen, the objects inside are anachronous. For example, there's a pastel pink icebox like something out of the mid-1900s, but no oven or stove that I can see. There's a fireplace built right into the wall like it's the 1800s or earlier.

Meela doesn't ask about Sol's planet. "Intriguing! Until now, the stylings of my trials have primarily reflected the values of *my* world, everything constructed from ethically sourced materials with natural color palettes. This artificial home is a deviation."

"How do you know these aren't naturally occurring colors on some other planet?" Sol asks.

Meela ignores him. "Shall we open the crates?"

My eyes narrow in annoyance. I don't like when the others are rude to Sol.

Without waiting for alternate opinions, Meela waddles to a crate as tall as her, taps on the wood with a thin middle finger, and sets an oversized ear to the side. Satisfied with whatever she hears, she tugs at the box's wooden lid until her little feet lift off the ground. It's not tacked down particularly well, but enough that she can't get leverage.

After a moment of amused observance, Sol locates a crowbar on a countertop and uses it to pry the lid off. To thank him, Meela gives him a suspicious glare before diving in headfirst.

My eyes meet Sol's above the crate, and he gives me a little bashful smile before examining the room. He seems content as he glances around, as if he's the one unboxing his things and moving into a new apartment.

If it were me, I'd repaint it.

"Oh my! What are these?!" Meela cries while emerging with sugar and flour jars. The ceramic jars have identical stylized paintings of a crowing rooster on the front. "Feathered lizards, perhaps? Is this the home of an explorer?"

"Those are farm animals," Sol corrects.

Meela holds the containers in her knobby hands and addresses me instead of him. "What should I do with them do you think?"

That's a good question. I'm guessing we're meant to unpack the crates, but the challenge has to be more than that. My gaze darts from a smattering of rune-like shapes painted on the countertops to a note taped to a pink cabinet.

"One key will be awarded to the eagle-eyed observer once everything is in its place," I read. Sounds like another pattern-matching game. "I think we need put everything exactly where it belongs in the house. Are the bottoms of those jars painted with runes?"

Meela checks. "Why, yes! Purple and blue!"

She lifts them to show me the undersides, which do have colored runes on them, but of a style that doesn't match the others. The ones on the counter are made of straight lines, while the ones on the jars are groups of circles. Oof. This will be rough.

I once again retrieve my sketchbook and scan the countertop until I spot two runes in purple and blue, side by side. They look the correct distance apart for the size of the ceramic jars. I scribble down the shapes from the counter, then pair them with the ones from the jars.

"I think the jars go here," I explain to Meela, "based on the color of the runes. But I still have to figure out—"

"Mmm. I don't think so."

I can't help furrowing my brow, and Sol tries and fails to hide a chuckle. How does Meela know where the flower and sugar jars belong in an *alien home*?

The confidently clueless hierophant twitches her whiskers and spins around to look at the kitchen. "That location feels incorrect. There's a slight breeze moving my whiskers in the direction of these cabinets, instead."

"Another divination?" I ask.

"I believe so. The Wondrous Grapefruit often directs my

movements in this way."

She sways on her feet as she stumbles toward the counters, head swiveling back and forth as if picking up on small currents in the room.

"What is the Wonder—" Sol begins, but he's once again ignored by Meela.

"Aha!" She nods to the handle of the icebox. "Can I get a hand?"

If I'm honest, I've suspected all along that the hierophant's divinations are baloney, but this one has me totally convinced to never bet my safety on Meela's premonitions. Sol's reaction is even worse. I watch, internally begging him to stop, as a mischievous grin spreads across his face and he bends to open the icebox door.

"Not that one!" Meela whines, addressing him for the first time since we entered the house. "That door is for the ice. Open the one to its right—and I'll need you to place these containers for me."

It seems talking to Sol is fine, so long as the talking involves barking orders. Sol's grin morphs from the jackal variety into a hospitality smile, and he does precisely as Meela asks. That delights the hierophant but annoys me to no end, despite my desire to gain her trust.

If the goal is to put all the objects from the boxes into their correct locations before any of us can escape, *someone* will have to go behind Meela and move everything back to where it belongs. Either that or confront her—which is out of the question if we want her to trust Sol enough to share her diamond. How do you tell someone like her that they're wrong?

As soon as Meela turns her back, I catch Sol's gaze and shake my head—giving him a stern look that I hope sends the message I intend. I want Meela on our side, but not if it traps us here for hours. He pouts but returns a subtle thumbs-up.

"We should all pitch in," I suggest, and pry open a box on the countertop.

To my dismay, it's packed with glass spice jars—enough to fill an apothecary, rather than a stocked kitchen. Fortunately, the antique spice rack is easy to locate in the room, as it takes up an entire wall panel. Unfortunately, its painted runes barely vary in size and position.

This is going to take forever.

While I stress about the spices, Meela plunks a kettle on the table and shoves dried flowers into it. That's enough to make my hands twitch with the urge to snatch things away from her. The kettle isn't even the right color on the bottom for any of the placements on the table—and the table should be set up for a meal!

"You doing okay?" Sol whispers.

Crud. I'm not hiding my distress well.

When I turn to whisper my frustrations, I'm caught off-guard by the juxtaposition of his medieval jerkin with rolled shirtsleeves and the chicken-themed oven mitts on his hands. They're not just decorated with chicken imagery. Oh no. They're quilted in such a way that his thumbs resemble misshapen beaks and the tips of his fingers form a lumpy comb. An involuntary smile creeps across my face—which is obnoxious, since I'm trying to be cranky.

"What?" he asks before following my gaze and wiggling the gloves to make the chicken heads bob. "Oh, these? I couldn't figure out where they went, so I put them on and kept unpacking."

I fight a laugh with everything in me, my mouth twitching despite my efforts. He looks ridiculous: black curls strewn about, wearing a blue jerkin and puffy sleeves as if costumed for classic theater, and holding up his chicken hands. Even his dark eyes look puppy-like when paired with his apparent confusion. He's . . . he's adorable.

I find my mind wandering to a conversation with Alex where they asked me to define my *type*. At the time, I had no idea at all. I don't think about people as types, and usually gravitate to folks who make me feel comfortable in my own skin. Jayden was an exception to that, and maybe the first time I felt something for someone in a purely physical way. But from now on, if anyone asks, my type is STEM-loving costume nerd with kitschy domestic chicken mitts.

"What?" Sol asks again.

My ears heat. "Uh." Why is my mind all static? Where are the words I was trying to find? Is this the way Sol feels all the time, unable to locate the thoughts he wants? Oh! There's the word. "Pegs!"

"Pegs?" His expression is goofy, too.

My mind rapidly snaps into focus. "There were pegs on the walls near the fireplace. Maybe the oven mitts belong on them? Though, why does the house have oven mitts at all if it doesn't have an oven?"

He shakes his head. "I looked. All the peg-paintings are the wrong color. Nothing like this."

He lifts the mitts to show me the runes, and this time I fight back laughter.

"A drawer, then?"

Happy for a reason to look anywhere else, I hustle toward the nearest drawers, nearly tripping over Meela in the process. She shakes her head and tuts at me but carries on with whatever she's placing—likely in the wrong location. It takes me three tries to find the drawer with mitt-matching runes on the inside, which is three too many when hunching down.

"Found it," I say. "Give them here."

Sol uses the opportunity to bend closer and whisper in my ear. "Seriously, what's bothering you?"

I draw in a breath and tuck the oven mitts into the drawer. "I'm worried we might have to redo a bunch of work before the star lets us out of here."

His glance at Meela tells me he understands. "Want me to say something to her?"

"No." That's the last thing I want. "Leave it to me. I was going to talk to her, anyway."

Sol nods. "Would it help if I gave you privacy? I could carry on ahead and double-back later when you're done with this room."

"Really? You'd do that?"

I'm kind of torn. On the one hand, that eases the building stress I feel for our zero-sum work. On the other, I'll be separated from Sol. That bothers me more than I want to admit.

"I'm going to the next room," he announces, robbing me of the opportunity to object. "I'm only getting in the way here. June, can I borrow a copy of your notes?"

After a bit of scribbling, he's gone, retreating into the adjacent room with a casual wave over his shoulder. I didn't even get a chance to teach him my methods. I hope he's okay on his own.

Meanwhile, Meela wastes no time waddling over to gossip with me. "I understand now! You're enamored by the scarecrow."

As usual, she's far too loud. It takes every ounce of civility in me not to stuff her in the tiny sink.

"Shh," I say instead. "That's not true."

Okay, she may be right. Sol makes me comfortable when I should be scared, and every time someone makes a jab at him, my skin prickles with the urge to fight. If I could bottle these feelings and examine them, maybe I wouldn't need the star's help. Maybe. There's one thing I'm certain of, though. I don't want Meela's opinion about it.

Unfortunately, her mind is made. "Oh, dearie, it's nothing

to be ashamed of. Why, if the star had targeted me and built a scarecrow with branching antlers and powerful scent glands, I, too, would have succumbed to temptation."

Ugh. Until this moment, I had not realized the levels of embarrassment I could attain. There has to be a way to escape this conversation.

"Speaking of Sol," I interject, making up the rest as I go along. "I noticed you spoke to the carnival staff."

Meela blinks her bulbous yellow eyes and twirls a saltshaker in her fingers. "Yes?"

"You asked them questions as if they were real people, even knowing they were created by the star."

She scoffs. "Because they *are* real people! Knowing your creator does not make you less alive!"

"So, then, why do you give Sol a hard time?"

"Because he's a scarecrow," she repeats as if it explains everything.

"But—"

"He's empty—his thoughts not inside his head. His mere presence upsets the balance. You would see this easily if you opened your mind to the Wondrous Grapefruit. Would you consider joining the order?"

Unprepared for the swift change in subject, I stammer, in search of a polite answer. "Right now? But I should probably, you know, the spice rack and all."

"Never fear! I have an abbreviated speech prepared that you can listen to while you work!"

The hierophant gathers up her robes, takes a deep breath, and raises one hand. It's then that I realize the mistake I've made in isolating myself with the lemur-like woman.

I settle in for a great deal of discomfort.

Twenty-Four

"In the year O-1-50-34, a second moon appeared in the sky. This moon was larger and brighter than the first, and had a rather surprising habit of hanging around in broad daylight. Having not yet invented astrology, the early inhabitants of the planet did not grasp the impossible nature of the moon's relationship to their orbit. Nonetheless, they knew its presence was special."

Meela takes a deep breath like an audiobook narrator encountering a run-on sentence with no punctuation.

"From this knowledge bloomed a new science, one focused on measuring subtle differences in nature after the new moon's arrival. Changing tides. Altered seasons. Strange shifts in mood. At first, it was a curiosity, but as the scientists connected the all threads between moon-related changes and the turning of fortunes, their roles matured from gatherers of knowledge to dispensers of impossible wisdom."

I interrupt. "The Wondrous Grapefruit is a moon?"

"A moon? Oh no! It is so much more. Perhaps a celestial ancestor of the very star upon whose creations we stand! But not a mere moon! No. No! That's only what people thought at the time!"

Noticing the woman's growing agitation, I apologize and

attempt to put away jars without drawing too much attention. Scribbled and crossed out rune combinations mar the surface of my sketchbook page, and individual jars line the counter.

"From those simple scientists grew an order that eventually encompassed the entire globe. It was impossible to deny the accuracy of the divinations performed by the fortunate few who synchronized completely with the Wondrous Grapefruit."

"Is that what you wished for?" I interrupt again, setting a spice jar down on the rack.

"Synchronization? Don't be ridiculous! I'm certain the meager star is incapable of granting such a request. Compared to the Wondrous Grapefruit, it is but a helpless infant."

"I see."

I do not see, but understanding is not worth extending the lengthy lecture. If Meela manages to anger the star over the course of her recruitment speech, I'll flee the room and hope for the best.

"I suppose this is jumping ahead a little, but my wish is to bypass my examinations and become a high-ranking member of the order through a special selection process."

"I thought you already were a member."

Meela shakes her head. "Sadly, I am only a member in training. It takes most trainees thirteen years or more to absorb enough to pass exams. I'm on year four of the stone-casting course, and believe between my natural talent and a friendly nudge from our friend the star I may exhibit enough promise to be selected for the leadership track."

"Thirteen years for one exam?!" I balk.

Meela crosses her arms. "*You* seek enlightenment and tell me how long it takes you to find it!"

"Are they charging you money for the education? It sounds like a scam."

Meela waves a hand. "We stopped using currencies for

trade a century ago. I pay my way with community service, which brings me closer to synchronization. It's a win-win!"

"If you say so."

The order sounds more like a cult to me, but Meela's descriptions of the moon and star are starting to worm their way into my thoughts. What if the star *is* infantile for its species—whatever that species is? Would that make Sol the imaginary friend of a temperamental child? I don't like that.

Meela snaps her fingers. "You're distracted by the scarecrow again, and I haven't finished my pitch yet. Are you interested in the order or not?"

How did she . . . ?

"I, uh." Oof. Lying is hard. "Sorry. I was thinking about . . . my own wish. Have you ever been in love?"

It's a desperate bid to change the subject, but I realize I might be on to something when her eyes brighten like high beams. "Oh yes! All the time!"

"Really?"

"Of course! My people are loving to a fault. Though, I understand other species are monogamous and get along fine, like Councilor Squirntoes for example. No judgement from me! But our way is superior."

"Wait. Yvit is—"

"Partnered, yes! With four little Squirntoeses of his own! That's why he wished for an insect farm!"

I nearly drop the spice jar in my hand, but catch it and set it onto the rack. "A farm? I thought he wished for political power."

Meela laughs. "No, no, no. That's what he wagered! Some folks, like the emperor, seek out power for themselves. Others feel burdened by authority, but responsible to those they govern. The councilor wishes to retire and place the safety of his people in more youthful hands. Were his goal not in conflict with my own, I would help him achieve that wish."

"That's kind of you," I mumble while opening a second crate. "What did you wager?"

"If I'm unable to escape this place, I will go back to mending clocks." Meela sets the saltshaker in her hand down on the table with a decisive thud. "I'll deserve it, too, if I'm unable to escape with all the tools of wisdom I require." She shakes her stone pouch to illustrate.

Afraid she might launch into her grapefruit speech, I intercept the conversation again. The subject of love really seemed to excite her, and that common interest may be just what I need to loosen her grip on her diamond key—without having to enroll in a cult.

"Can I ask another personal question? What does it feel like when you're in love? How do you know when it's the real thing?"

Meela tucks her stones away and raises both arms above her head. The robes slide down her wiry arms and clump up around her furry armpits.

"Like the Wondrous Grapefruit itself has shone all its light upon a single person! Suddenly, all the tiny flaws I might have found unattractive in others—twisted teeth, veiny claws, one antler snapped off in a fight—become the features I moon over. I want to put on all their clothes and roll around to absorb their scent. I want to steal their precious belongings and hoard the objects in my nest, wrapping myself around them as I sleep!"

I blink. "Wow. That's pretty intense."

"I told you, we're a loving people."

I've never considered stealing anything from Jayden . . . or Sol. Nor would I want to wear their clothes. I'm not sure Jayden ever washes his, and Sol's jerkin looks uncomfortably warm. Hot on the torso and cold on the arms? That's the opposite of what I want.

"Do you think it's possible to love someone before you really get to know them?" I ask.

Meela tuts. "You mean the scarecrow."

"No, I was thinking of someone else."

It's the truth. My mind has wandered back to Jayden and the things Alex said tonight. Tonight! It feels like it's been forever. Meela gives me a one-eyed squint as if she doesn't believe me at all.

"Members of the Order of the Wondrous Grapefruit love everyone equally. Speaking of which . . . where was I?" She digs through her latest crate, emerging with a double boiler. "I've lost my place in the memorized speech. Anyway, it's important that you know, the Order makes every major decision on my world. Becoming a member is a great honor and a great responsibility."

"Every decision?" I ask, doubtful, while glancing into my new crate. To my dismay, it contains loose utensils. "The Order is your government?"

"I don't believe that question translated properly," Meela says. "But if I understand correctly, yes, the Order creates regulations and oversees disciplinary cases."

"And everyone is okay with that?"

The hierophant slowly searches the room, nose wriggling as she does, until she settles upon the fireplace and shoves the double boiler inside. "Sadly, no. There are some disbelievers. But never fear, they are always cast out. It takes an open mind to understand that the Wondrous Grapefruit knows best for us, even when its decisions seem unpleasant. Some folks are simply incapable of understanding why they can't have their way."

I hold my tongue. I can imagine the rules enacted by a deity who speaks to unelected leaders through itchy feet or whisker wind. If I were born on Meela's planet, I'd likely be among those cast out. There's too much room for corruption in a cult.

Meela herself seems sincere, if obsessed, and there's nothing I can do to help her world, so I play along as best I can for the sake of civility. "Do the disbelievers ever return?"

Meela peers into her empty crate, topples it, and moves on to another. "Not a one. I've heard rumors that the other side of the planet is crawling with deadly predators. As much as it saddens me, I must assume the worst."

Oh! I get it now. If the Wondrous Grapefruit shines day and night, it's not orbiting the planet. It's possible there's a civilization living on the other half of the world, free from the rules of Meela's Order. At least, I hope such a place exists.

"Oh my! Treasure!" Meela cries, and dives face-first into a crate of junk.

Apparently, the concept of a junk drawer is a multi-planetary tradition. That's good, though. A box of junk will keep her occupied and should be easy for Sol to re-sort.

I lift two spoons—one short and bulbous and the other thin with a decorative handle—and note the runes painted on them. Meanwhile, Meela squints at my spice rack and replaces a jar with a pair of scissors.

That's it. I'm going to scream. We will never get out of this place if she keeps messing everything up.

"I shouldn't have sent Sol away," I mutter—apparently not quietly enough.

The hierophant's head snaps toward me. "As a wise and mature abecedarian of the Order of the Wondrous Grapefruit, I advise you get over your apparent fixation." Her look softens. "But it's not been so long since my thrill-seeking days, and I've had my share of whirlwind romances. Perhaps we ladies can swap some gossip about past conquests to get your mind off this?"

The offer makes my stomach turn.

Except, hmm, that's not true.

Something else is causing my stomach to turn. Something so subtle I hadn't noticed until I stopped to focus on it. I drop a set of forks back into my crate and set a hand down on the counter. It vibrates gently under my palm.

"Meela, what are you sensing right now?"

The hierophant stops digging and raises her head, holding her body entirely still as if feeling the same rumbling I am. "It is as I said, we've upset the balance."

"Is the balance literal?" The tremor in the counter gives two sharp bumps that subtly rattle my cutlery.

"Oh no," Meela chides. "Don't be ridiculous. The balance is a state of being. For you or me it manifests differently than for the universe or the Wondrous Grapefruit, but—ah! Are you sensing it as well? That is progress! Yes! We may convert you yet!"

The tremors are strong enough that I can feel them in my feet, and for a moment, I start to believe Meela's claims that starlike deities can speak in vibrations. It's at that point I happen to turn my head and see a crate slide across the adjacent room.

"Hold on," I say with a waver in my voice. "I need to go check on Sol."

"Of course, of course," Meela mutters as her long fingers sift through garbage.

It's unclear if she's giving me permission to leave or mocking me for my supposed fixation. I don't care which, because something is wrong. I step through a rounded archway, expecting to find Sol in the adjacent room. He isn't there, nor are most of the crates. It appears they're already disassembled, reduced to pallets of wood in a corner, their contents placed on various surfaces around what could be a family room.

Except, some items haven't yet settled. I gape as they place *themselves* around the room, floating about like we're in a movie with a witch who hates to do manual chores.

I can still hear Meela muttering in the kitchen as if giving herself a pep talk. "The girl is hopeless, Meela, darling. This is not a reflection of your talents, but rather the Wondrous Grapefruit testing you. Never fear. You shall be rewarded for your efforts."

Rude.

The rumbling grows in intensity, and I pitch myself onto a tiny couch as porcelain rats whiz by my ear and land like bookends on a shelf. Seriously, what is going on? I straighten and cautiously cross the room.

Off the family room is a wood-paneled hallway with three doors—all open. Unease sets in as I note that the first room is already unboxed, like the family room. It's a child's bedroom with a shiny pink desk and drawers that match the counters in the kitchen. Dolls, puzzles, and other toys dot the shelves and line the singular bed. Like before, the crates are flat.

Across the hallway, I find an adorable bathroom with perfectly placed towels and toiletries. There's no way Sol has completed all this in the time it took me to unload some jars. Even using his perk to cheat, it would take him time to solve the runes. Concerned, I fidget with my sleeves and creep toward the final door. What I see makes my breath freeze in my lungs.

Sol is *not* rushing about the place, unpacking items at the speed of light. He's hovering, cross-legged, a foot above a bed, while objects in crates sort themselves out. A multi-level wooden bookshelf slowly fills itself with books that hop obediently out of their crate while family portraits leap onto the wall. Oblivious, Sol hovers like a ghost, slowly flipping through a photo album.

He starts when he notices I'm in the room. "June!"

The sudden shock breaks the spell over him, and he falls abruptly to the bed. Likewise, the books that are halfway to shelves drop to the floor with a loud thump. He glances over as if noticing them for the first time, then looks back at me.

"How were you doing that?" I ask.

It's not exactly what I mean. I know he's able to move some objects in the trial without touching them, but there's a chasm of difference between shifting an object and making a trial complete itself.

Sol tugs at his curls with one hand while gripping the album in the other. "I didn't realize I was. Your conversation sounded private, so I made my way in here where I couldn't overhear, and found this book sitting on a crate."

Oh no. How much did he hear, and why does this keep happening to me? I fight the urge to literally slap my forehead. I need to learn to be more discreet.

"That was—" I begin, but he mercifully interrupts.

"You have to see this."

With effort, he rights himself on the bed and scoots over to show me the album. It's modern compared to the rest of the house, but still an antique by Earth standards. Tacked onto the craft-paper pages are black-and-white photos that have yellowed and faded. Instead of images of total strangers, however, the photos depict competitors.

I first identify Yvit, who's admiring an industrial planet from a balcony somewhere high above. He looks straight out of film noir in his sharp pangolin business suit, only lacking a fedora. Next, I see Meela in an overgrown garden, both arms raised toward the sky. I imagine she spends a lot of time like that. Finally, I spot myself, standing on the rooftop of the old Victorian—with a blazer-clad Sol.

I frown. "Why would the star make this? You weren't there

with me."

I bite back the rest of what I'm thinking: that nobody who looks like he does in that photo would spend time alone with me at all. Come to think of it, I'm not sure idols go anywhere without a bodyguard and groupies. It's mean of me to think it, but I'd forgotten how intimidating he was when we first met. I'm glad he changed his look.

Sol frowns. "Logically, I know the image is fake, but I can't shake the feeling that this really happened. It's the closest thing to a memory I've had since we started."

He flips the page and shows me more photos: The emperor lounging by a pond wearing nothing but his plant-based hot pants. Death crouched alone in the dark while soldiers march outside their window. I notice a bright drink in their hand and open notebooks on the ground, full of astronomical charts.

I look at Sol. "These are the star's memories of when it first encountered us—when we made our bargains. I was on a rooftop alone, because my friend Alex met me there and left to go play video games with their partner."

"Then why does it feel like *I* was there?"

Out of the corner of my eye, I see the books lift back off the floor to re-sort themselves on the shelf. Sol's perk is acting without him again, and I worry that it's psychologically triggered. Does he think I'm lying about the picture? Does he think I lied about what the star said? Why would I do that?

"When I spoke to the star," I say gently, "it said it created you to play my role in the trial when I first rejected its offer. The other competitors said you were unresponsive when you arrived. Maybe the star created Earth memories for you and then stopped when I changed my mind."

"No," he argues, and flips the page back, pointing forcefully toward the picture. "I was there. I remember this exact moment. It was cold and breezy on the roof, and dark except for a couple streetlights. You had your hands curled up in your sleeves, and you looked so sad and confused. I wanted to do something to fix it. Oh! And the hatch to the attic smelled nasty."

My eyebrows shoot up. "The greige paint! Yeah! That must be the star's memory."

"No," he says again, but quieter. "That can't be right. I was excited to be there with you. The star . . . It wouldn't . . . It doesn't feel. Not like us."

I smile as warmly as I can, though my insides are all jumbled up between delight, concern, and pity. "You weren't there. You're not from Earth. And if you were, you wouldn't be hanging out on a stranger's rooftop with someone like me."

I meant the last bit as a self-deprecating joke, but a flash of anger crosses his eyes.

"What's that supposed to mean?"

The floating books miss their mark and smash into others on the shelf, bent pages fluttering as they plummet back down. I take a shuddering breath, and the room does likewise, a deep tremble that reminds me of a growl. There's only one window, and through it, I see the shimmer of holographic scales, as if the massive snake is slithering by.

When I focus on them, the scales disappear.

A warning?

"I-It's just," I stammer, "when we met, like I said, you didn't look like someone who would—" I stop myself, searching for words in my head that might calm him down rather than make him angrier. "You'd outclass me. We'd travel in very different circles that would have no reason to intersect, and there's nothing about me that would draw your attention."

Anger flashes in his eyes again, and he leans forward to glare at me. "I disagree."

I chew my lip, and the room rumbles again. This time, I see

the lit spine of the snake slither past the window along with the scales. To my relief, something in Sol's expression softens, and he looks down at the album in his hands.

"Sorry," he mutters. "This isn't your fault. I know the memory isn't real, but I want it to be. Is that wrong?"

I sit down on the bed, remembering how I argued for Sol's humanity before I learned the truth. "I want it to be real, too. Though, I doubt I'd have made a wish at all if I had you on the rooftop with me."

I mean it. Something about being with him quiets all my nagging questions about love and relationships.

The rumbling in the house also quiets.

Which makes it all the more startling when a bloodcurdling scream interrupts our conversation.

"Children!" Meela's shouts ricochet through the house, and without a thought, I vault toward her. "Children! Help! Come quickly! Please!"

When I tear through the archway and into the kitchen, sliding to a stop on the tile floor, I see Meela standing on a chair, pointing to the counter like she's seen a spider. On the counter are the sugar and flour jars with painted roosters on the side.

"Those were not there a moment ago," she says with a shaky voice. "The lizard jars have become sentient!"

It takes me a moment, but I figure it out. "You're saying the sugar and flower jars moved from the icebox to the counter on their own?"

"Yes! Yes!"

Sol appears behind me, rubbing the back of his neck. "That's my perk. I can move things with my mind. I'm sorry if it frightened you."

The hierophant squints and scoots her chair toward him with tiny hops like a potato sack race. She stands on her toes to look him in the eyes. "No, it is *not* your perk!" There's venom in her voice. "It is something else. Something wrong. It's upset the balance and angered the star. I do not wish to partner with you again!"

"Meela," I begin.

The hierophant rounds on me. "You would do well to listen to the Wondrous Grapefruit before it's too late. This one's card was not one of fortune. He is a bad omen. It does not matter how large his antlers. You must cleanse your feelings if we're ever to restore the balance."

Sol crosses his arms. "How large my *what*?"

Meela does not answer, because we're all distracted by a click and rumble in the family room. I turn in the archway to see what's happened. "It's the exit. We must have completed the trial. Wait. No. It's two exits!"

A bookshelf has rolled aside, exposing two pastel doors. Each has a series of symbols upon it, and there's a message above them in the opposite runes.

"I've got this!" I say, tugging my backpack from my shoulder. "We just have to match the symbols on the door to the ones in the message above!"

Something behind me clatters, and I turn just in time to see Meela scoop her stones up from the counter and bolt for the doors. She's through one before I can even react.

"Pretty sure she just got the key," Sol says.

I groan.

There are only three trials left.

Twenty-Five

"It's obvious they cheated!" the emperor screams as we exit into yet another lobby between trials. "How can you not see that? I thought you were on my side!"

"I don't remember choosing a side," Yvit snaps back. "I thought we were all competitors."

The latter has somehow managed to find himself a dress shirt since I last saw him, and looks almost exactly as he did when the competition began. Where did he get it? It's possible he's using his magician's perk to pull the clothing from his bag. If so, that seems a terrible waste.

"The final question," the emperor growls, "was which of us was wealthier on our home planet. You and I both know it's me. So, how did they bet on themself and win, if not by cheating?"

"I don't know. Ask them."

Death ignores the conversation, choosing instead to run their gloved hands through the leaves of a weeping willow. The doors have deposited everyone in the center of a mushroom circle beside a picturesque lake, and Death seems enchanted by the lush nature. That makes sense. I suspect the emperor lost because, though he is financially wealthy, Death is basically a war profiteer on a dying planet with no food.

There's no comparison.

It's odd. In any other situation, I would loathe someone like Death. Any war profiteer on Earth would get a quick block on social media, regardless of their excuses. Somehow, between Death's story and the surreal nature of our surroundings, I gave them more grace than I normally would have. I'm not entirely sure that's wise.

"Never again," Meela announces, jarring me from my speculation, "will I partner with the scarecrow! He is everything the Wondrous Grapefruit warned of. Beware. Beware!"

Sol shakes his head. "That's a bit much, even for you."

It's nice to see him stand up for himself, rather than leave and hide in the shadows. The competitors' behavior hasn't changed for the better since the competition began, but at least he can let it roll off his back. Hopefully, that means he's gaining confidence in himself, not hatred for his peers.

Death releases the willow and approaches. "What has he done? Are you all right?"

Realizing the potential for drama, I jump in to put a stop to it. "He moved a jar of flour from an icebox to a countertop."

"With his *mind*," Meela adds.

"Terrifying," the emperor says. I really hope he's being sarcastic.

"On purpose?" Death asks.

Sol shakes his head. "Subconsciously. It completed the trial. I wasn't trying to spook her."

"Hmm." They reach behind a pauldron at their hip and retrieve an object from their pocket: another key with a diamond-shaped bow. "Do you still need this?"

Sol's shock mirrors mine. "Yes. But I don't have anything to trade."

I nearly leap out of my boots. "I do! I can trade!"

"Stop." Death waves me off and sets the key in Sol's hand.

"There's no reason to hoard or trade now that everyone has three of four keys. We should be helping each other escape."

"To what end?" the emperor snaps. "One more qualified person is one more person to challenge my win."

"That's so selfish," I complain. "You'd let someone else lose their wager to improve your chances of winning?"

"Yes."

Yvit crosses his arms. "I have to agree with the lady. I wouldn't enjoy my win as much if I knew I left her to rot here forever."

"I do not agree!" Meela declares while clutching a silver spade key to her robes like someone present might try to rob her. "The scarecrow is not one of us. He has nothing to win or to lose. Aiding him will only upset the balance and will gain him nothing in the end!"

"That's not true!" Sol snaps. "June's helping me escape to her planet."

Everyone's jaws metaphorically drop, save Death, who could not emote if they tried.

"So, you admit you aren't real?" Yvit asks. "No more pretending you lost your memory?"

Bolstered by Sol's confidence, I chime in. "He's real. He was just born here. That's not his fault, and he's not trying to hurt us. He's just trying to survive. Who knows what happens to someone like him when the competition ends? We should help him get out. It could save his life."

"And upset the star as well as the balance?!" Meela cries. "No, no, no, no, no!"

"We still don't know what that means," Yvit argues. The pangolin politician throws his hands in the air, once again untucking his dress shirt. "Fine. I don't know when this event changed from a competition to a rescue mission, but I'm in. I'll help the guy get out, but not at anyone else's expense. Hope that's clear. Now, where do we go from here? How do we pick the doors?"

While the others search the lobby, I dig in my bag for my sketchbook. As quickly as possible, I scribble in my edits.

June: 2 Clubs, 1 Spade, 1 Diamond
Meela: 1 Club, 3 Spades, 2 Diamonds
Death: 1 Club, 1 Spade, 1 Diamond, 1 Heart (?)
Yvit: 1 Club, 2 Spades, 1 Diamond
Emperor: 1 Club, 1 Spade, 1 Diamond
Sol: 1 Club, 1 Spade, 1 Diamond

It feels pointless to jot down keys when we all need the same one to escape—everyone but Death, I assume. Still, there are three trials remaining, and anything could be revealed in that time.

That's what I tell myself, but in my heart, I know this will be a struggle. Twenty-four keys came from six trials, with only one heart showing up among them. The odds are hopelessly stacked against us, and the chances that anyone will give a heart to Sol are zero, unless we all have one first. It's up to me to save Sol's life.

"The only door has been here the whole time," the emperor scoffs. "You're standing on it."

Everyone looks down.

"You're speaking of the ring of gray mushrooms?" Meela asks. "Is it some kind of fungal portal?"

The emperor rubs his brow, impatient. "Step out of them and look again."

Skeptical, we all stand back. It's not until we're outside the ring with no one blocking the view of the grass that we notice what he already has. In addition to the mushroom circle, there's a pattern in the moss that coats the ground—one that resembles a person with a sword. A page, maybe? It doesn't look like royalty.

"I see," Death says. "And how would we open this door?"

"We step back over," the emperor explains as if he's speaking to a child.

Meela gathers her robed sleeves to her chest as if scandalized. "All of us? Together? No, no. We're incompatible."

Yvit sighs. "Knowing the star, that's the point."

I don't feel great about this, either. Through sheer luck, I've managed to avoid pairing up with the horrid emperor until now, and everyone paired with him regrets it. How Yvit manages to put up with the guy round after round, I have no idea. The pangolin must have built up a tolerance to jerks over his lengthy career.

"At the same time, or individually?" Death asks, still focused on the specifics.

The emperor rolls a hand in the air impatiently. "Whichever. I'll go first."

He steps back over the gray mushroom circle, and nothing happens. He looks smug about it.

"See?"

"I don't—" Yvit begins, but I notice a subtle change.

"Look at the mushrooms," I tell everyone. "Are those spores?"

Wispy smoke rises from the mushrooms almost imperceptibly, twinkling like the dust that forms the star's ever-changing snake body. The emperor may not know much about equality, empathy, or manners, but he apparently knows his mushroom doors.

"All right, let's go," Yvit concedes, despite a dramatic cringe from Meela.

"No, no no," she continues to mutter as Yvit and Death stride into the circle.

I glance to Sol, who smiles back. The smile betrays a hint of the mischief I saw when he humored Meela in the kitchen.

"Looks like we're together again," he says, looking directly at me, but Meela reacts to the comment instead.

"We are not! You must cease your disruptive manipulations. It's unnatural. It disrupts the—"

The emperor clears his throat. "If you wish to exit the competition here, I'm certainly not going to stop you."

Meela mumbles, "Mm. I do not," but still hesitates.

For my part, I hop across. There's no point arguing if there's only one door. Though, that fact in itself is suspicious. Setting aside the previous trial where the emperor chose the number for us, this is the first lobby since the start without an option to pick the number of doors.

I wouldn't put it past that weasel to lie about the mushroom circles or to have kicked some down before we arrived. There's a creepy gleam in his eye that makes me worry he's gathering us together as part of some twisted strategy. Come to think of it, he didn't even take the opportunity to shun Sol when he had the chance. That's out of character. He's up to something.

The mushrooms continue to release their spores, which drift upward and across the grass, creating a twinkling band of fog. Sol steps across after me, and everyone stares expectantly at Meela.

"This is a mistake," she declares, but hitches up her robes and crosses the circle.

The spores twirl around us like a cyclone, until I once again see nothing but stars.

Twenty-Six

Thanks to Meela's rude outburst when first stepping into the retro kitchen, I don't immediately comment on the alien nature of the new trial. Instead, I slowly turn in a circle to examine the mountain that rises before us, inhaling a breeze that smells like fresh peaches.

Meela, meanwhile, has learned nothing. "From whose planet is this bizarre terrain?"

When no one answers, she bends down and runs her fingers through the eggplant-colored soil that holds a sheen like an oil slick. Growing from that shiny soil are thousands of pronged, crystalline trees that reach for the sky like saguaros. Bioluminescent flowers with petals as delicate as glass wind through the shimmering quartz forest. Their vines meander through fiber-like grass and strangle gorgeous amethyst shrubs. None of the plants feel alive.

"The soil is moist," Meela informs us as she tries to shake sticky clumps from her fingers, "but the plants are dry. Living stone. I can't comprehend it."

Yvit sets his hands on his hips. "I've seen crystals grow in wild shapes, but never imitating flowers."

"Perhaps, the star has more imagination than it lets on," the emperor suggests. "Then again, we're not its first victims.

This could be something from a prior world."

Death clears their throat. "Is anyone else interested in the trial, or only the geology?"

I'm surprised to see them standing next to Sol, as if the two have been whispering while the others were distracted. Both are examining a twisted glass bottle half as tall as one of the trees. Inside, dangling from a thin stem, is a smaller bottle containing an oval capsule. There's no question what's inside the capsule.

My gaze darts desperately along the mountainside, searching for identical bottles. There's no way this trial has only one key—not when we're so close to the end. To my relief, at least two more bottles are visible through gaps in the crystalline forest. Three keys aren't as good as six, but our odds are better than if there was one.

"This seems simple enough," the emperor says. "We smash the glass and take the key."

Death raps their knuckles on the outer bottle, which makes no sound upon impact. The thin glass inside is unaffected.

As if the pair are professor and assistant, Sol explains Death's demonstration. "The outer glass is indestructible. It looks like we have to find a way to break the inner glass to drop the capsule in this chute."

He points to a sealed hatch near the base of the bottle which is connected to a glass chute and trigger plate.

"Nonsense," the emperor says, digging into his regalia for his scepter. "Get out of my way."

I flinch as he waves the thing around, afraid it might affect Sol's mind like the creatures he forced to dance, but Sol easily sidesteps the fairy and backs up to let him humiliate himself. The emperor winds up like a batter, then takes his hardest swing at the glass. The resulting sound is not a ping or a crack, but a thump—and a series of frustrated curses.

"That's no natural glass," he complains while retrieving his filthy scepter from the mud.

"It's well dampened, at the very least," Death agrees.

Yvit joins them in their examination, while Meela extracts her bag of stones. She searches the muddy ground until she spots a flat rock large enough to dump the contents on.

"It seems this one is not for me," she says before stumbling toward another bottle. Every step squishes purple mud between her toes.

Death watches her go. "I should follow her."

"Why?" I ask. "Will she need your help?"

"The opposite. She hasn't lost a single trial, and none of you can afford to sacrifice a key."

That's true, now that I think about it, and a bit annoying as well. On the bright side, Death accidentally confirmed my suspicion that they already have a heart.

"Shouldn't we figure out the puzzle before we wander too far apart?" I ask.

"You'll get there," Death says with a casual wave. "You know what you're doing."

Do I though?

The emperor crosses his arms and frowns. "If we're claiming bottles, this one is ours."

"Ours?" Yvit asks. "You also claiming people?"

To my shock, the emperor points to Sol. "This time, I'll be partnering with *it*."

Alarm bells go off in my head.

On the one hand, splitting up gives Sol and I the potential to win two keys in one trial. On the other, it risks losing both. And that creepy look is still in the guy's eyes. There's no way I'm leaving Sol with him.

"He's not an it, and he's with me," I declare while making myself look big in the same manner as an alley cat. I want him to know that I'm on to him.

Yvit glances back and forth between us like he's watching a tennis match, then sets a stubby hand on the emperor's cloak. "Let's let the couple here do their thing, why don't we? I think we'll be fine without them."

The emperor glares down at him, eyebrows arched as if he might argue, then takes a deep breath and smiles. It's a queasy grin, and he pairs it with a sickeningly saccharine tone. "I was merely giving the young lady a chance to avoid whatever curse is on this creature. You know, the balance and what not. But if my generosity isn't appreciated—"

"It isn't," I growl, not believing him for a second. "We're out of here."

I turn on my heel—a squishier process than I envisioned—and storm toward the final bottle. Sol hurries to keep up.

"Is it just me, or is that guy exhausting?" he asks.

Exhausting is an understatement. When I go home—assuming I make it—I'll spend as much of the weekend as possible avoiding the rest of humanity. Normally, that means two days straight alternating between naps and crafts, but if Sol is there, that changes things. A brand-new human can't appear in the world without causing complications.

"Is everything okay?" he asks.

I bite my lip. Why can't I have a poker face?

"I just realized how rough it's going to be for you when we get to Earth. My planet's not always friendly to strangers."

He blinks. "I don't mind. I'll be with you. You can help me blend in."

The words make me feel like I'm in carbonated water: tingly with joy, yet drowning in worry for the real-world implications of his freedom. I can picture us sitting together in school, catching jealous glances from Jayden and blowing them off without a care. But then I think of what it would take to enroll Sol in my public high school without a local house or parents.

"I'll do my best, but I don't have my own place or a real job. If my folks refuse to help you, I don't know where you'll live."

It's not like he's a cat. My mom won't let me keep him.

"Does this mean you don't want me to come with you anymore?" His expression is so pitiful, my chest aches with the urge to say anything that will make him smile.

Curse those puppy eyes.

"I do. We'll make it work."

His brow smooths, but he doesn't smile. "If I get out, I won't be a burden. I promise."

Another peachy breeze drifts across the mountain, creating a lovely wind chime effect as glass and crystals clink together. It would be romantic if I wasn't such a downer. What's wrong with me?

"*When* you get out," I tell him. "I'm bringing you to roleplaying night. It's basically the only social thing I do other than hanging with my bestie. You can make some friends there. Plus, I'll help you create your character so you don't make any newbie mistakes."

I'm babbling, but it's working. The puppy eyes look thoughtful, not sad.

"Create my character?"

Finally reaching the third bottle, I run a hand along its surface. "Yeah. When you're roleplaying, you invent a person based on characteristics in a rule book. Then you act out that character and adventure in fictional worlds with your friends."

"Like we're doing here."

"Not exactly. You don't *really* travel. You just pretend."

His nose scrunches up in confusion. It's cute. "Everyone pretends together? Do you all have telepathy?"

That gives me a genuine laugh. "No! There's a storyteller—like a referee. They describe the world and the people in it and come up with the story that we play through."

"Wouldn't that person's character always know what was coming?"

I shake my head. "The storyteller can't also be a player. That would be a huge conflict of interest. I mean, sometimes they have to take over a character if somebody who's missing has a skill the group needs. But they usually overcompensate and make that character totally useless. Like this one time, when my friend was on vacation—" I stop jabbering and cringe, realizing I've moved from mood lifting to infodump territory. "Sorry. I'm oversharing."

He smiles. "It's okay. I like when you talk about things that make you happy. You make funny faces."

I'm too embarrassed to keep going. "Um, we should probably figure out the bottle. How do we break something on the inside if there's no way to get through the outer glass?"

He shrugs and taps on it. "I was hoping Death would stay around long enough to give us a hint. Do you also get the impression they're some kind of genius?"

"Eh." I crouch down to pry at the hatch where the key will fall if the glass inside breaks. "They're book smart, but not as wise as you think."

"Oh?"

He crouches down as well, peering at a mechanism that looks like it might lift the hatch open when the capsule strikes a plate. Meanwhile, I consider how to clarify what I'd said. It's not my place to tell Death's story, but now I've got my foot in my mouth.

"They get too focused on solving problems and miss the things that really matter in life."

Sol stops staring into the glass long enough to shoot me

a smirk. "Unlike us."

"What do you mean?"

He pauses to think, then looks at me like he did when taunting Meela in the kitchen. "Like, why sit here and solve this? We could take a walk in the forest and wait for the others to figure it out."

I panic. Okay, not actual panic, but a familiar, tense discomfort that always happens when someone goes off-script. It's the same feeling I have when stuck in a car with a driver who ignores GPS.

"Why would we do that?" I ask.

"To focus on what really matters: a beautiful day, crystal trees, spending time with good company . . ."

I scowl. "Okay, I get it. But we shouldn't mess around. If we fail, you might not be able to escape."

This isn't the time for jokes. I still haven't figured out how to convince the star to let me take Sol to Earth with me, and I can't even start if we don't have keys. The literal rules of the game seem to be the only thing the star respects.

"Or," he offers, ignoring my distress, "I might never get out, no matter how hard we try, in which case these are my final moments. Shouldn't I be allowed to enjoy them?"

"That's not funny."

"Maybe not, but the look on your face is."

"Sol!"

He moves as if dodging a punch I haven't thrown, slips, and falls perfectly onto his back. It makes a comically wet sound.

All right, now *that's* funny.

"What's that?" he asks, pointing straight above his head.

I follow the gesture to the branches of a two-pronged tree standing next to the bottle. Upon one of the prongs, someone has clamped a heavy stone. It looks familiar.

"Oh!" I cry, staring up at it. "I know what that is!"

Sol wobbles to his feet, trying to look over his shoulder at the condition of his filthy jerkin. When that move predictably fails, he picks up a stick and attempts to scrape off the mud. I yelp.

"Give me that stick," I say.

The look he returns is pathetic, but he hands it over and I march to the tree. Perhaps the emperor had the right idea all along. He was just striking the wrong object. I wind up and swing the cylindrical stick into one of the pronged branches. The resulting sound is louder than expected, filling the air with a lengthy ring.

"The tree is a tuning fork," I explain.

He cups a hand over his ear. "A what?"

"A tuning fork! We can break the glass with sound!"

"Should something be happening, then?"

The ringing slowly dies down while Sol and I inspect the bottles. Sure enough, the inner bottle is undamaged. I hadn't expected it to be that easy.

A distance away, Death shouts "Brilliant!" and repeats my experiment, sending another ring back across the forest.

I lean close so Sol can hear. "I think we need to adjust the weight to find the right frequency. Like we did with the dancers in the first trial."

"Gotcha."

Without waiting for instructions, he climbs up to the center of the prongs and gingerly unclamps the weight. "Up or down?"

"Down, I think."

He lowers the stone, clamps it back, and hops to the ground. "Strike away."

I smack the tree with the stick again, and the resulting ring is higher pitched, but still doesn't affect the glass. It's not even vibrating like I might expect. Meanwhile, across the forest, someone hits a much lower note that clashes and buffets my eardrums uncomfortably. Death swings their hands in the air, signaling for everyone to stop.

They shout in the emperor and Yvit's direction, but all I can make out is "Too low!"

The emperor shouts back, and again, I hear only one word of his reply. "Working!"

"He's wrong," I tell Sol. "On Earth, we have this experiment that folks like to do with a wineglass—"

"Where they sing at the natural resonant frequency of the glass and cause it to shatter. Yeah. It's a higher frequency than this."

I blink. In all the excitement of the trials, I'd forgotten Sol's talent with physics. Why am I telling *him* what to do? I should just let him do his thing. Maybe, between his mind and his perk, we can coast through this one.

"I'll lower the weight again," he says, climbing into the tree.

As he does, the emperor and Yvit strike another low note, which vibrates my eardrums like a dump truck passing over a suspended bridge. Death stops messing with their tree and bolts toward the emperor.

"Hold on," I say to Sol, gesturing for him to get down. "Something's wrong."

We watch as Death races toward the duo, arms raised as if starting a fight. But when they reach the other group, they instead throw their arms around the nearest tree and hug it as if greeting a relative. Inexplicably, the emperor and Yvit do the same.

I can't even hear Sol's boots hit the ground over all the low humming, and barely make out when he says, "I don't like this."

Unsatisfied with the hugging, Death climbs into the tree and grips the branches. It's then that I realize the low ring has not quieted despite their efforts. It should have slowed naturally in the time we've been watching, if not earlier with the help of the hugs.

"That sound isn't coming from their tree anymore, is it?" I ask, already knowing the answer.

"No," Sol replies, glancing left and right. "They found the resonant frequency of all the trees on the mountain. It's hopping from tree to tree."

The whole forest has started to vibrate, making my organs shake like my eardrums. Even worse, though, is the second sound—a low rumble coming from above.

"Oh," Sol breathes as up the mountain, crystalline trees are torn from the ground, snapping and smashing their way downhill, along with rapidly sliding soil.

"Landslide!" I scream, as if that's not the outcome Death had specifically been trying to prevent. "Get away!"

But there's nowhere to go. There's no shelter, and every direction is mountain. Nothing is safe from the landslide above, not trees, stones, or the ground itself.

A flash of light catches my eye, and I watch as a terrified Yvit soars into the air on a rocket pack, still gripping his magician's bag. The emperor flies up after him under the power of his mothlike wings.

"Help!" Meela screams, still alone with her bottle.

The hierophant grips the indestructible glass like the surface might protect her from what's coming. There's no way, though—the landslide will drag her away. Perhaps the star has finally grown bored of jettisoning competitors into space and has decided to bury us all under mud. If that's not disqualifying, I don't know what is.

Sol clenches his fists. "She's not going to like it, but I can save her with my perk."

"Then do it!"

He nods and gestures in her direction.

Meela, her bottle, and the tree beside her vanish instantly into the earth. If she screams, it's impossible to hear over the roar of the oncoming landslide. My heart thuds as Sol turns his gaze to Death, who holds out a hand and waves him off. Carefully, as if there's all the time in the world, they remove their glasses and store them in the trouser pocket beneath their tasset.

The landslide doesn't wait for them. It crashes and crunches through the trees, growing closer by the second. I grip Sol's hand as the tumbling mass of dirt and trees approaches our position.

The ground opens up beneath us, and we plunge rapidly into darkness.

Twenty-Seven

It's not as dark underground as I expect, but it's twice as chilly and damp as I prefer. Bioluminescent flowers—some shattered, but most of them still whole—dot the glistening purple cave in which I find myself after my tumble. Water and mud grip my boots and threaten to pull them off my feet, but I trudge forward in search of Sol. I'm not sure how we separated in the fall.

"Sol?" I call, but it's a wasted effort.

Nothing is louder than the rumble above. It's like a train passing overhead or one eternal thunderclap. I march on, imagining the squelch my boots must be making as they squish and pop in the muck. The air doesn't smell like peaches anymore. Without foliage, the soil takes on a scent that's closer to sharp cinnamon. It stings my nostrils.

"Sol?" I call again as the rumble fades and I reach a branch in the tunnel.

A faint response directs me to the left, though it's hard to tell if the sound is a voice or the deceptive clatter of crystalline debris.

"Sol!"

I no longer have to imagine my boots squelching as I hop along. My gait is more like a distressed flamingo than a graceful gazelle in the mud, but my pace has officially picked up, and the corresponding sound is like a toilet plunger. Something is moving in the tunnel ahead. I can tell because it's obscuring the light from dozens of tiny glowing flowers.

For a second, I imagine a grizzly bear or fantasy monster at the end of the cave, drool dripping from its sharp fangs as it turns on me like—

"There you are."

Sol doesn't have any fangs. He does have a lot of mud, though, and a face lit by flower light like a beautiful ghost in a horror movie. I don't care. I'm happy to see him.

"I'm here! I'm good!" I shout, and squelch over. "Thank you for the rescue."

"Don't thank me yet. I don't know how to get us out of here without bringing the tunnel down around us. Everything I shift threatens a cave-in."

I frown and glance around the tunnel, wondering how it's holding at all. The walls look like the same soft soil with a rainbow sheen that we walked through above. Though, now that I'm paying attention, I see a repeating geometric pattern. It reminds me a little of bismuth crystals, beautiful and alien.

I see something else, too, and fail to hold in my excited squeal.

"The inner bottle! It broke in the fall!"

I flail toward the larger bottle that no longer contains a smaller one. The stem has snapped and the glass has shattered—but where is the capsule that was inside?

"I know," Sol says, with no joy in his voice. "Sorry I didn't wait for you. I figured I should grab it before someone else did."

He holds up his hands to show the opened capsule, in which rests another spade key. All the excitement drains from my body and into the chilly sludge at our feet. Two trials left, and still no heart. The logical part of my brain struggles to find a way to make that work.

The realistic part sets off panic alarms.

"It's fine," I say, not believing it myself. "We'll split up for the last two trials. It'll improve our chances of getting two hearts."

"Or we stick together to make sure at least one of us gets one. We're a team, so we can share." His poker face is as bad as mine.

I glare. "You mean if you get one, *you'll* share it with *me*, and if I try to share with you, you'll refuse like before. Am I right?"

He doesn't answer.

I know what he's doing, and I'm not in the mood for an existential crisis while uncomfortably damp. How much more evidence do I need to prove to him that he's a real person? Does the star have to fly out of the muck and tell him directly to his face?

Apparently, I'm not the only one getting grumpy. The frustration I saw in the kitchen trial flashes across Sol's face again. "And is that wrong? You need to get home. You have a whole life waiting for you. Real people, remember?"

"And what about your life?" I dig my heels in the mud—literally. It's actually kind of gross. "If I lose, I get to read books all day. If you lose, you get *deconstructed*. I'd rather get stuck here while you live than go home knowing I've sentenced you to death."

Sol musses his hair with both hands as if trying to rip the curls from his head, then lowers his arms and sighs. "Look, I didn't mean to eavesdrop on your chat with Meela, but you were loud, and I heard what you said about love."

That stops me cold. I can't remember what I said.

He looks away. "You and me, well, we've only been here one night. Both of us know that's not enough time to fall for someone. Not really."

Oh.

A chill seeps into my skin. Now I remember Meela's constant taunting about my *fixation*. Had he heard all of that? No wonder he was so upset when I found him with the book in the bedroom. He must have been wondering how to let me down without losing his chance to escape. And now that everything looks so bleak, he's going to use it to push me away.

I can't deal with this. Not twice in one day. Not with *him*.

If I can just stop him talking, I can pretend it was all a misunderstanding. Pretend I haven't been dreaming of our future, and my heart doesn't flutter every time he smiles. I can swallow the pain and be a good friend till we escape. If he'll just . . . stop.

"But," he continues despite my silent pleading, "in the heat of the moment, with all this pressure on us, things can feel more intense than they are. It can make you believe you care about someone so much that their safety is more important than your own—even knowing that's irrational. I appreciate your help more than I can say, but prioritize getting yourself out. Please."

He's trying to be kind, and that makes it hurt more. My heart doesn't crumble—not exactly. It's more like a pair of invisible hands has reached inside my chest and twisted until I can feel the tension in my throat. I can't breathe or think. My pulse pounds in my ears.

"That's . . . I . . ." What is there to say? I'm furious with myself for falling so hard and embarrassed that he knows, and— Oh, there's the flush. I want to lie. I want to say whatever it takes to get us back to the way we were. But who am I kidding? Things will never be the same.

My voice catches. "Fine. Whatever. You're right. Maybe I got carried away. But it's not like I can un-love you just because you want me to. You can insult me to my face, and I'll still leap into the stars to save you—because I'd rather you survive and hate me than miss you every time I see the sky. There's nothing you can say to change that."

Oof. The words just tumbled out, and now I have to grapple with their truth. Somewhere along the line, I stopped caring about my wish as much as I care about saving Sol. Maybe that means I'm leaving here twice as broken as I arrived—but a little voice in my head says, "Worth it."

I expect more frustration and hair-pulling, but Sol steps back with his mouth ajar as if I just hauled off and slapped him. He blinks once before saying, "I was talking about myself. I thought you were into some other guy. You've been bringing him up all night."

The invisible hands squeezing my insides give one last twist before letting go, unleashing a rush of hot and cold that fills my head like helium. He thinks . . . because I said . . . What is *wrong* with me?

"No! I can't even remember why I liked him!" I blurt before Sol's words sink in. He wants to sacrifice himself for me? On purpose? Even believing that's he's real?

I try to compose myself, though he isn't making the same effort. "Huh" is all he manages.

For the first time since my arrival, I allow myself to really look at him without fear or embarrassment. Even smeared with mud and backlit by flowers, he's more handsome than anyone on Earth. And it's not his style or charming face that makes him so beautiful. It's the way his smile spreads and his eyes shine as he examines me the same as I do him.

Meanwhile, what does he see? A muddy girl with self-cut bangs? How long would someone as gorgeous as him stay interested in someone like me?

"You don't need to worry about other guys," I assure him.

"Me, on the other hand, I'm doomed the moment you meet literally anyone else on Earth."

His eyes narrow as if I've struck a nerve, and I catch a glimpse of the sourpuss he was when we first met. "Stop. It was hard for me to tell you all that, especially thinking you didn't feel the same. Don't make light of it. If I had my choice of anyone on your planet, I would pick you. That's the end of it."

I swallow and nod. "Sorry."

"So." His expression softens. "What happens now?"

What, indeed? I fidget with my sleeves. "Well, like you said, our feelings probably aren't rational. It's just the excitement of the trials."

He's right. I've seen the leads in a play get together only to break up when it ends. Maybe this is something like that. Still, I want to believe it's authentic.

He nods solemnly. "Maybe."

"But," I add, "what if we never get out of here? These could be your last moments alive. It would be awful if you didn't get to live a little before it all ended, right?"

"What do you—" His mouth snaps shut, his eyes widen, and he takes a tentative step closer. "That would be terrible."

I squelch closer as well, then pause to chuckle at the goofy sound. It's hard not to feel a little self-conscious while figuring out how to make the first move with a guy who's inexperienced. He silences that fear with a hand on my cheek and a quick kiss just beside my lips.

It's so childish it makes us both grin, but his hand is warm and the spot he kissed tingles as though his lips have lingered there. I don't hesitate to dive forward and give him his first real kiss.

It doesn't feel like a first. It feels electric, like tiny galaxies are swirling everywhere our skin touches, lighting up my nerves with pinpricks of pleasure. His hand on my cheek moves to cup my jaw while the other slides behind my back to pull my hips closer to his.

Taking his lead, I wrap my arms around him and grip the curls at the back of his neck. My head and heart are fizzy with joy, and just when I think the rest of the world has literally melted away around us, a voice cuts through the darkness of the cave.

"June? You down here?" It's Yvit. He tries to lower his voice for the next bit, but we can hear him all the same. "I've forgotten what the guy's new name is."

Meela's voice chimes in. "She calls the scarecrow Saul."

"You mean Sol," Death corrects.

"Sol? June?" Yvit calls again.

I reluctantly break away from the kiss, but Sol moans and tugs me back again. "Ignore them. There's more living I want to try."

I let him pull me into another kiss, but the grating voice of the emperor breaks through.

"See? They're not in here. Can we go now?"

"I'm not leaving while people are still buried underground," Yvit snaps. "What's your problem?"

Finally, someone said it.

"Besides," Meela adds, "the circle won't work without everyone standing in it. I've tried."

I gently push back and set a finger on Sol's lips. "They're not going to stop. We have to go."

"Do we?"

I laugh. It's like he's reading my mind. But if either of us is going to make it, we need to get out of this muddy cave.

"We're here!" I call, and gently tug him in the direction of all the shouting.

"I told you," Yvit says. "I saw them fall."

We don't have to squelch too far before we see the spot

where the tunnel caved in and the four figures backlit by the sun. Sol squeezes my hand and helps me climb collapsed piles of rough crystal back up to the warm surface. It's way brighter than I remember, and flatter without any standing trees.

"The mushroom circle is this way," the emperor says with a gesture. "I suggest we all hurry before we cause another landslide."

I glare at him in annoyance—we all know who caused the landslide—but trudge after him, stomping my feet to clear mud from my boots along the way. The dried spots are now a violet dust that easily brushes off my clothes. Miraculously, it leaves no stains.

"Here we are," Yvit announces. "End of the ride."

The new circle consists of mushroom-shaped crystals in a lime green, like uranium glass. They're a little creepy, but I hop right in, because—well, what else can I do? Sol follows me, and when no one is looking, he leans close and lets our fingers touch. I get a rush from the tiny contact.

"That's all of us," the emperor says. "So where's—"

He doesn't get a chance to finish.

Twenty-Eight

"I cannot contain my excitement any longer!" Meela shouts before I even get my bearings.

We're in some kind of snowy chasm, surrounded by icicles as thick as my arms—some twice as long as my legs. They're clumped up on sagging tree branches and topped with blobs of pristine snow that make the trees look like ghosts reaching out. It's beautiful and spooky at the same time. What word would that be? Spookiful?

Meela whips something from her sleeve and holds it up. "I have the final key! My faith in the Wondrous Grapefruit has led me at last to victory! You should all consider joining the order. Your rate of success may improve."

She's moving her hand around too fast to make out the heart-shaped bow on the key, but it's golden, and Death isn't correcting her. The visible scowl on the emperor's face tells me he was not so lucky.

"You're not the victor yet," he snaps. "There can only be one winner."

The way his fists clench and unclench makes me worry for Meela's safety, despite knowing we can't hurt one another. I insert myself in the conversation before it devolves into a fight. "We got another spade. Did you . . . ?"

"I got a diamond," he grumbles. "Worthless."

Oof. The odds are not improving. I pull out my sketchbook to record the keys, though my hands are going numb from the cold. Hopefully the next trial is warmer.

June: 2 Clubs, 1 Spade, 1 Diamond
Meela: 1 Club, 3 Spades, 2 Diamonds, 1 Heart
Death: 1 Club, 1 Spade, 1 Diamond, 1 Heart
Yvit: 1 Club, 2 Spades, 1 Diamond
Emperor: 1 Club, 1 Spade, 2 Diamonds
Sol: 1 Club, 2 Spades, 1 Diamond

"I'm growing impatient with these intermissions," the emperor declares. "Someone help me find the die."

I very badly want to reply that *growing* implies he had patience to begin with, but that would likely start a fight, so instead I say, "I've been calling them lobbies."

"What word was that?" Meela asks.

"Lobbies. Like when you're in between matches in a video game or movies in a theater."

"Vision games?"

I frown. "Never mind. Translation issue."

"Hmm," Death mutters while kneeling in the snow to brush off a large circle.

Meela hurries over to join them, pawing at the snow like she's digging a burrow. Meanwhile, the emperor and Yvit stalk the trees, presumably searching for a die. Sol takes the opportunity to slide his hand into mine and pull me aside.

"You look cold," he says, cupping both my hands in his. "Do you want my jacket?"

"It's a jerkin. I mean—no thanks."

I'm torn; do we go right back to making out with everyone around to see, or pretend nothing happened in the cave to keep things from getting awkward?

Sol makes the decision for me by wrapping his arms all the

way around me and kissing me once on the forehead. "How about this?"

He's warm, but before I can nuzzle in, Meela expresses her opinion. "*Tsk*. Hopeless girl. The balance is irreparable now. Let's hope she only endangers herself."

I turn my head, ready to glare at her, and instead get an unexpected pang of shame when Death crosses their arms and lowers their glasses. Last we spoke, I was torn up over Jayden and denying any interest in Sol. I must look so immature.

"We've found something. Come take a look" is all they say.

Upon approach, I wish they had been more descriptive. What they found is a human skeleton dressed in a moth-eaten parka and buried under a thick layer of ice. On its forehead is a carving of a question mark, and its bony hand points off to the right, where Meela has uncovered a river.

The river that flows beneath the ice is not filled with salmon or minnows, but rather with free-floating pirate treasure. Sparkling jewels and sun-bleached skulls tumble through coinage at random intervals, and I marvel that the skulls haven't smashed to bits as they whiz through the water, pinging off rocks. Every jewel is a bright shade of blue or green, making the river shimmer and glint, but that doesn't improve the morbid theme.

"This reminds me of home," the emperor says, startling me. I hadn't noticed his return. "The jewels I mean, not the skeleton. My company owns the only mine that produces gems of this color. They also happen to be the only gems capable of powering the— Well, that's a trade secret. Suffice to say, having the market cornered is beneficial to my bottom line, so long as the workers continue to behave. I can't afford to lose that advantage."

His gaze slides to Meela as he speaks, expression wolfish and a little scary. I remind myself again that we can't be injured, and he's not the only one getting nervous.

"I don't understand the parka," Yvit says, bringing the level of tension back down. "If the flesh rotted off the bones, why would the parka be intact?"

"Perhaps it's an artificial material," Meela suggests. "If left alone, flesh dissolves to dust in only a handful of years. Artificial materials last much longer. That's why we've outlawed them on my planet."

"Then why make the parka ratty? Oh! No offense."

Meela sets a hand to her chest. "I'm not a rat! Did you think I was a rat?!"

I keep my lips zipped.

"I don't suppose anyone has a spare ice saw?" Death asks. They're still examining the river, focused on the task, as usual.

To my astonishment, Yvit responds, "Yeah, I got ya."

I've once again forgotten his magician's bag.

He thinks for a moment, then reaches in. When he pulls his hand out, an impossibly long swordlike saw comes out with it. Each point on the saw's blade looks like a hooked dagger aiming toward the pointed tip. There's no way such a thing could fit in the bag. It's just like one of my roleplaying games.

So cool!

"Stand back. I've never done this before," Death warns before striking the ice with a rock to make a big enough divot to insert the blade.

The rest of us take several healthy steps back, just in case the ice splits apart. The river isn't small, and it's moving very fast. Fortunately for Death, the ice remains firm, and they're able to carve away a large square before slicing it diagonally to dig the ice out.

"The next step is less pleasant," they say. "Someone's going to have to grab a skull."

"You know what?" the emperor says. "I think it's time I give someone else a turn."

"Not it either," Yvit adds.

Meela looks confused. "I thought you were cold-blooded? Shouldn't this be easy for you?"

"Nah," Yvit snaps back, "and if I were, I definitely wouldn't stick my hand in there. I don't think cold-blooded means what you think."

"Oh! My mistake."

I feel a little better about my own confusion. At least I knew pangolins were mammals.

"I'll do it," says Sol, and before I can object, he's rolled up a sleeve and shoved his hand in the water.

It takes a moment for a skull to pass, but when one does, he snatches it up and yanks it out with a dramatic splash. The drips that roll off its surface freeze before they even hit the ground, and I want to reach out and warm his hand. Unfortunately, everyone has gathered around to stare at a carving in the skull's forehead. There's a jagged number four just above the eyes.

Before anyone can utter a word, four large rectangles of ice crash upward from the ground, spraying everyone with snow. Each one houses a carved ice door with a gemstone handle and tarot theme.

I can't honestly say I'm any better with the cards than I was at the start of the competition, but the one right beside me has a gorgeous woman in a flowing gown with a crown and a scepter. It's hard to tell when she's upside down, but she's holding it a bit like a microphone. The text says she's the high priestess.

It's a promising card, and Sol needs all the luck he can get. I'm not waiting for Meela.

Speaking of Sol . . .

I gently brush the skull from his fingers and draw him

near so I can warm him without fear of missing out on door selection. He smiles as I bring the hand to my face and try to warm it with my breath.

"It's not that bad," he whispers. "The cold can't hurt us. But don't stop. I like this."

I laugh.

Meela dumps her stones on the skeleton ice and clucks her tongue before choosing a door with a seated man surrounded by goblets—the nine of cups. I wish I'd seen it before I chose the high priestess. It looks promising, too.

"Which one is better when both are upside down, the nine of wands or six of wands?" Yvit asks.

"Six," Death responds without hesitation. "I'll take nine."

"That's not what my stones said," Meela objects.

Death can't shoot her a nasty expression, having no face with which to express, but I imagine that they would if they could. The emperor, meanwhile, prances to the door with six staves and a figure on horseback.

"Six looks fine to me. Come on, Councilor. Let's go."

Yvit crosses his arms and shakes his scaly head. "Again, you're just assuming I'm joining you. What if I want to team up with someone else?"

The emperor snorts. "Really? Death gives you the creeps, the girl wants to partner with *it*, and Meela will win and won't share the key."

"That's true," Meela confirms.

Yvit huffs. "Fine, I'll go with you again. But you're going to be real mad when I win."

"Don't be ridiculous. I'll only be angry *if* you win."

When the emperor wrenches his door open, cheers of adoration pour out and echo around the frosty chasm. I don't wait for the rest to leave. I open my door and tug Sol inside, only realizing my mistake when the door shuts behind us.

Twenty-Nine

It's not the lights that set me on edge this time, though they are uncomfortably bright. Nor is it the empty stage with an old-timey microphone and piano. Not even the audience in their beaded dresses and sharp tuxedos qualifies for the scariest thing in the latest trial. It's the massive Nixie tube clock counting down from twenty minutes with the backlit phrase *Entertain to win* that makes me want to run.

"I don't see any mirrors this time," Sol whispers.

It's not particularly quiet in the room, and yet we both instinctively hush as if speaking too loudly will attract trouble. The similarities to our first trial are impossible to miss, to the point where I suspect the restless crowd are the same NPCs as the ballroom dancers.

I have to admit, the star has leveled up its dance-hall-decorating game. The costumes are straight from the 1920s, more flapper-style club wear than fantasy formal, and the lighting is electric, if a little peculiar. Everything's black and gold and geometric, from the line art on the walls to the outrageous chandeliers. I wish I could say there was an obvious puzzle—a key dangling like a piñata or a pattern of symbols and shapes to decipher—but all I can see are the crowd and stage. The countdown clock is at nineteen minutes.

"This isn't like before," I whisper back. "I think we're the entertainment."

Sol's eyes widen. "I don't know any songs. I've *never* known any songs. What are we supposed to do?"

The room is starting to feel small and stuffy despite the high hexagonal ceiling, which is even more dizzying than the walls. I want to leave, but the door behind us is gone. We're trapped. This isn't what I expected.

A painful screech reverberates around the room, and the noise of the crowd fades to whispers and coughs. On the stage, a tiny figure drags a metal stool and plunks it down in front of the mic. I recognize the alien immediately, though its top hat is shinier and lacks a bird.

The ringleader from the carnival climbs onto the stool and adjusts the mic downward.

"Who's ready for karaoke?!"

I blink. Karaoke? They didn't have karaoke in art deco dance halls. I mean, I'm not a historian, but I'm pretty sure that came along much later. Besides, how can you have karaoke without something to play the music?

As if reading my mind, the ringleader leaps off the stool and onto the piano bench. It dramatically cracks its knuckles in the air, then plays a quick scale followed by a chord. The lighting in the dance hall dramatically shifts from incandescent bulbs to a rainbow of LEDs. Geometric patterns appear on the walls and many of the dancers' clothes, along with details that weren't there before. Some of the LEDs must be ultraviolet.

"Invisible ink! Maybe there is a puzzle!" I desperately search the surreal line art that now enhances the dizzying decor, but no patterns emerge from any of them.

Behind the ringleader, holographic screens lower, each displaying the empty microphone from a slightly different angle. They fade in and out of transparency, obscured by the stage decorations behind them. Above the mic, a similar but smaller screen displays a list of karaoke songs.

My stomach twists. The list looks long, but that doesn't mean it includes songs I know. What if it's all alien music? What if there's no way for us to win? Is this a disqualifying trial, or just another chance to miss out on a key?

The piano lights up with a final screen that occupies the space where sheet music should be, and Sol perks up at the sight.

"I think I can read music," he says, "and play the piano. It must be like math; the star knows how it works, so I do, too. You'll have to sing, though."

I pale. "I can't sing, and I don't know many songs!"

It's a half lie. I can technically sing. I do it all the time while dancing around my empty house with headphones on. I just can't do it in front of people. The second my parents walk in the front door, I pretend I'm getting a snack from the kitchen and slink back to my bedroom like a startled crab. I'm not sure if they've caught on, but if so, they've been kind enough not to ask.

"Besides," I whisper, "look at us. We're still in ren faire clothes. We fit in even less than before."

"Performers wear costumes," he argues. "We don't have to blend in."

He's right, and I hate it. I also hate that the clock is still ticking.

"Any volunteers?" the ringleader asks, as if there's anyone in the room unaware that the two poorly dressed strangers are the ones who have to get onstage.

They all know. They've always known. It's been clear since my encounter with the squirrels that the NPCs are self-aware. They're playing their roles in the competition, hoping to make the star proud. Maybe they believe that if they do a good job, the star will bring them back for a repeat performance.

It's like when I draw an original character and later recycle them in ten more drawings that may or may not be related to each other. The star has its favorites and uses them often. Does that mean it might give Sol another chance if I fail to get him out of here, or is he doomed for his unchecked perk?

An awkward silence falls over the room, and the ringleader claps its tiny gray hands. "Would it help if I explain there are no losers in this game, so long as the crowd is entertained?"

It reaches into its tiny tuxedo and pulls out two golden pouches. *Two* keys.

"We'll do it!" I shout before I can stop myself.

The odds are twice as good that one of us will get a heart. What if it's both? This could be what we need! Of course, we still have to entertain, and the crowd looks . . . sophisticated.

"Wonderful!" the ringleader shouts. "Come on up and select a song!"

"I thought you couldn't sing?" Sol whispers as I drag him by the hand toward the stage.

I lie and say, "I have an idea."

I don't. Not yet. I'm terrified—but it's the kind of terrified where you realize you're cornered and can only fight or give in, and I'm not going down without a fight.

"It's just like last time," I explain. "They want an entertainer? I'll be an entertainer."

I let go of his hand and spin my backpack around, digging out the leather mask that had transformed me in the ballroom. As I pull it over my head, I think as hard as I can about the most popular entertainer I know.

There's no sensation or sound to tell me if the mask has done its thing. Only Sol's disappointed, "Mmh."

I lower my hands and look down at my dress, only to find

it's hard to see past my overflowing push-up bra. It's worked! My arms are pale and painted with bloodred roses that resemble lace. My nails are bright and impeccable. My heels look like they have enough gemstones to transport me home if I whack them together. I'm the famous pop star Vivid Shock.

The look on Sol's face says he's not a fan, and to be honest, neither am I. But my musical tastes have always been a little bit outside the mainstream, and I'm trying to wow this crowd, not bore them. Besides, her tunes are repetitive enough to sing without memorizing . . . I think. In any case, she'll entertain the crowd better than a nerd in a fairy skirt.

The collective gasp as we climb the stairs to the stage reinforces my theory. Sol slowly takes his place at the piano, and I check the holographic screen for easy to sing Vivid Shock songs.

To my infinite relief, all the tracks are familiar, and it takes me no time to scroll to her section. I select one titled "Eat My Exes" and grin. I already know the refrain by heart because folks love to use it in videos. Granted, I never did figure out if the ex-eating was positive or negative.

"Are you ready?" I ask Sol.

He replies with a snarky "Nope."

"Neither am I," I admit. "Let's do it."

I poke at the holographic screen to start the "Eat My Exes" song. The intro Sol taps out on the piano is clunky, but that isn't his fault. The music was written for a cycling synth, not a live human performer.

"You say I chew them up and spit them out," I sing—or rather, read from the screen with what I hope is the right tune. "You say I use them and throw them away."

The tune is wrong. My voice is wrong. I can't match the cocky confidence of the woman I've only heard in the background of dance videos. Also, the microphone is too low, and when I go to raise it, the sound of my hand touching it is like a boxing glove to the ear.

Even with the mask—the crowd judging someone else—I can feel my muscles tensing up. My armpits are warm, my arms move stiffly, and my legs won't even shuffle back and forth. This isn't what a performer looks like.

The audience agrees. Little neon frown faces light up in red above several people's heads as if I'm in a musical video game, about to be booed and booted from a level.

"Baby, you wish you had a meal half as tasty as my leftovers."

The line makes me cringe. I've never said *baby* in my life outside conversations about infants. The word doesn't feel right in my mouth. Worse, more frowns are appearing in the crowd, and the temperature is rising in the dance hall.

"Are you okay?" Sol asks. His voice is distant. "We can stop, if—"

"No, we can't!" I try to cover the mic with a hand, but it's suspended in a metal cage that makes it impossible to block. "We have to make it through this."

If I can't get this right, we lose both keys. Sol keeps playing the music in a loop, waiting for me to jump back in, and I try to get my breathing under control. Finally, it's time for the refrain.

"Baby, are you starving? You can eat my exes. Baby, are you greedy? You can eat my exes. Baby, are you desperate? You can eat my exes. You know you'll never beat me to a meal."

That was okay, right? It sounded the same as I remember. Why are more frowns popping up? What did I do wrong? The tune? The dancing? This is too hard. I'm going to scream.

Nearly tripping over the ringleader's stool, I stumble off the stage and hunt for somewhere I can go to hide myself for a moment. There's nowhere. The dance hall has no backstage or restroom signs that I can see. The best I can do is curl up in an empty corner and bury my face in my arms. To my shame and horror, a sob catches in my throat.

"It's okay." Sol is beside me in a flash and crouches to share the corner with me. "You don't have to do this."

I sniffle. "Yes I do, or we won't get out. I just need to figure out what the audience wants. Maybe the song is wrong for the setting? Or maybe I'm supposed to be dancing."

He frowns and grips the edge of my mask, pulling it up and off my head. "Maybe we won't get out. At least we're here together now. I'd rather lose the competition than watch them torture you."

"It's not torture," I fib. I'm getting better at fibbing. That may not be a positive thing. "I'm just not good at performing in front of people. I wish my friend Alex was here. They know how to walk me through things like I'm five so I can feel more confident."

Maybe that was cruel to say with Sol sitting right next to me, but I suddenly miss Alex a lot. I miss the way they always take the lead in scary social situations, without me even having to ask. It's like having a tour guide or a human forcefield. They absorb everyone's attention, and nobody bothers me at all. I need them now.

Sol chews his lip, then points at one of the holographic screens and twitches his finger like he's beckoning it over. Unsurprisingly, it obeys. He gently turns me around and slides the screen between me and the crowd, positioning himself to block them out.

With another tap of his fingers, the screen starts beeping and lights up with Alex's name displayed in the center. I gasp, and only two beeps later, an image of their worried face pops up.

"Hey, you okay? You never call."

The sound I make in response is both a laugh and a choked

sob. Alex hasn't changed their clothes. They're still sitting in an office chair with a headset slung over their neck as if the game is still going, hours later.

"I'm having a really rough night," I mumble.

"Because of Jayden, or something new?"

Sol grunts, but it's quiet enough I don't think Alex is able to hear it. How do I explain what I'm going through without sounding like a total weirdo?

"It's not that. I started playing a game, and now I'm stuck. I guess I need your advice."

They look confused. "Oh? What kind of game?"

"Karaoke. It's, uh . . ." I peek around Sol's legs at the still-angry audience. "It's multiplayer."

"Who are you, and what have you done with June?" Alex demands.

I laugh and wipe my eyes. Just talking to them is grounding me, and it's making me feel worlds better. Unfortunately, thinking that makes my eyes well up again. What if this is our last conversation?

"I tried a pop song," I squeak, "and I thought I did okay, but nobody liked it."

"Sounds like trolls. What game is this? Is it on your phone? Want me and Sudo to join you after we finish?"

"No!" There is nothing I want less than involving my friends in the star's nonsense. "I just want to know what you would do."

"I'd put my phone down and go to bed."

"Liar."

Alex smirks. "I'd pick a song I like and sing it at the top of my lungs, as obnoxiously as I can. Forget the trolls."

I nod. "A song I like. Okay."

"Then I'd hang out with my friends tomorrow. Maybe around eleven?" They pause, and I can see the flicker of their ongoing game reflected in their eyes. "Actually, maybe later. I'll text you."

"Okay." I can feel their attention slipping away and try to catch them before it's gone. "Alex—I love you."

"Sorry, I'm taken."

I laugh. "Not like that. You know what I mean."

"I know. We'll talk tomorrow, okay? Promise."

"Okay. Thank you. Bye."

"Ta."

The screen flickers, then returns to an image of the empty microphone. Sol bats it away.

"Did that help?" he asks.

I wipe my face again. The eye makeup I had on when I started the competition is long gone. "Not really, but I feel better. Thank you." He nods, and I force a smile. "You sure you don't want to try singing? I can't be any worse on the piano than I am on the microphone."

He looks genuinely remorseful. "I'm sorry. I literally don't know any songs. The star didn't give me any memories of them. Maybe it was hoping to experience Earth music for the first time through me in this trial."

"Wait, hold on." I furrow my brow. Experience! That's right! In all my stress, I'd forgotten the whole purpose of this competition was for the star to experience emotions. "I know what I have to do!"

"You do?"

I jump to my feet. "You figured it out!"

"I did?"

"Yes!" I lean forward and plant the biggest kiss on his lips. When I pull away, his eyes are wide.

"Go, me," he says.

Thirty

I KNOW WHAT song I'm going to pick. There's this indie band called Buttons and Squish that writes soft tunes about hope and love. They're not popular or showy like Vivid Shock, but they make me smile—and I think that's what matters. I want the musical equivalent of a warm blanket and a good book.

As a bonus, Sol might enjoy the lyrics.

He stops me before I can reach the stairs, still confused about my plans. "So, wait. You're going to sing a song you like? Like Alex said?"

"Not exactly. I'm not belting something out to annoy the haters. I'm singing something to make me happy. You too."

"I don't understand the difference."

I point to the clock, which is dangerously low on time. "It says entertain to win, so I tried to entertain the crowd based on what I thought they'd like. But they're not here to judge my performance. They wouldn't know what to judge me on, because the star's never experienced a song as a human. They're going to determine if the act is going well based on how we feel about it."

He tilts his head. "So, we need to enjoy ourselves to win? There's no other requirement?"

"I've got this great song in mind," I say at top speed while hurrying back up the stairs. "It's sweet and silly, and I think you'll like it. The original is acoustic guitar, so I'm not sure how piano will sound. Oh! And I'll have to tap the drum beat with my feet. But I think if—"

"Wait."

I reluctantly halt my dash to the mic and turn to see him fumble with something. It takes me a moment to work out that he still has my mask in his hand.

"Do you mind if I destroy this?" he asks.

I hesitate. After all, it's come in handy in the trials. Plus, it's my mask from home and if we break it here, it may stay broken. Ultimately, though, I trust him.

"Sure," I say. "But why?"

"I need to break it down to understand how it works."

"Huh?"

There's no response. Whatever Sol is doing, it takes all his focus. I'm curious if he's sifting through the fog for some old star memory of the mask or if he can see the inner workings like a human X-ray machine. Either way, I don't want to interrupt.

"Aha!" he shouts before clapping his hands and crushing the mask like tissue paper.

I blink. Okay, that's new.

When he moves his hands apart again, a swirling mass of tiny stars occupies the space between them. Several thoughts crowd my head at once. First, that was super hot. Second, I don't know if I should worry that he's graduated from moving objects to disassembling stuff outright. After all, I'm also stuff. Third, that was super hot.

"Do what you did before," he says. "Think of how you want to look."

I nod.

Sol twirls his fingers through the stardust and flings it at me so quickly I wince. The sensation is like the pins and needles of a waking limb all over my body. When it fades, my outfit has once again changed—this time to a replica of the dryad dress I always imagined for my roleplaying character. In place of the hand-sewn layered skirt are soft leaves in greens and blues, and the top has a pattern of twisted vines that come together in the shape of a star. For fun, I added some of the glowing crystal flowers from the cave where we kissed.

Other than the dress, though, I'm me. Same hands. Same face. Same hair as far as I can tell by looking at myself on the floating screens. He did it.

"Hey—" I turn back to find that Sol has given his outfit the same treatment, and I have a hard time finding my words.

He's swapped his bulky jerkin for a dark green tunic that perfectly matches my dryad dress. To that look, he's added all the accessories an over-ambitious cosplayer might, including extra belts and a baldric. Yet, he's mixed up his fantasy and sci-fi by pinning LED card suit pips to his baldric—complete with a visible battery pack—and stringing blue and green lights through his curls.

When I smile at him, he shrugs.

"You said to enjoy ourselves."

I suspect what he's enjoying is the view of my backside, and give a little shimmy to make the dress flutter. A few of the glowing red frowns in the audience melt away when I do. It's already working.

"No more looking at them," he instructs. "This is for us, remember?"

He pinches his thumb and index fingers together, then flicks them apart again. When he does, my tiny screen expands to completely block our view of the crowd. The screen still fades in and out of transparency like the other ones behind us, but it's enough to isolate the stage.

"All right," he says, sitting at his piano. "I'm ready."

I'm not. I'm still checking out every inch of his goofy but adorable costume. Is this what Meela was talking about when she mentioned broken antlers and teeth? Features that are inexplicably attractive? Oof. I need to turn around.

"I think you'll like this new song," I say, unsure if I should be addressing Sol, the audience, or the star itself. "It's called 'Stars Like Fireflies.'"

I select the song, wait for the intro, and am surprised to hear acoustic guitar. When I turn, Sol is playing piano over top of the looping strums. Somehow, he's managed to turn the keys into some kind of synthesizer so he can play all the instruments at once.

I'm so impressed, I almost miss my cue, but manage to sing the cute song about a boy who encounters his true love after wandering into a field of fireflies that turn out to be fallen stars instead. His lover starts out as a twinkle of starlight but soon becomes human to remain with him. The song is sweet and magical and the music is soothing. Sol even adds a touch of harmony that makes my voice sound angelic in the hall. Every time I hit the refrain, I watch a grin spread across his face.

"I found you, my heart, my soul, among the stars like fireflies."

I knew he'd love these silly lyrics. They make the song sound like it's written for us. And I know . . . truly know . . . I love him. This isn't a crush, or a special interest, or me getting caught up in excitement. I want to keep reminders of him when he's away like Meela squirreling things in her nest and make irrational, lifelong decisions like Death wanted with their true love. This is it. I finally get it!

Forget the wish! I need to get Sol home.

As the song progresses, he amuses himself by toying with

his abilities: coloring the lighting, adding drums, and producing camera effects on the screens that make it seem like I'm surrounded by fireflies. I amuse myself by singing to him rather than the crowd. With every word, my heart screams, "This is us!"

By the time the song ends, I'm so absorbed in the moment, the applause from the audience startles me.

"Bravo!" the ringleader cheers.

It climbs the stairs and beckons us close, producing the two golden pouches from its tux. That's when I realize all the frowns in the crowd have been replaced with green smiles, and many of them are wiggling around as if their owners are still mid-dance.

"Thank you," Sol says, reaching for his key.

I quickly do the same, not wanting to be rude.

"Jeffrey was worried you wouldn't make it through," the ringleader tells us—like a total gossip, "but I had a feeling you'd be just fine."

"Jeffrey?" I pull a face and scan the audience. "Jeffrey the squirrel?"

"Squirrel for now," the ringleader answers, leaning in conspiratorially. "He's one of the star's favorites."

Aha! The NPCs *are* like an artist's original characters. I knew it!

"And there's your exit," it adds at a much more reasonable volume. It points to a door slightly offstage that hadn't been there when we began. "You'd better be off before the timer runs out."

That's it? I can hardly believe it. All the other trials were struggle after struggle, and now we're handed one where all we have to do is make each other happy and collect two keys? It feels fake, like the star is messing with us. Was this what it was like for everyone else who didn't choose the trials Meela's stones warned against?

I glance at the clock, and though it's ticking down, it still shows five minutes remaining.

"Augh. I can't wait!" I exclaim, and tug open my golden pouch.

The tip of the key I slowly slide out is just as gold as its packaging, and my heart takes off like a released dove. Could it be?

Sol steps closer, both watching me and flicking his fingers to restore our old outfits. It's for the best. I don't need that gross emperor ogling me in a beaded gown. The rest of the key slips into my palm: gold bit, gold shank, and . . . a heart bow! My scream of excitement nearly blows Sol over.

"We got one! We got it!"

Sol's smile is as bright as the stage lighting. "Let me check mine."

He tugs the strings on his pouch to open it, and I hold my breath. The tip of his key is gold, like mine, but as it slips out, I can already tell the bit is different. My soaring heart plummets.

"Another diamond," he says with a frown. "One heart is better than none, though. Right?"

I'm not so sure. Staying here while Sol leaves for Earth is starting to feel just as awful as leaving for Earth while he dies. I have to get us both out, somehow.

"Time's almost up!" the ringleader squeaks.

Sol grabs my hand and tugs me toward the exit. "Come on. We still have one trial left."

One more. There's still hope.

I follow him.

Thirty-One

Calling the new lobby dramatic would be a terrible understatement. The energy we step into is more like fireworks viewed through the windshield of a crashing race car. Everyone is mid-argument, but we lack any context for it.

"Exactly!" Yvit shouts, sounding legitimately angry rather than his usual state of annoyance. "You were supposed to appoint the most qualified person for the job, not step in and do it yourself!"

"There was no better qualified person! I did everything correctly. I commanded more authority than you did. I earned more profits than you did. It's because of me that we won! That key should be mine, and you should be the one with this worthless diamond."

Yvit jabs a stubby finger toward him. "The keys were random! And you didn't earn a cent. You swindled that money and stripped a healthy store for scrap. I don't know why you keep saying you're a businessman when you're clearly no good at maintaining a business!"

"Why you nasty little—"

The emperor whips his scepter from his sleeve and swings it violently toward Yvit, who manages to dodge and roll away. The scepter strikes a wooden apparatus, taking a chunk out of a support beam.

I step back, not only to get out of the way, but also to take in the device he hit. It's as tall as my house and full of gears, with a large wooden crank sticking out of one side. Judging by the flat panels that have various numbers carved into them, I'm guessing pulling the crank makes the device spin and select a number. It's basically a complex die that's big enough to crush me if it falls.

"Be careful," Sol says, setting a hand on my back to keep me from stepping any farther.

Behind me, there's a gaping canyon with whitewater rapids rushing through it. I assume, based the depth of the canyon and the ridiculous speed of the traveling water, falling in is disqualifying. And here I am with one heel at the edge. This last trial is starting out well.

"Let me guess," the emperor snarls, turning his vile glare upon us. "Both of you got hearts as well? I'm the only one who didn't?"

Sol frowns. "I got a diamond."

"Oh, well look at that. I'm on par with the star's little plant."

Meela squeals, "You must step away from the scarecrow. Remember the balance! It's terribly broken!"

The emperor spins on her, face as red as his regalia. "Will you shut up about the balance?!"

Death takes that opportunity to step in. They're just as tall as the emperor and wearing armor that can absorb a good impact. It's enough to make the fairy think twice.

"We need to focus. There's still one trial left, and we have to pick our doors and partners. Also . . . we should say our goodbyes."

My eyes widen. "Goodbyes? Why?"

They gesture to a sign on the wooden device that reads

Complete your final trades. "I take that to mean, wherever we go next, we won't be reunited after."

"Oh." My skin prickles, and I look at Sol, then around at everyone else. "So, this is it?"

Sure, there are some folks here that I'd rather not see another time—like the emperor, who's starting to fume like a steam locomotive leaving a station. But Death? Yvit? Even Meela? I still have more questions to ask them.

What's Death's plan if they win their redemption? How do they know whatever they try won't turn out as bad as the first time? What will Meela do with her power if she becomes a member of her order? Will she use it to help oppressed people on her planet, or do whatever her itchy feet tell her?

I'm never going to know the answers. That's weird. It feels wrong, like reading a book without an ending. And Sol . . .

"Get over yourselves!" the emperor snaps. "We're not friends! We're competitors! It's all of you against each other! And I, for one, don't intend to leave any part of this to chance!"

He dives for Meela, who yelps and scrambles up the side of the wooden device. She's surprisingly quick for someone laden with far too many drooping robes. With a crack, he brings his scepter down just below her foot as she climbs. The whole device shakes, and something snaps, barely giving her time to leap before the section she's on collapses.

Gears spin, numbers whirl by, and several doors appear on the cliff. At first, there are four. Then six. Then three. The device picks up speed and the doors start to blur—five, six, two, one. Control is rapidly lost, and six flickering doors remain, all cycling far too quickly to get an idea of what card they are—not to mention where they might lead.

Meela scampers far away from the emperor and pours her stones out onto the ground. "There's no incorrect answer! That man has destroyed the trial!"

Everyone turns on the emperor then, fuming and livid, but he lifts one arm, pointing his scepter directly at Sol. "Nobody move, or *it* goes off the cliff."

My breath catches and my limbs stiffen in a desperate attempt to move nothing at all. I want to order my pounding heart to stop beating so impossibly hard. *Don't mess this up. Don't even twitch.*

"Emperor," Death says, calm as a hostage negotiator, "what exactly are you trying to do?"

"What do you think I'm doing?" he snaps. "This scepter lets me control the star's minions, and the boy here is one of them. I've been waiting for the most opportune moment to take advantage of this knowledge, and it seems now is my final chance." He looks to me. "You, girl, toss me your heart key."

"Don't," Sol whispers.

I move my hand slowly to my backpack. "I have to. He's going to make you jump."

"He can't."

The emperor rolls his eyes. "I can hear you! This little gadget hasn't failed me yet, I assure you."

"He's not bluffing," Yvit confirms. "What he did in the last trial wasn't pretty. Didn't help him win, though. That was all me."

"Thank you, Councilor," the emperor hisses through his teeth. "I don't believe for a moment that this one has wished for or risked a thing, but I'm sure the punishment for disqualification will be severe, nonetheless. Wouldn't you rather give him a chance in the next trial than see him jump here?"

I clench my teeth. If it were possible to set someone on fire with the sheer power of my rage, the emperor would spontaneously combust. Unfortunately, that's not my perk, so I retrieve the key with the heart-shaped bow and move to toss it to the jerk.

"Don't," Sol says again. "I have a feeling his perk won't work on me."

I eye him. "If you're so sure, why aren't you moving?"

"I'm scared of what it means if I'm right."

Ugh. Not now! I can't risk everything for another existential crisis.

"I'm sorry," I tell him, and toss the key, sealing one—or both—of our fates.

No. I can't think like that. I'm saving him right now so we have another chance. There's still one more trial left, and we got two keys in the last one.

The emperor catches my key in one hand, grins in triumph, then glares at Yvit. "And you, give me that magic bag."

"Are you kidding me?" the pangolin asks.

"Never. I don't need your strategies to win, and I certainly don't need your sass. I would enjoy your perk, however, so toss me the bag or the boy takes a swim."

I hold my breath and watch Yvit, afraid he won't sacrifice his perk for someone he considers fake. He opens and closes his tiny mouth before saying, "Sure, fine. Take it."

It should not be possible to want to grovel in thanks and apologize at the same time, and Yvit must see the conflict on my face.

"Don't worry." He unties the little bag from his belt and tosses it at the emperor's feet. "I can get along just fine with my wits."

The emperor scoops it up and sneers, scepter still leveled at Sol's face as he backs toward one of the doors. "I'll get along better without your so-called wit. Farewell, my former partner in—gah!"

Something long and flailing launches from the bag and wraps itself around the emperor's throat. It makes a wet slurping noise as it squeezes, dripping slime down his chest. He releases the bag and reaches up to try to pry the sticky thing off, when another thing—a tentacle, I realize—shoots out of the bag and wraps around his torso, pinning down his wings.

With the emperor distracted, I quickly lead Sol away from the edge. Both of us watch the struggling fairy in horror as more tentacles shoot from the bag.

"What is this creature?!" the emperor demands as he twists and tugs, stumbling back and forth. "Call it off!"

"I'm gonna go with giant squid," Yvit says. "I'll be honest, I didn't have time to think about it all that well, since I was under duress. And I only decide what comes out of the bag. I don't control what happens next."

The emperor's struggle intensifies, and he tries and fails several times to get his scepter pointed at the bag. "You, you backstabbing, scaly, corrupt—aah!"

We all collectively gasp as he stumbles to the very edge of the cliff, then over. There's no bloodcurdling scream as he falls, like in a dramatic action movie, only more thrashing as if he might deploy his wings and save himself. It's no use. We don't even hear the splash above the roar of the rapids when he lands. His squid-entangled regalia is visible for only the blink of an eye before he's carried out of sight.

My blood chills. It's hard to watch someone fall so far and comprehend that they're unhurt. It's even stranger to think that the only consequence will be his workforce going on strike. Compared to an eternity with the star, it doesn't seem like a punishment at all. Is it wrong of me to want worse for him?

Yvit shakes his head slowly. "You see what I mean? Any businessman worth his title knows not to trust a politician."

I want to respond that Yvit is probably the most trustworthy politician I've ever known, but a rumble and a crunch behind us distract me.

"That's not great," Death says while backing up.

The device is not only spinning out of control, it's breaking down at an alarming rate. Splintered chunks of wood snap free and fling out across the tiny plateau, barely missing Death and Meela. The grating and grumbling of the gears make dirt and rocks shimmy around.

Meanwhile, the six flickering doors become even less stable. Stone arches form and crumble around them, only to be replaced by fancy molding that rots as vines grow through it and perish.

"Do we pick doors now?" I ask. "Is it safe?"

"I don't know," Death replies. "I think we should—"

Whatever they're about to say is cut off by the earsplitting crash of the device breaking loose from containment. By some miracle, it launches over our heads instead of rolling directly through us, but the chaos that ensues when it smashes in the canyon is as mind-melting as a surrealist painting.

All at once, the six doorways lose control. Instead of cycling through possible options, doors form inside doors like a long hallway in an infinity mirror. Physics and perspective are so broken, I can't tell what I'm looking at.

"Everything's coming apart!" Meela shrieks.

She's not being metaphorical this time. Space itself appears to warp around the doorways, bulging and bubbling to a breaking point. At that moment, the interior doors blast outward like socks that have suddenly turned inside out, exposing the hidden worlds between them like cars in celestial passenger trains.

Instead of portals with mysteries behind them, each door sits in front of a morphing blob, an encapsulated trial viewed from the outside with an ever-shifting interior. After each trial is another door with another trial and so on. They spew impossibly far into space.

"I recognize some of the objects," I say, pointing to changing bits of material jutting out from one of the trials. "For a second, I saw part of the mansion maze."

Several of the train car blobs have details from the trials I remember. Others have objects that are completely foreign, with industrial or wildlife themes. It bothers me that they blur in and out while I stare at them, as if changed by observation.

"The ground is cracking," Death observes as casually as if they're noticing rain.

"It's time!" Meela cries. "Everyone select a door!"

Yvit squints into the distance. "What are those things at the ends of the tunnels? Are those the exits?"

I try to make them out, but the blurring shapes between me and them make it hard to focus.

"Come on," Sol says. "One door per person."

I grab his sleeve. "Wait. Come with me."

"What?" He stares at me, confused. "But there's six doors. The rules—"

"We made up those rules, remember? You're coming with me, and if that *is* the exit up there, you're coming through that door, too. This isn't where we say goodbye."

He looks like he's about to argue, then nods and follows me to a door. The others have already selected theirs, and just in time, too, as the plateau splits.

I wave an arm. "Death! Meela! Yvit!"

They all stop to look at me, with varying visible—or invisible—expressions.

"Good luck," I say. "I'll miss you."

"Same to you," Death replies.

Yvit only shakes his head. "Yeah, yeah. Mushy stuff."

Meela hops through her door without another word. I don't know why I'm surprised.

"Hold on to me, just in case," I tell Sol, and we wrap our arms around each other. "Ready? Three, two, one—jump!"

Thirty-Two

Everything in the room is glaring and loud, but the phrase that comes to mind is *déjà vu*.

Somehow, we've stepped back through the same door we just exited, and into the dance hall again. Members of the audience have taken the stage to blast swing music while the crowd raves. I shake my head in disbelief.

"Do we have to turn back?" Sol asks, but when we spin, the door we came through is already gone.

I am not doing this trial again. As delightful as it was to sing with Sol, this can't be what the star intends.

"If we came in through the exit," I say, while standing on my toes to see over the crowd, "then we should be able to leave through the entrance. Right?"

It's a total guess, but as I squint through bright lights reflecting off a dozen beaded gowns, I think I spot the top of the entrance door. Unfortunately, this isn't a quiet audience waiting to be entertained anymore. Everyone is shaking and twirling around, filling every corner of the tiny hall.

"We're going to have to cross through," I tell Sol, but the moment I grab his hand to lead him forward, a loud crunch cuts through the music.

With a rumble and crack, an entire corner of the dance hall

breaks away, tumbling into outer space. Oddly, the audience keeps dancing. The music doesn't even skip a beat. Everyone ignores the fact that a handful of people have just drifted into the night sky.

"The whole thing's still unstable," Sol remarks as if I haven't figured that out. "We have to hurry."

He drags me forward into the crowd, but someone else grips my other arm.

"It's the performers from before!" they shout, and everyone around starts to murmur.

"Sing another song!" demands a goat-faced creature in a tweed vest and newsboy cap. I don't recall seeing them in the audience before.

More hands claw at my sleeves, and several halt Sol's progress as well.

"It was so sweet!" a group of the gray aliens coo. "Sing another, please?"

I tug my arm away. "Sorry. We need to go."

None of them are moving. Their bodies block our path, and all of them are still swaying to the beat. Where's the ringleader? Where's Jeffrey the squirrel? There's nobody around I can call to for help.

"One more song," an impossibly tall and slender woman with large eyes begs.

Did everyone look so alien before and I never noticed because of the lights?

I squirm and squeeze as close as I can to Sol, who's started shoving people away. The music is blaring, and the lights are reflecting on every bead and rhinestone in sight. I close my eyes and cling tight, wondering if this is how things end—not with a mudslide or tumble into space, but pinned down by adoring fans.

"She said no! Back away!" Sol shouts, loud enough to be

heard over the music.

To my shock, all of the hands release me and the dancers shuffle away from us.

"Are you sure?" one of them asks. They're staring at Sol, not me.

I pause, confused by the creature's sincerity, but Sol takes charge and drags me forward. Inexplicably, the crowd parts before him, and we rush to the door as if cloaked in a force-field. I almost feel bad for the dancers when I leave. They're only doing what they were made to do, right? We didn't have to yell at them.

That sentiment rapidly flees my mind when I realize we've exited the karaoke trial and onto a thin web of stardust stretched between one door and another. I can hear the canyon collapsing behind us, and the snap of bits ripping off the previous trial. I glance at the trial train to my right and catch the tip of Yvit's tail vanishing through a shimmering door.

In all the chaos, I forgot this was a race to the finish line.

"Let's go," I say, shuffling ahead on the stardust as if it might disintegrate with a heavy step.

I'm not racing Yvit to the exit. Rushing will only lead to mistakes. Instead, I have to make it to the end and somehow smuggle Sol out with me, even if we only get one heart key. This plan has less merit than my former strategy to reach the end with two sets and argue over rules. But the star seems obsessed with correctness, so maybe the fact that it didn't specify one person per exit is a loophole.

We pass through a portal-shaped door and squelch into a familiar field of purple mud. Toppled and shattered crystalline trees dot the devastated landscape, and slick soil once again clings to my boots.

"Where was the entrance to this one?" Sol asks, his head

already swiveling around.

I inhale the peachy scent of the flattened forest and search the landscape for something familiar. "I don't know. Nothing looks like it did when we started."

We spin in place, searching for doors, mushrooms, or anything that looks like a way out, eventually trudging up the mountain for lack of something better to try.

"This is where we first kissed," Sol says, but the smile that accompanies his words is strained, like he knows we're out of time.

The edges of the mountainous landscape draw nearer, as if it was never a landscape at all, but rather a single chunk of terrain arranged to look like it had a horizon. Around us, sinkholes form in the mud, and I'm certain they don't lead to caves this time. The trial train is falling apart, one passenger car at a time.

I really hope the entrance wasn't over a sinkhole.

"First kiss of many," I say, trying to distract him from the hopelessness.

He stops hiking. "First kiss goodbye, more like. I don't think this will work out the way you hope."

I fix him with my best glare. It's not as intimidating as his sourpuss scowl, but I hope it sends a strong message. "No more talk like that. I have a new plan. The star technically never said two people can't leave through one exit. So, all we need is one set of keys. I'm used to debating vague regulations with storytellers in my roleplaying games, and they almost always let me win. The star will appreciate that I'm thinking creatively."

Sol bites his lip and runs a hand through his curls. "Yeah. Speaking of storytellers, there's something I've been thinking about since the last time we were here. Remember when you told me about your friends who missed games?"

I glance around the mountain and gasp. "Hold that thought. I think I found the mushrooms!"

We've nearly walked straight past the circle, because it isn't a circle at all! Some of the tiny amethyst fungi are sprouting directly from the soil, but others are poking out of snapped trees or clustered on the sides of boulders. They only form a circle together when looked at from this exact angle. What a dirty trick!

I dart toward the optical illusion, sloshing through the sticky soil and trying to ignore my squelching boots. The mountain above begins to rumble, threatening a second landslide, and near us, more of the ground falls away, sucking dirt and trees down with it.

Too late, mountain. We made it.

I wait at the very edge of the mushrooms until I'm sure Sol's caught up with me, then leap toward the center of the fake circle.

The star does nothing to break my fall as I land on my rear on the next stardust path, surprised by its solidity. Sol's landing behind me is much more graceful.

"So, this is it?" I ask as he helps me to my feet. "We're just going backward through the previous trials?"

"Only one way to find out," he replies, urging me on toward the third door.

In a flash, we're in the family room of the house with the tiny pink kitchen. Sol's gaze immediately drifts toward the hall and the bedroom where he found the photo album, but that whole side of the house is gone. It's splintered off into several pieces, which are drifting around weightlessly in space.

"I think I know why I was in the picture," he says, but the trial doesn't give him time to explain.

The half of the house we're standing in is tilting as if about to drift away. I curse. Not only are the trials deteriorating one train car at a time, they're falling apart faster than we're moving.

"Kitchen! Hurry!" I shout while I run.

Our feet skid on the pink tiles as the floor tilts dramatically to one side, sliding us into the cabinets and smashing empty crates near our legs. With a flick of his hand, Sol manages to stop the kitchen table from crushing us. On his command, it fills the space between the cabinets and the exit door, giving us a ramp to use. We scrabble up the table, climb through the door, and tumble back out into open space. At least that trial was relatively quick.

Once again, I cower on a path of stardust, catching my breath from the exertion. Behind us, the kitchen disintegrates, merging with parts of the dance hall and canyon. Swirling blobs of purple mud drift past like oil dropped into water.

To our left, Death deliberately plummets into space before rising on their skeletal horse, bypassing an entire trial.

"That's got to be against the rules," Sol mutters. "They can skip all their trials, but we have to run through?"

"It's a good thing the star allows it," I tell him. "Don't forget, we want to bend the rules, too."

Carefully, we wobble to the next trial door, and I brace myself for what I know is coming.

It's exactly as I fear: an empty white cube with black illustrations on the walls.

The mirror room has reverted to showing our nightmares instead of dreams. I recognize the four gossiping girls as well as the spooky version of Sol. They seem to have come together on one side of the room to hang out while we were away.

Every other surface is covered in mirrors. There are round ones, square ones, large ones, and small ones. I try my best to give them my focus—one of them must be the old entrance, after all—but the grating voices of the girls wreck my calm.

"The competition's almost over," the one with the pleated skirt informs me.

"But don't worry! The star's promised us fun next time," adds the one with cute glasses.

I glance up in time to see the white-haired girl twirl a finger through spooky Sol's curls. The fake Sol smiles and leans into her touch. He gently bites her exposed shoulder with his eyes closed in contentment. It's like a dagger to my gut.

I'm not jealous of the girls. I know their whole act is meant to distract us, and they're NPCs like all the others. They're doing what the star told them to. It just bothers me to see them enjoying something with Sol I may never get to experience. All the running and plotting and puzzle-solving hasn't left us any room to *be*. I want a quiet moment with him.

Actually, I just want a quiet moment.

"You wouldn't believe the fantasies the star can dream up," the white-haired girl coos while running her nails through fake Sol's hair.

I sigh. "I know you're just doing your job, but I'm tired and I just don't care anymore." I expect Sol to chime in and tell them to back off like he had before.

He doesn't.

He only stares, transfixed, at the spooky version of himself. Fake Sol's teeth elongate into fangs again as he lifts his head from the girl's shoulder. When he finally opens his creepy eyes, they're bright white, not black and gray. The real Sol staggers back.

"And where will you be for the next one, June?" the fourth girl asks, then tsks. "Oh, right. You'll be in a world full of books, amusing yourself, all alone. The star's lonely rat in a maze. You have no idea how much it longs to keep you. There's no way we're letting you out."

Sol flinches back another few steps and rubs his brow as if he has a headache. The shadow version silently cackles at him, mouth wide with terrible fangs.

"We need to check the mirrors," I remind him. "These people are illusions, and their words are lies. They're only trying to slow us down. One of these mirrors is our exit."

The wall behind the four girls cracks. Multiple mirrors on that side shatter, sprinkling images of glass shards down upon the pristine white floor. I can't tell if the crack is real or fake, but either way, it's motivating.

Sol sets his hands against the glass in each of the mirrors on our side, testing to see if he can get through. "You're right. We need to get out of here."

"Is she right?" the white-haired girl asks. "Are we lying? Do you think so?"

The crack widens, and I join him, pressing my hands against each smooth surface, ignoring anything I see in them. Too bad I can't ignore the girls.

The one with glasses targets Sol. "Do you think she'll enjoy life in her little—eep!"

Apparently, the cracks are real. They split the gossip girls' wall in two, forcing everyone into a corner.

"Enough!" the real Sol shouts. He clenches his hands and shuts his eyes, breathing hard through his nose.

The white-haired girl twirls a ringlet and bats her eyelashes in false concern. "Oh no, I think he's figured it out."

The others respond, "He knows? Are you sure?"

"Well, we weren't exactly subtle."

"Should we tell her, or will he—"

The entire room goes white. It's sudden enough to make me stumble, as if someone unexpectedly turned on a light. Everything is gone—even the sound—but the crack remains, as does one mirror hanging on the opposite side of the cube.

"Hurry! Now!" Sol barks. He doesn't wait for me to respond, which is annoying because I want to ask him what he did.

Half a second later, we're standing on stardust.

How many trials was that? Four of eight? That means we're halfway to the end. I almost start to feel a bit of hope—then I realize which puzzle lies ahead. The playing card stairwell isn't encapsulated like the other trials were, and some of the cards floating before us are already starting to drift away. That must have been why Death fell.

Sol picks up on my concern. "It's okay. We'll get on the first card, and I'll move it to the end, same as last time."

Last time—like when he moved a card and the star shut him off like a broken toy. *That* last time. I'm not comforted, but I don't get a chance to express my worry, because someone on one of the other trains screams.

Thankfully, it's not the shriek of someone plummeting to disqualification. It's more of a constant, angry swear that I'm happy I can't understand. A glance at all the trial trains answers my questions right away.

Death has reached their exit door, and Meela is having none of it.

Thirty-Three

DEATH PASSES BY something on a marble lectern—presumably, a final key, which they haven't needed for a while—and marches up to a solid door with four separate keyholes in it.

"We shouldn't stop to gawk," Sol reminds me. "Hop up on this card with me."

I climb onto the card that he's selected, trusting that his plan will work. But even as I wrap my arms around his waist and he pushes off toward the other side, I keep my gaze fixed on Death.

As I could have guessed, all four keys are needed to unlock the door and open it. Death turns briefly to take everything in and acknowledge the still-wailing Meela before they step through and the door dissolves.

A shudder runs through me, and Sol looks back. "You okay?"

"Yeah," I answer—unconvincingly. "I guess, if I could pick the winner, I probably would have gone with Yvit."

Sol pushes against the air with a hand as if rowing a gondola. "I thought you liked Death. You two seemed friendly."

"I do! I think they're a good person, deep down. It's just . . . complicated."

"Well, if I could pick the winner, I'd pick you."

I give him a squeeze and enjoy his warmth. "It's strange,

but I feel like I already won."

The smile that stretches across his face is just as beautiful as it is brief, like a candle lit and quickly snuffed out. "We have to get you out of here first."

"Us. Get us out of here."

He looks away and pushes the air again. Meela's stream of curses falls silent just as our card bumps against the next door.

"Hold on," I say. "What's stopping us from rowing this card all the way to the end?"

"You haven't looked back yet, have you?"

The moment I turn, a card behind us tears in half and flutters into space. Bad plan. Terrible plan. I scramble onto the stardust bridge and turn the handle of the train car door, mentally reciting the remainder of our path.

Pinball. Mansion maze. Ballroom. Home.

Except, the room beyond the door isn't pinball.

"Oh no," Sol breathes. "Not this one."

As far as I can tell, we're outdoors, but it's a different kind of world from the tuning fork mountain. It's dark and foggy, and it seems we've appeared between two chain-link fences with razor wire. I stumble forward over uneven ground lit only by tiny slivers of light blinking on and off in the fog.

"Is this another haunted maze?" I whisper.

"No. Worse. If I tell you to run, you need to run. Understand?"

That doesn't make me feel great. I nod and creep along with him, noting the peaceful chirp of crickets and something that sounds like cracking wood.

"Is that part of it, or is the trial breaking down?"

"Shh!"

One hand clamped over my mouth, I follow him to the edge of the fence. Roughly a dozen yards beyond, blobs of colorful light flit about. They remind me a bit of wild rabbits hopping around in thick grass. Sol shrinks away from them.

"This way," he whispers. "We'll go around."

With our backs to the fence, we continue on, both of us flinching when the blobs hop near. He relaxes a little as we put them behind us, and I assume that means we're in the clear. I'm wrong. The whole fence suddenly lights up cherry red as if shoved in a fire and turned to lava. In the light it creates, I can see Sol's terror.

"Run! Now!" he screams, making a beeline for something I can't see.

I try to keep an eye on where he's going while glancing back at the melting fence. It dissolves, cools, then reforms in the shape of a sprawling maple tree.

"What was that?" I ask through gasps of breath.

"Terraforming," he replies.

"What, like in sci-fi novels?" I take a calming gulp of air. "Changing the atmosphere and biology of a planet so some other species can survive there? I thought that was done with, like, algae and stuff."

"This is a more direct method."

"And how is that a trial?"

He sighs and comes to a stumbling halt at the edge of a dense forest. "It's not. When I first came here, this was some kind of prison escape game. I was trapped in a military complex and had to manually break myself out."

I glance around the fog-filled forest, unable to see any lights within. "That sounds kind of fun. I would have enjoyed that one."

"I didn't. I got stuck and searched the barrier in my mind for helpful memories like you taught me. When I did, these things came out of it."

"The light things? Out of the barrier *in your mind?*"

"Yes. Kind of. They were in my memory, and something

told me they could get me out. Next thing I knew, they were real. They tore down the complex and turned it into . . . this."

I stare into the silent forest. When he mentioned he could see the star's memories, I never questioned how alien they might be. But now that I'm thinking about it, the terraforming thing makes total sense. The star's abilities seem perfectly suited to tearing down and rebuilding worlds. I wonder if that's what it did before it changed its vocation to studying emotions.

"Are these things dangerous?" I ask.

"Very."

"Will they terraform us if they catch us?"

"They'll certainly try."

I exhale. "That sounds pretty disqualifying. Let's—"

An electric blue critter flashes by my leg. The thing is maybe two feet long and slithering like a snake. Sparks fly from the tip of its tail as it whizzes off into the trees.

"This way," Sol orders, leading me forward.

More lights bounce and zip through the trees. Some are up high, as if bounding on branches, and some are low and buzzing like bugs. Any time one heads directly toward us, Sol turns and dodges to avoid it. Eventually, we locate our door, which sits alone on a concrete slab with no human structures around it.

"We made it." I pant and stumble forward.

The blue serpent whizzes into my path.

"Get away!" Sol commands, putting himself in front of me.

A green frog bounds up on our right, and a red dragonfly swoops in on our left. I gasp, realizing we're surrounded, and my lungs decide that's enough air for now.

"I said get away!" Sol demands again, but the things aren't as accommodating as the dancers. They creep closer, as if savoring our fear. "Fine," he declares, "this is on you."

I barely have time to shriek, "Don't!" before he dives straight for the blue serpent. His hand snaps around the glowing thing's throat faster than a house cat with a fly. To my relief, he doesn't dissolve like the fence and turn into a maple tree.

The serpent, on the other hand, twitches and pales, electric blue fading to brilliant gold with tiny white lights along its spine. It's a perfect replica of the star. Sol releases the baby serpent and it hisses, snapping at the dragonfly.

"Now we really need to go," he says. "I've just made this a whole lot worse."

The things in the woods lose interest in us, instead lashing out at the star, which strikes each in turn, turning them to dust—and absorbing them into itself. It's growing larger with every kill.

"Now!" Sol shouts.

I can't tear my gaze away and trip several times while I stagger toward him. The star elongates, and I worry what will happen if—no—*when* it escapes. Somehow, I feel even more nervous as I pass through the door to supposed safety.

"It's okay," Sol tells me as I stand on stardust in the tiny pathway between two train cars.

I know it's not. Everything is coming apart. I want to put on a brave face for him, but the best I can do is shake out my limbs and try to put the baby star out of my mind.

"I'm sorry," he says. "I should have warned you before I tried that."

I don't know what to say. All my mental gears are grinding, trying to understand what I saw. "You terraformed the terraforming creatures."

"I guess I did, yeah."

"Can you do anything the star can do?"

His face goes pale. "That's hard to answer. I—"

Yvit's voice cuts in. "Hey, you two!"

I look up to see him standing at his exit door. It's already open, but he hasn't stepped through. Meela's door is already gone.

"You need to hustle! This place is coming down around your ears!"

I shout back, "I know! Thank you!"

"No problem! And, uh, goodbye, I guess."

"I hope you get an insect farm one day," I call.

"Yeah . . . not likely." He fidgets with the door, and I wonder if he's dallying because he thinks we aren't going to make it. I can't tell how bad things look from his perspective. "Anyway, I gotta go take care of my kids! Bye, you two!"

"Goodbye, Yvit!"

And just like that, he's gone forever. It's so strange. He's right, though. We need to keep moving before everything breaks.

"I've memorized the wallpaper patterns in the next trial," I tell Sol, who still looks pale. "All you have to do is follow my lead."

It's cocky to say, but of all the trials, I feel like my talents shone the most in this one. Even Death hadn't figured out how to navigate the maze. Riding high on that burst of self-esteem, I wrench the door open, take a step through, and realize that I should have stayed quiet.

The mansion maze is nothing but rubble. That's bad, because I can't navigate floating chunks of mansion. It's good, though, because I'd completely forgotten the number of trapdoors and slides there were. How did I think I would climb back up? I couldn't even jump the widest crevice.

"Oh" is all Sol manages.

"We could, um . . ." I start, then stop.

Even if I could jump onto one of the drifting chunks of

mansion wall, I'm not sure I could find the foyer—assuming the foyer even exists.

Sol straightens his spine and lets out a breath so large it makes his cheeks puff out. "You asked me if I can do anything the star can do. The honest answer is, not yet. The barrier of fog is almost gone, but there are some things I still can't access. I can't make a door. I can't make a key. I can't wish you right out of this place, no matter how badly I want to. But I can work with what we're given."

With that, he clenches his fists tight and glares at the rubble that was once a mansion. Bits of crumbled wall that were drifting ever so slowly into space change their minds and return to the trial. The mansion doesn't re-form as it was, which is both a shame and a blessing, but all the pieces slam back together into one continuous stairwell.

At the top of it are the foyer doors.

"One more trial after this," he says as we both clamber up the rubble.

It's a wonder I don't twist an ankle as I scrabble over beams and plaster. I'm going to miss this impervious body when the star puts me back in mine. Imagine taking a martial arts class with no fear of breaking any bones. I'd be a menace.

The foyer doors are heavy and wooden, but I grab the handle of one and yank, practically tossing myself outside. We don't even speak as we bound across stardust and into the last trial—the first we did together.

When we enter, I think we've outrun the destruction. The basement and stairwell of the ballroom are intact and the table by the door is undisturbed. However, as we climb the stairs, we discover that the dance floor has buckled and split. I hold my breath and shimmy through a haphazard pile of boards, then wriggle around a toppled pillar to make my way to the remnants of the hall. Sol has an even harder time and moves with half my enthusiasm.

"I wish I could feel nostalgia right now," he says, "but this place is trashed."

No kidding. The domed ceiling is gone, and the refreshment stand is floating away.

He continues, "I enjoyed solving this puzzle together. I mean, I was caught up in my head at the time, but in hindsight, you were amazing. You made me want to be part of a team when I was determined to be alone."

That's sweet, but my whole body is energized, ready to bolt straight through the door, and I can't understand why he's slowing down.

"The entrance is over here!" I tell him while gesturing at it wildly. "Come on!"

There's no reply, but he speeds up. I wait until he frees himself from the rubble, then fling the door open and stumble out onto a surprisingly healthy patch of grass.

Grass! Normal, green grass. It's not purple or crystal or scented like lavender. It's a boring chunk of regular earth. I've never been so happy to see dirt. And there, directly in front of me, is a marble lectern with an open book that's hollowed out to conceal a key.

I creep toward it, taking calming breaths and squeezing my hands into excited fists. Sol follows close behind, then leans over my shoulder to peer into the book.

The key is not a golden heart.

Thirty-Four

I don't know what to do. I freeze for what feels like an eternity, staring at the diamond-shaped bow of the very last key we're going to get. I can't believe it. The competition is over. I'll never see my family again *and* Sol is going to die. It's the worst of any of the possible outcomes, and I'm entirely responsible. My brain fills with static.

Sol's reaction is more explosive. "No!" he shouts, first at the key, then into the midnight sky. "That's not what's supposed to be there!"

He paws through the rest of the book, then spins around in desperation as if searching for a miracle. For a second, I even think he's found one.

"The unused doors still have keys," he explains. "If I can bring them over here, you can— Oh, come on!"

I watch in a daze as the scaled tail of the star-serpent rises up from below and dashes the unused doorways to dust. In my fuzzy-brained state, I find myself wondering if the tail belongs to the original star or the one Sol set loose—though logically, I understand they're the same.

"I have to fix this," he says. "It's wrong. It wasn't supposed to end like this."

He doubles over, fists clenched, and I realize he's not

panicking—he's fighting. The doors aren't the only thing the star is trying to reclaim now that the game is over.

"Sol!" Concern breaks me free from self-pity, and I throw my arms around him like I can hold him in one piece. "I'm so sorry. This is all my fault. If I'd just let you pick your own door—"

"You still wouldn't have made it out. You couldn't have passed those trials without me."

"Maybe not, but you might have made it."

He strokes my hair, then gently pushes me away. "No. I never would have. This is *my* fault."

I refuse to cry. That is not going to be the last thing he sees before he's disassembled. I'm also not going to let him take the blame when all he's ever done is try to save me.

"I should have listened to you, every time," I confess. "If I'd tossed the gem in the mansion or refused to give my key to the emperor, it might not have turned out this way."

"Please, listen to me *now*. I could never have escaped, even if you had done all those things. I can't leave, because I'm part of the star. This—" He gestures all around us, at the bits of broken trials and swirling stardust. "This is me."

I shake my head. He's confused. "If the star has the power to terraform a planet, it has the power to leave one guy behind when it flies off to ruin more people's lives."

"One guy, sure. But not me. Hold on. I need some space."

Sol steps back and lowers his hands toward the ground. With a flick of his fingers, the bit of grass he's standing on breaks free from mine and floats several feet away. His little chunk of land joins pink tiles and green mushrooms in globs of purple mud, all tumbling and sloshing around in a sphere that's closing in all around us. The star is putting away its toys.

"What are you doing?" I ask.

"I can't be so close when you decide you hate me. It'll break me, and I'll come apart before I can find a way to save you."

The flash of heat that hits my face is more frustration than despair. "I could never hate you!"

Why would he say that?! I need to snap him out of this. Maybe we can take a chunk of debris and file away the bit on the diamond. We could make a skeleton key! Except, wouldn't the star have made the keys as impervious as our fake bodies? It seems like something that snake would do.

Sol clenches his teeth as if in pain, then runs his hands through his hair. It's whipping about on a warm breeze that makes no sense in outer space. "I was hoping this wasn't true, but I can't deny it after these last few trials. Everything that's happened to you is literally my fault. Everything."

"It isn't—"

"You know when you told me about your roleplaying games and the friends who didn't show up to sessions? Remind me—why shouldn't the storyteller also be a player?"

My face scrunches up reflexively as I try to make the question make sense in the context of everything that's happening. "Because it's too easy for them to tip the scales in their favor. Even when they try to be fair, they usually overcompensate and give their character a disadvantage. It's impossible to maintain that . . . balance."

Oh . . . my . . . grapefruit.

I understand now! Sol isn't an NPC like the squirrels or the ringleader. He's the storyteller's player character. He's . . . the star.

"How?" I blurt. "Why?"

Even as I say the words, the pieces come together in my mind: the empty version of Sol everyone saw before I arrived, the barrier of fog blocking his access to his memories, the way the star had declared it would be difficult for it to make decisions while Sol was awake. They've been the same being all along, thinking with two very different brains: one human and one alien.

No wonder the star wanted to stop us. If we'd figured all this out earlier, it would have ruined the competition. Sol, reasoning with a human mind and all the wacky chemicals that come with it, would not have agreed with the star's decisions.

"I'm sorry," he says again. "If I'd known, I would have told you. I swear."

"It's not your fault," I say, without thinking.

Do I mean it, though? It *is* his fault, because he's the actual star. My head and heart kick off a battle over which can cause me the most pain. It doesn't matter. Sol, the guy I grew to love, moans in anguish and falls to his knees in the grass, gasping for air.

He's fighting *himself* for control of his consciousness. He's fighting for his life.

"I still love you!" I shout, afraid I'll never be able to say it again.

Sol's head snaps up, and I choke on a scream. His eyes are no longer black and gray. They're lit from within, bright and white like the serpent-star when it's deep in thought. Twinkling tears streak down his cheeks. He's losing the battle—or burning up from inside.

"That only makes it worse," he says, brows pinched in agony. "Because I don't want to lose you. I want—have always wanted—to keep you here forever. You're fascinating. You make me *feel*. I don't want to let you go."

I take a step back toward the door, caught between the heart-melting desire to stay and be with Sol forever, and the understanding that it's the star itself that wants to keep and analyze me. He groans and reaches toward the remnants of the self-destructing trial-train. A snap and a crunch tell me that he's torn a piece of one away.

The wind picks up, dashing stardust and debris violently against my skin. I raise a hand to protect my face, even though I know it can't harm me. Around us, scales flash and slither in the wind, which is building into a nasty storm. Whatever Sol's doing, it's making the part of him that wants me to fail fight back even harder.

"I love you, too," Sol says through gritted teeth, "And that's why I have to get you out of here."

A chunk of the ballroom trial smashes out of its containment and rushes toward me at an alarming speed. Before I have a chance to react, it smashes into my tiny field of grass, toppling me onto my side. When I push myself up, I realize I'm looking at a jagged section of the dance floor.

Other than the splintered edges, the wooden floor is still smooth and shiny. There's even a hint of glitter between boards, especially around the edge of the stairwell where Sol used his perk to clear—the keyhole!

I don't hesitate to leap for the key, despite the wind whipping me in the face and a low growl emanating from the sky. When I wrap my hand around the tiny thing and yank it up to look it over, joy and relief wash over me.

It's gold. It's a heart. It's a trial key!

"You did it! We can get out!" I call while rushing back to my exit door.

My fingers fail me repeatedly. They tremble and make it difficult to dig the other keys out of my bag. Still, I get the club key into its keyhole and turn—then the diamond, spade, and heart. A loud click signifies the release of the mechanism, and I'm able to turn the knob and push.

There's nothing beyond the open doorway except a thin holographic film with an image of Earth in the center, yet I know the moment I step through, I'll be disassembled like the others. I'll go home.

A loud, rattling hiss joins the growl. I'm not sure if it's the sound of the hurricane wind or the star's rage at what Sol's done.

I spin. "Come with me! There's still a chance it might work!"

He's on his hands and knees on his tiny chunk of grass, fingers digging into the dirt. "I can't run away from myself."

"But—"

His bright eyes are pleading. "You need to go now. If you don't, I *will* try to stop you."

"I can't just leave you."

"June!" he screams so suddenly I wince. "Go!"

What I see next will haunt my nightmares forever. As soon as he speaks his final words, Sol's body bursts into sparkling stardust that catches in the terrible gusts and blows away in a swirl of light. In that same moment, the star-serpent strikes.

Its face alone is as big as my house. When it soars toward me—jaw impossibly wide—I know it plans to eat me whole. Me, the door, and everything nearby. Its scream of rage is a blaring echo of Sol's final, desperate shout.

There's no time to think or move. Only my own clumsiness saves me.

My body instinctively jerks backward when the serpent's unhinged jaw shoots toward me, and my shoe catches on the doorframe. Before I know it, I'm tumbling backward through the film and into darkness.

I make it out.

Thirty-Five

When I open my eyes, I'm in my bedroom, lying in my warm bed. But this is not like a fantasy novel where I'm left wondering if I was dreaming. The star is here with me, like a creepy stalker. Its serpentine body is smaller now—three feet long and coiled on my nightstand—and it's staring at me with those flickering eyes.

"This is new," it says in its spooky two-toned voice. "No one has ever fulfilled their wish without winning the competition before."

I sit bolt upright and glare at it, holding back an enraged scream only to avoid waking my parents.

The thing on my nightstand is not Sol. I tell myself that repeatedly. Sol was just a piece of this creature stuffed into another body. He reasoned with a human brain and experienced life with human senses. The serpent is no more human than the hairbrush and stack of books beside it.

"What are you doing here?" I demand in a whisper.

"It is customary to inform competitors that I may revisit your planet in the future, should you wish to try again. Your situation, however—"

"Not a chance."

I'm not going to cry. My nails are digging into my bedsheets, and for the first time in my life, I understand what it means to bristle with rage. But—I am not going to cry.

The star's eyes flicker in deep thought, and it tilts its head. "Are you certain?"

Of course it would ask me that, after last time when I changed my mind. Worst decision of my life. I could be pining over boring Jayden right now instead of mourning Sol.

There will never be another Sol.

"I won't let you use me like that again!" I snap before realizing I've raised my voice. One quick glance out the window tells me the sun is already coming up. I spent the whole night in outer space. Literally, this time.

The star continues its unnerving stare. "Did you not receive what you desired? Knowledge of the emotion called love?"

A memory comes to me, unbidden—an image of Sol in the little pink kitchen wearing those goofy chicken mitts. I know, in that moment, he was confused, but in the memory, he's smiling. Laughing. Why couldn't he stay that way forever?

Tears are stinging my eyes now, and it feels like my chest has been hollowed out.

"Yeah. I understand love," I say. "It's horrible, and it hurts. Just like Death said it would."

The serpent's head tilts the other direction. "Interesting. That was not my experience."

Its experience? *Its experience?!* Does it mean the feelings it siphoned off me? The ones it manipulated me into? Or does it mean . . . I made Sol happy?

Ugh! Now I'm actually crying. I try to turn the sorrow back into anger.

"You would know what I'm talking about if you checked Sol's feelings now," I growl. I don't even care if I wake my parents. "Oh, wait. You can't. You turned him to dust!"

Based on the speed of the flickering, I can tell the star is totally lost before it even opens its mouth. "The emotion of love has become a painful sensation. And yet, you still use the same name. Is this not grief instead?"

That's it. I lose my temper. "You don't get—no—you don't *deserve* to understand. You will never figure love out, and I'm glad! I hope that lack of satisfaction eats you up as long as you live! I hope you suffer for what you did!"

I don't, really. I mean, I hate the star right now, but technically . . . it's still Sol. I don't want him hurt. This is so confusing.

The star doesn't respond at all, nor do its eyes flicker with light to indicate some inhuman response lingering on the tip of its tongue.

I shake my head. "You need to leave."

"You have not yet confirmed your response to—"

"Get out! Go away!"

The star's little body jerks back from the nightstand so quickly it scatters my stuff on the floor. Its response is calm as ever, though. "Very well."

There is the tiniest twinkle of light before it spins in the air like an ouroboros, vanishing into its own tail. When it's gone, my room feels colder. The hollow pit in my chest where Sol used to be expands even more.

The inevitable comes immediately after. A gentle knock on my bedroom door.

"Sweetie?" my mom asks. "Are you okay?"

Crud. I'm not getting away with a fib while my eyes are red and the contents of my nightstand are strewn all over the bedroom floor. I reach into my pocket to grab my phone—the internet is always upsetting, so I could load up the first news I see and blame it for my lousy mood—but there's nothing in my pocket. The star never picked up my phone from the roof.

"June?" The door creaks open a crack, and my mom's concern-lined face appears. She's already dressed. I didn't even wake her. "What's going on? We heard you yell."

"I—" I look at the floor, then my bed. "I think I lost my phone."

"Oh." The deep breath she takes tells me she's torn between pity for my tears and frustration over the cost of the cell phone.

"I mean, I'm pretty sure I left it with Alex."

Phew. Quick thinking.

My mom smiles. "Aww, don't worry, honey! I'll just give their dad a quick call."

"No!" Oops. That may have been too much. "I'm gonna walk over there. We were supposed to hang out today anyway."

The forehead creases appear again. "Are those the same clothes you wore yesterday?"

"Yeah. I guess I was really tired last night. I'll change, then I'll visit Alex."

"You should clean up and eat breakfast, too. A shower will help you feel better. Then you can go."

"Sure. Thanks."

She nods. "You'd tell me if something else was wrong, right?"

"Of course."

See? I can fib now.

The moment she shuts the door, I wriggle out of my narwhal clothes and ponder the contents of my dresser. After a pause, I pick a near identical outfit—this time, without jousting water cows—but add a few accessories that I had tucked away for special occasions and never found the courage to wear. Forget occasions. The best time for an ivy-wrapped headband and glittering dice necklaces is now.

I shower, brush my teeth and hair, do my makeup the way I like—not how an internet trend says I should—and eat an excruciatingly slow breakfast before I gingerly excuse myself. It feels like hours are going by, even though I move as fast as I can.

Turns out, time feels much slower when you're putting on makeup in your own bathroom and not racing through a crumbling maze.

I don't head to Alex's when I leave. As soon as I'm out of my parents' eyesight, I bolt straight for the Victorian, hoping to get inside and out before the neighbors notice me. If I manage to lose my phone for real, my parents are going to be livid.

Oddly, when I reach the porch, the front door is slightly ajar.

Maybe Alex left it open last night, expecting me to follow behind them. It seems risky, even for them, but I'm grateful to not have to mess with the lockbox in broad daylight where I might be seen.

I channel the heroes of detective novels and enter the house as if I'm meant to be there, then shut the door behind me and exhale. The old Victorian is pleasant in the daytime, with sunlight streaming through its tall windows. The stairs don't even creak when I head upstairs and climb the ladder to the roof.

My phone is exactly where I dropped it and, thankfully, not cracked or wet. The lock screen catches my attention, though. It looks like I have a whole series of texts from a number that isn't in my phonebook. Upon unlocking, I see it's a group chat.

Happy Saturday, autocross fans!
Thanks to a generous donation for spark plugs
the rustmobile is back on the road!
Catch us on our stream at 9
Or head to the course to cheer us on live!

I almost block the number, assuming it's spam, before I recognize a couple recipients in the group. They're people from my school.

It takes a few minutes of internet sleuthing while pacing back and forth on a stranger's roof to find out that autocross is an amateur race that people enter with their own cars. There's a local one at a private airport that started a race at nine o'clock—and they have a participant list.

I'm not surprised by the names I find. Jayden and Gabe are on the list.

This is the part where I should feel relieved—joyous even. Jayden and Gabe weren't laughing at me. They think I'm a fan of their racing stream! Sure, this means I'm probably the worst flirt in the entire world, but it also means I wasn't rejected. Or, at least, not publicly mocked.

I should be happy! This would have meant everything to me several hours ago.

But I don't feel anything at all. Not even bitterness for the pain I suffered after spiraling from Jayden's laughter.

I wonder how long this is going to last.

"You!" a man's gruff voice barks. "What are you doing up here?"

I shriek and jump at the sight of the man standing halfway up the ladder. He has ginger hair, a bushy mustache, and paint-spattered overalls with a name tag. A contractor! On a Saturday? They never work on this house on Saturdays.

I am in so much trouble.

"I'm sorry," I babble as fast as I can. "I'm not a burglar—I mean—my phone was up here. The door was open. I just wanted to get it back. My friend, uh, they—"

They what? How can I explain my phone being up here without confessing this isn't my first trespass? This guy won't believe it survived being thrown to the roof without a scratch. I am *so* going to jail.

"As long as you weren't looking for my stash again," he says.

I stop jabbering. "Stash?"

"Stash. It hasn't been that long, has it? Feels like only a few hours to me. Then again, I never know how much time has passed when I'm out of commission. It's a good existence, when I exist, but sometimes it's a little confusing."

I step toward him and read his name tag. "Jeffrey?"

"Aye, that's me. You do remember!"

"Jeffrey the squirrel?"

"Not at the moment. The boss altered our design to blend in with the locals. Apparently, they're afraid of squirrels."

"Only ones that talk," I respond. "What's going on? The boss?"

"That would be me," someone says from below. "Jeffrey, if you don't mind."

The voice sounds so familiar that my heart starts pounding, but I bite my lip, afraid my hope will only break my heart again. If the NPCs are here, does that mean—

"Oops! My mistake!" Jeffrey says. "Ma'am, if you could come this way."

He wriggles back down the ladder, and I cautiously follow him.

The room I step into when I descend is nothing like the one I left. All the gray-beige paint is gone, replaced with colorful wallpaper that reminds me of the mansion maze. The windows are draped with luxurious fabric that matches the canopy over a bed—which I'm sure was not in the attic earlier.

Even with the number of contractors whizzing about in the tiny space, the amount of change is impossible for a single day, much less a few minutes. I scan the room until I find the "boss," and my breath catches in my throat.

He's back in his dark blazer, but it's no longer paired with accessories that cost as much as a compact car. Instead, there's a homemade Buttons and Squish tee, and a pair of familiar muddy boots with a golden ring painted around one ankle. He clasps his hands and looks at the doorway, then the floor—anywhere but me.

"Sol?" I ask. "How is this possible?"

He takes a shuddering breath as if he's afraid he might upset me. "I took your advice and spoke with myself. It's difficult when you're the same person thinking with two different brains."

I step closer. "And?"

"And we—I—agreed. I can't take the deal you offered to remain in this body forever. It would be like severing part of who I am."

I find that strangely relatable, but all I can say is "Then why are you here? For how long?"

I can't do it. I can't have him back and lose him again.

"Not forever, like I said. But one human lifetime . . . that's nothing to me." His hands squeeze together so hard I can see the tendons in his wrists. "If you don't mind having an alien for a neighbor, that is. I know you asked me to go."

There's a moment where I can do nothing. Every single possible emotion is trying to squeeze into my head at once, preventing any from getting through. Then the flood gates open, and I rush toward him, flinging my arms around his neck and pulling him as close as I can.

"That sounds perfect," I breathe.

He lets out a sigh of relief and wraps his arms around me as well. My phone buzzes in my pocket, but I ignore it and nuzzle his cheek. It buzzes again, and I pull back, apologizing before I notice something.

"Your eyes! You left them black."

His brows knit. "Should I change them to blend in?"

"No." I smile. "They're perfect, too." My phone buzzes

again, and again. "Sorry. Hold on. I need to see who this is."

I expect to find more advertising for Jaden and Gabe's autocross livestream, but what I see are texts from Alex—who should not even be awake yet. Oh no. I hope my mom didn't call their house.

"It's Alex," I tell Sol, and unlock the phone.

> *Someone's moving into the OV*

The texts get less hinged from there.

> *Wake up! You have to see this*
> *My dad is losing it. These people are loaded*
> *He said he saw a mini grand piano*
> *Dude. The place is crawling with movers*
> *Hey!*
> *This is wild. Get your lazy butt up!*

Sol chuckles. "Maybe I overdid it a bit?"

"A bit." I smirk. "You mind if I—"

"Go for it."

He leaves one arm around me, and I lean against him as I think of a response.

> *I know. I'm in the Victorian now*
> *You should come over and meet the new owner*

I pause and glance at Sol, who gives me the warmest smile.

> *I think you're really going to like him*

Acknowledgements

THIS BOOK LIVED many lives from conception to print. After penning my early drafts, I spent over a year trying to wrangle this odd little story into something that could fit in the current market. In the end, I couldn't bring myself to sacrifice the weird bits for a better place on a shelf, so my gratitude goes first to YOU, the reader, for giving this strange book a chance.

As is the case with all of my writing, this book would never have made it to print without the support of my wonderful husband and daughter, who made time for me to write and even created a special space for my desk. Yes, there are chicken oven mitts on the wall.

Connolly Bottum, my Developmental Editor, deserves all the credit for wrangling this complex story into something understandable. Her insight has been invaluable both for this book and those I will write in the future.

I would also like to thank my Copy Editor, who rescued me from messy punctuation, embarrassing typos, and immersion-breaking confusion. She is a true professional and it shows.

Rowan Pierce went above and beyond as a sensitivity reader, pointing out not only individual passages I could improve but thematic elements throughout the story that could be hardened to make the character arcs more impactful. Thank you!

And likewise thank you to Mel Carubia who gave me a second set of sensitivity reader eyes. I am so appreciative for your time and feedback.

Many thanks to Terri Lambert for her encouragement and praise throughout my writing career. Thank you for keeping me going!

And finally, a shout out to the Loons, whose constant companionship and feedback throughout the process has pushed me to be a better writer. If I could give one piece of advice to any aspiring creative, it would be to find your people. They will be the reason you continue when things feel hopeless, improve when you could stagnate, and find joy when you could become jaded.

About the Author

L. N. CLARKE is a video game production director by day and word nerd by night. In the past, she designed comic books and studied computer science. She loves strange old books, antique lockpicks, and pen and paper cryptography. She lives in the Eastern U.S. with her equally nerdy spouse, cool kid, a dog, a cat, and a flock of chickens.

www.ingramcontent.com/pod-product-compliance
Lightning Source LLC
LaVergne TN
LVHW091621070526
838199LV00044B/888